Operation Dagger

By

Ro

Carter's C... ...k 3

© 2019

Having purchased this eBook from Amazon, it is for your personal use only. It may not be copied, reproduced, printed or used in any way, other than in its intended Kindle format.

Published by Selfishgenie Publishing of, Northamptonshire, England.

This novel is entirely a work of fiction. All the names characters, incidents, dialogue, events portrayed and opinions expressed in it are either purely the product of the author's imagination or they are used entirely fictitiously and not to be construed as real. Any resemblance to actual persons, living or dead, events or localities is entirely coincidental. Nothing is intended or should be interpreted as representing or expressing the views and policies of any department or agency of any government or other body.

All trademarks used are the property of their respective owners. All trademarks are recognised.

The right of Robert Cubitt to be identified as the author of this work has been asserted in accordance with sections 77 and 78 of the Copyright Designs and Patents Act 1988.

Cover Design

The front cover of this book was created by Hammad Khalid, who can be contacted at **https://www.fiverr.com/hmdgfx**

Other titles by Robert Cubitt

Fiction
The Deputy Prime Minister
The Inconvenience Store
The Charity Thieves

Warriors Series
The Warriors: The Girl I Left Behind Me
The Warriors: Mirror Man

The Magi Series
The Magi
Genghis Kant (The Magi Book 2)
New Earth (The Magi Book 3)
Cloning Around (The Magi Book 4)
Timeslip (The Magi Book 5)
The Return Of Su Mali (The Magi Book 6)
Robinson Kohli (The Magi Book 7)
Parallel Lines (The Magi Book 8)
Restoration (The Magi Book 9)

Carter's Commandos Series
Operation Absalom (Carter's Commandos Book 1)
Operation Tightrope (Carter's Commandos Book 2)

Non-Fiction
A Commando's Story
I'm So Glad You Asked Me That
I Want That Job

Contents

Author's Note On The Language Used In This Book
1. Edinburgh
2. Night Raid
3. Fight Night
4. Bishopstone
5. Briefing
6. The Channel
7. The Himmler Battery
8. The Hill
9. Kasmire's Ambush
10. The Battle For The Hill
11. The Defence Of The Battery
12. The Final Fifteen Minutes
13. Nurse Duckworth

Historical Notes

Preview -Operation Nightingale

And Now

In memory of all the Commandos of World War II
and in memory of one commando in particular. The truth is often stranger than any fiction that can be written.

Author's Note On The Language Used In This Book

This is a story about soldiers and to maintain authenticity the language used reflects that. There is a use of swear words of the strongest kind. It is not my intention to cause offence, but only to reflect the language that was and still is used by soldiers. Apart from the swearing there is other language used that may cause offence. I don't condone the use of that language, but it reflects the period in which the story is set. While we may live in more enlightened times and would never consider using such words, the 1940s were different and the language used is contemporary for the period. We cannot change the past, we can only change the present and the future and I'm glad that our language has changed and become more sensitive to the feelings of others but we must never forget our past. We should, however, seek not to repeat it.

Abbreviations of rank used in this book (in descending order of seniority):

Lt Col – Lieutenant Colonel (often referred to simply as Colonel by their own subordinates)
Maj – Major
Capt – Captain
Lt – Lieutenant
2Lt – Second Lieutenant
RSM – Regimental Sergeant Major (Warrant Office Class 1)
CSM – Company Sergeant major (Warrant Officer Class 2)
TSM – Troop Sergeant Major (Warrant Officer Class 2) as used by the commandos.
SMjr – Sergeant Major (generic)
CSgt – Colour Sergeant
SSgt – Staff Sergeant
Sgt - Sergeant

LSgt – Lance Sergeant; a Brigade of Guards rank, but sometimes used by the commandos instead of Corporal.
Cpl – Corporal
LCpl – Lance Corporal
Pvt – Private
Tpr – Trooper, a cavalry rank equivalent to Private but used by the commandos.

Cdo – the abbreviation used when naming a specific commando, eg 15 Cdo.

Other military terminology is explained within the text where the narrative allows, or is explained in footnotes.

1 – Edinburgh

Carter awoke with the bright Edinburgh sunshine streaming into his eyes. He must have neglected drawing the curtains the previous evening. He looked to his left where her hair was flowing across the pillow like spun gold. Her eyes were tight shut in sleep, or perhaps she was pretending, not wanting him to catch her watching him as he was watching her.

She was even more beautiful in daylight than she had been the night before, if that was possible.

His mind was still in a turmoil, wondering how he had got from there to here. It had seemed so innocent, standing there in the Troon branch of F W Woolworths, trying to choose between brands of razor blade, when he had found her standing there next to him. Fiona Hamilton the farmer's daughter, well, farmer to be correct seeing as she was running the place now. She had asked after him, commenting that he must have been away on another raid, which he confirmed without going into details.

Then he told her that he was, rather reluctantly, taking a few days leave in Edinburgh. She had offered to recommend a hotel; this hotel. They'd gone to a café for a cup of tea, just for a chat, or so he had thought.

"Make sure you ask for room four oh one." She had advised. "It's the one my parents always ask for when they stay there. It has a wonderful view over the city, from Castle Rock all the way to Arthur's Seat, in Holyrood Park."

"A double room? That's a bit extravagant on a soldier's wage." He replied. Had she planned this all along? Their relationship had ended, at her behest, when he had been sent to carry out a raid on Jersey, just a few weeks earlier. But here they were now, in bed together.

He had been out walking in Princes Street Gardens, enjoying the unseasonably warm air as the city bustled around him. Returning to the hotel he was surprised to find her sitting in the lobby, a small suitcase at her feet.

"I shouldn't have come, I know." She had said as he had approached. She seemed flustered. "What will you think of me? Proper ladies don't go chasing men across Scotland and to their hotels."

"Well, you did recommend the hotel." He smiled warmly at her, telling her that her visit wasn't unwelcome.

"But it isn't the done thing, is it? What would people think?"

"The war has meant that the rules have changed a lot." He replied.

"Not according to my parents, they haven't" She said, a rueful smile on her face.

"More to the point, what are you doing here anyway?" he asked, getting to the more serious issue regarding her sudden appearance.

"I didn't really 'just bump into you' in Woolworths." She had said, looking at her hands, twisting her gloved fingers into knots of anxiety. "The truth is I've been finding excuses to go into Troon, looking for you. Looking for an opportunity to speak to you. Mrs Bliss, your landlady, has been keeping me up to date on your movements, ever since you got back from Norway in January. See, she even told me where you had been. It wasn't deliberate." Fiona gave him an anxious look, worried he might think she had been spying on him. "I told you, she's a sort of cousin. I'd gone to commiserate with her on the loss of her son and the talk turned to her lodgers and your name was mentioned.

After I had sent you on your way, before you went on your next trip at the end of January, I regretted it deeply. We have no idea what's going to happen in this war, so it's foolish to worry about it; foolish to let it stop us living our lives. I heard about a farmer and his wife in Fife, just ordinary folk like me and my parents, killed when a stray German bomb fell on their house. A bomber crew must have jettisoned it, they think. They lived miles from anywhere, no other houses anywhere nearby. What were the chances of that? And there was me berating you for doing dangerous things when it might be me that ended up dead. It seemed stupid.

So I took to visiting Mrs Bliss more often, on some pretext or another. Usually I brought her something from the farm; eggs or a few slices of ham. She thought I was being kind but I suppose I was manipulating her. I don't think I fooled her, but she was kind enough not to mention my real reasons for visiting. I watched you when you were out training with your men, doing your PT on the beach or running around the fields like a bunch of Neds[1]. Anyway, she kept me up to date with your comings and goings. I'd visited yesterday morning and she told me where you were.

It took some doing, but I plucked up my courage and spoke to you. I was so frightened you might not want to talk to me."

"You have no idea how many times I wanted to go out to the farm to see you." Carter said. "But I was also afraid you wouldn't want to speak to me. Besides, your father has a shotgun and you might have sent me away with more than just the sharp edge of your tongue."

She laughed her bright, tinkling laugh. "Actually, my father would have welcomed you. He likes you. My mother thinks you're the best thing ever. When I told them that I'd sent you away my father told me how stupid I was being. He got quite angry about it, which is very unusual for him. He reminded me about all those middle-aged spinsters around the area who had refused to marry when the young men went away to the last war, because they were so fearful of losing them.

They were afraid of becoming war widows, and goodness knows, there are enough of those around along with their fatherless children. I think that was what coloured my thinking. I didn't want to end up lost and alone like them. Then he reminded me of the young men who had come back safe and sound. I told him it was a risk I wasn't prepared to take and he told me that the only risk I was taking was being unhappy because I'd sent you away. He was right, of course. I could feel it eating at me, the regret, the pain of losing you.

I went to your lodgings that night to speak to you, to tell you I'd changed my mind, but Mrs Bliss told me you'd already gone. By the time you came back a couple of weeks later I'd lost my nerve."

"But you found the courage to follow me all the way to Edinburgh."

"It was that cup of tea we had in the café. I could see that you still had feelings for me. I thought that if I came here, at least we could talk. If you don't want me to stay …"

He placed a hand on hers. "Of course I want you to stay. We'll have dinner then see if they have a room for you for the night." He would have preferred her to stay with him, but to even suggest such a thing would be scandalous.

"Thank you. That would be lovely. My parents think I'm visiting an old school friend. They won't be expecting me back tonight."

Only they didn't see if they had a room for her. After dinner she had insisted that they change the occupancy of the room to two people, as Carter's 'wife' had unexpectedly decided to join him for his short holiday. The receptionist managed to keep her face expressionless. Fiona had put her gloves back on so that the young woman wouldn't notice the lack of a wedding ring on her left hand. While Carter was delighted at the turn of events, her suggestion had taken him by surprise.

"Penny for them?" Her soft voice broke into his reverie.

"Ah, you're awake. I was just thinking about the last twenty four hours. They've been such a whirl. Yesterday morning I didn't even have you in my life, now I have you in my bed."

She blushed from the roots of her hair down to where the crisp white sheet was pulled modestly up to her shoulders. "You must think me a terrible trollop." She whispered.

"I do not. Besides, if you're a trollop, what would that make me? Some sort of Lothario?"

"It's different for men." She pouted. "You get to sow your wild oats. We women are expected to be pure."

"In that case, we had better do something to maintain your reputation. When I came up to the farm that last time, I was going to ask you to marry me." He took a deep breath, summoning his courage. "Fiona Hamilton, will you marry me?"

"Oh no you don't." she laughed. "You're not getting off that lightly. I want the whole thing. Down on one knee, Carter, or I shall refuse."

He struggled out of bed, remembering that he was still naked from the previous evening. He hunted around on the floor for enough clothing to make himself respectable. He settled on a pair of trousers and a vest. Going to her side of the bed, he went down on one knee. She slipped one arm out from under the sheet and offered it to him. He took her hand gently in his fingers.

"Fiona Hamilton, will you marry me?" he asked, putting all his sincerity into the question.

She sat up, holding the sheet across her body. "I will." she replied.

He stood up and bent over her, placing his lips on hers to seal the bargain.

"It will have to be soon." She said after they broke apart. "I don't think we can have a long engagement."

"How about tomorrow?" He said. "We can get a special licence."

"Really? That soon?"

"Why wait?" His face darkened a little. "When I get back off leave, we start training for our next op. I don't think I can ask the army to schedule things around our wedding day. It will either have to be now, or it will have to wait until after we get back from wherever we're going." He didn't want to spoil things by reminding her that he might not make it back at all.

"OK. Well, my parents always had in mind a big do for me. I'm afraid they're going to be disappointed."

"We can still have the do. We'll plan it for later in the year. The only difference will be that we will already be married. I'm sure that we're not the only people in Britain today who have had to do things a little less traditionally than before the war."

"You're right. And now that I have you, I'm not going to risk letting you get away from me." She laughed. "So, what happens now?"

"I guess we have breakfast and then go to the Registry Office and start filling in forms. Then we must go and buy you a ring."

"Not quite yet." She said. "I have something else I want to do first." She drew the sheet from around her body, revealing her nakedness.

"Trollop." Carter grinned, pulling his vest over his head.

[1] Neds – Scottish slang word for hooligans, possibly originating as an acronym for 'non-educated delinquent'.

* * *

It turned out to be forty eight hours before Fiona Hamilton could become Fiona Carter, under Scottish law. They spent the intervening time buying those few things they could to make the wedding more of an event. A new dress was out of the question, but Fiona had enough clothing points on her ration card for a new hat.

Carter found the branch of a Scottish bank that dealt with Cox's and Kings, the bank that most British Army officers used. Through them he was able to cash a cheque large enough to cover the cost of a wedding ring and some of the other expenses. Although army officers weren't paid a great deal, Carter had benefited from the estate of an aunt that he didn't recall ever having met, but who seemed to be very fond of him if the size of the legacy was anything to go by He had been saving the money to buy a car after the war but decided that the happiness of his bride-to-be was a higher priority. He'd also had very little opportunity to spend any of his pay since the middle of the previous November, so that had mounted up as well.

The ring wasn't expensive, just a plain gold band. Fiona, however, said that it was as much as she had ever wanted.

They spent the rest of the time exploring Edinburgh, Fiona acting as tour guide around the city that she had visited many times as a child. Carter was surprised to find that despite the Army's use of the castle[1], they were still able to wander around it.

On the Friday morning they returned to the Registry Office promptly at ten thirty. "Where are your witnesses?" The Registrar, a severe looking middle-aged woman, asked them.

"We don't really know anyone in Edinburgh." Carter replied.

"Well, Y'll no be getting married without witnesses. I probably shouldn't suggest this, but the firemen[2] at the station next door have been known to stand in. Mind, now, you're not allowed to pay them."

"Would buying them a drink at the end of their shift count as payment?" Carter asked.

"I wouldn't think so." The woman allowed the faintest of smiles to play around the corner of her mouth.

So it was that the marriage of Fiona Hamilton and Steven Carter was solemnised with two Edinburgh firemen as witnesses.

Afterwards they went up to the castle and had their wedding photograph taken on the northern battlements. Behind them was the magnificent panorama of the New Town[3] and, beyond that, the Firth of Forth. The photographer, Mr Jerome of Leith Walk[4], promised that the photo would be ready for collection before he closed his shop that evening.

The previous evening Carter had written a letter to his parents, announcing his marriage. He kept it short and to the point and worded it in the past tense, as a fait accompli. However, he didn't want to jinx things, so had kept it in his pocket. As they left the castle, Carter dropped it into the post box next to the castle's guardroom.

"Happy, Darling?" Carter asked as they strode along the cobbles[5] of the castle esplanade.

"Ecstatic." Fiona had replied, gripping his arm tightly. "You look so handsome in your uniform."

Carter was wearing his Number 2 uniform, the one worn by most officers when not engaged in operations. As he was engaged on an HO[6] basis he wasn't required to buy the formal dress uniform of his regiment[7]. It was one of the other things that had been a bone of contention between him and the commanding officer of his previous regiment, especially as some of the other HO officers had purchased the uniform.[7]

"I'll soon be back in my battledress. We have to go home tomorrow."

"But we still have tonight, husband." She said, trying to keep her tone light. "And I am going to make sure that receptionist gets a really good look at this." She said, holding her left hand up so that the sun sparkled off the gold of her wedding ring.

[1] Edinburgh Castle – The castle was no longer in use as a military installation by the time of the Second World War, it was under the management of the Ministry of Works and Buildings, later known just as the Ministry of Works. However, captured Luftwaffe pilots were imprisoned in the castle for short periods after capture and the large amount of office space available leads the author to suggest that parts of the castle may have been used by the army. The castle is now under the care of Historic Scotland.

[2] It is true that this often happened. The marriage of the author's own parents in the Edinburgh Registry Office was witnessed by two Edinburgh firemen from the fire station next door.

[3] New Town – Prior to the Jacobite Rebellion of 1745, most of the city of Edinburgh was centred along the south side of Castle Rock and along the Royal Mile, which connects Edinburgh Castle with Holyrood Palace. To the north of the rock was a large lake, called the North Loch, which was used as a sewer and waste dump by the residents above, hence the lack of houses or businesses on that side of the castle. After the '45 Rebellion the lowland Scots started the construction of the New Town to the north of the lake, laid out in broad streets and squares based on the Georgian architecture that was already in vogue in London and other English cities. Construction work took place between 1767 and 1850. In

1820 the North Loch was drained to allow construction of Princes Street Gardens and, later, also became the site of Waverley railway station and the route west out of the city for the trains. The city then expanded north as far as the Firth of Forth, influenced by the growth in importance of the Port of Leith during the Victorian era.

[4] Jerome's of Leith Walk – This was a real establishment and the author, as a child, was taken there to have a photograph taken. The business no longer exists but was well known in its heyday.

[5] The cobbles of the Castle have now been tarmacked over to allow the area to be used for display purposes, such as the annual Edinburgh Military Tattoo. Drivers used to be able to park there as well, but that is no longer permitted.

[6] HO – Hostilities only. This was a class of enlistment into the armed forces that guaranteed a return to civilian life at the end of the war. As such it was different to both regular and reserve service. Volunteers could enlist on HO terms but it was also the standard term for conscripts.

[7] Officers in the British armed forces are required to purchase their ceremonial uniforms and accoutrements and have them tailored at their own expense. There is an initial grant paid on enlistment, but the cost of maintenance and replacement is met by the officer. On being commissioned in the RAF in 193, the author's grant was £700 to cover the cost of No 1 Home Dress and No 5 Mess Dress (worn in the Officers' Mess on formal occasions) and the tailors got every penny. Combat equipment and working uniforms are provided free of charge by a grateful taxpayer. ORs (other ranks) have their uniforms provided free but certain items, such as dress uniforms, have a 'life' attached and personnel who need to replace theirs early may have to make a financial contribution.

2 – Night Raid

Serious training for the next operation commenced on the following Monday with the Long March, as it had become known. It was a twenty five mile route march from Troon to Irvine, inland to Kilmarnock and back to Troon again. Even the fittest of the commandos found it a challenge.

For Carter it was something to be endured, more so because he was still suffering from the remnants of the hangover he had woken with the previous day. On the Saturday night his troop had practically kidnapped him to take him on the bachelor party he hadn't had because of his sudden and unexpected marriage. He was taken to the neutral ground of the Atlantic Hotel, where many of the Commando's officers also joined the revelries.

The following morning had been spent in recovery, while he packed up his kit at Mrs Bliss's house and moved it to Home Farm, where the Hamilton's lived. The property had once been part of a much larger estate which had been sold during Queen Victoria's reign to pay off gambling debts John Hamilton, his new father in law, had told him. The farm had then been split into two by his grandfather, creating Hamilton Farm for John Hamilton's uncle, though the property had been unified once again when the uncle had died without an heir.

"It will all be Fiona's one day." Hamilton had told Carter over a glass of whisky one night. Carter suddenly realised that his new wife was probably quite a wealthy woman; or at least she would be one day.

In the afternoon Carter had run the five miles from the house at Home Farm to the derelict building at Hamilton Farm and back again, trying to get the last of the alcohol out of his bloodstream. It had made him feel nauseated, but seemed to do the trick.

When he returned to the farm Fiona had been waiting at the gate holding a rather rusty looking bicycle; a girl's model, lacking a cross bar. "This was mine until I learnt to drive." She had said. "I found it at the back of the barn. It needs a bit of cleaning up and some maintenance, but it will get you to work in the morning."

They spent the rest of the evening working on the bike between them, exchanging cheesy smiles over buckets of soapy water and greasy bicycle parts. One of the Land Girls had come in, seen them staring into each other's eyes over the frame of the bike and left, muttering something about young love.

As farmers, the Hamiltons were in the habit of going to bed early, which was fine by Carter. What he should have done, he realised after about ten miles of the route march, was actually go to sleep. Even so his wife had been up first, heading for the milking parlour to take care of the herd. By the time Carter rose, Mary Hamilton, Carter's new mother-in-law, had a huge cooked breakfast ready for not just him, but for John Hamilton, Fiona and the two Land Girls. While living at Mrs Bliss's Carter had been as well fed as it was possible to be, considering the rationing, but he decided that living on a farm was going to be far more enjoyable when it came to the matter of food. Then there were the other attractions.

The route march was just the start of the training regime, something to point them in the right direction. Over the following weeks they practically re-lived the curriculum of Achnacarry House, the Commando training school north of Fort William. Added to that was the climbing training that Carter had suggested. Volunteers were trained first, learning the wide range of skills and techniques that would keep them safe as they climbed. The volunteers then took groups of commandos out into the Scottish mountains and passed on their newly found knowledge to them.

No one had time to be bored.

* * *

They could hear the sound of hammering coming from the large hanger that lay off to the right. A pool of light showed where the entrance was.

"That gives us a bit of a problem." Sgt Chalk said. "The backwash from that could end up giving away our presence."

"I know. The alternative is to go around the other side and cut our way in there and cross the runway to get to the objective."

"It would take at least two hours to get there. And there's always the risk of us being spotted by that patrol we saw earlier."

They were interrupted as a twin row of lights came on, marking the edges of the runway. Something was about to land.

"We'll wait, see what they do when this aircraft is down. It may be why the hanger doors are open." Carter said, keeping his voice to a whisper.

The sound of aero engines split the night sky and the dark silhouette of the aircraft passed in front of them. There was a squeal of tortured rubber as the tyres touched the concrete and the aircraft was down. It was a big one, Carter could see that. Probably the biggest he had ever seen. It taxied around to come to a standstill outside the hanger, where its nose was lit up by the light from inside.

Other than the aircraft's size, the other thing that Carter noticed was that it had a tricycle undercarriage, the third wheel being at the front, under the aircraft's nose, rather than under the tail, which he was used to seeing on British aircraft.

He wondered what the advantage was. As he watched, the crew climbed down through a trap door under the aircraft's fuselage, dropping luggage down ahead of them. It wasn't a full crew, just a pilot, co-pilot and navigator, enough to bring the aircraft from the factory where it had been built. A figure walked out of the hanger and came to a halt under the nose of the aircraft. Two others followed, carrying chocks which they placed fore and aft of the wheels. The first figure saluted, a gesture that was returned by the crew as they gathered up their luggage, their task complete.

A small tractor appeared and a mechanic connected it to the nose wheel of the aircraft by a long metal pole, while one of the other mechanics clambered up into the bomber's cockpit to take control from within. The chocks were removed and the tractor drew the aircraft into the hanger and out of sight.

As they watched, the pool of light in front of the hanger grew smaller and smaller as the hanger doors were pushed shut. As though at a signal from the hanger, the twin row of runway lights also went out, leaving the airfield in almost total darkness.

"Thank goodness for that." Carter breathed. "OK, I'll go and get the men. You wait here. I think we can get in here and make our way to the control tower."

The men of Carter's half troop were lined up under the hedge on the far side of the road that led to the airfield. Travellers in a vehicle wouldn't have seen them, despite a vehicle's headlights. A foot patrol would only find them if they tripped over them. Even Carter, who knew where they were, had trouble locating his men.

They had studied the map of the airfield in detail, so they knew where they were going. Through the fence, around behind the back of the hanger, across the open hardstanding and then to the control tower, their objective. He found one of the men and whispered his order to advance, which was passed from man to man along the line. Turning, he led them across the road at the run.

They dropped to the ground, listening for any sound of the alarm being raised. It seemed unlikely. The nearest sentry post was at least half a mile away, at the main gate. But there was always the possibility of an unseen foot patrol hearing them.

There was nothing. Just the sound of the hammering from the hanger, muffled now that the doors were shut. Carter wondered what it was that required such an extensive beating. As they got to the perimeter fence, Carter passed the word down the line to summon two of his men. "Mills, Mitchell, do your stuff." He backed off from the wire so that the two soldiers could get at it with their wire cutters. For the next few minutes all that could be heard was the steady click, click, click of the wire cutters severing the strands of chain link, along with the occasional rattle of the wire as it vibrated under their hands. It sounded thunderous to Carter, but in reality he knew the noises wouldn't be heard more than a few yards away.

A hole large enough for a man to crawl through was eventually completed. Carter was the first to enter, the two men holding the wire apart so he could do so without snagging his clothing or equipment and causing the fence to rattle again. He was followed by the four sections, in alphabetical order, seven men to each section, led by their corporal. They spread out along the line of the fence, lying flat on the ground so that their bodies seemed to melt into the grass. Two of the last troopers through replaced Mills and Mitchell at the wire, so that they could crawl through themselves, then Sgt Chalk was the last to complete the journey.

So far, so good. There was no sign that they had been detected. Carter would have been extremely disappointed if they had been. They trained hard for night incursions such as this. It should be second nature to them by now.

Carter led them along the fence until they were at the closest point to the hanger, its sides offering deeper pools of shadow in which they could hide. There was a half moon, but that was mainly hidden by clouds, making only the briefest of appearances in the gaps. But during those few seconds it gave the defenders time to see them, if they were alert and watching. Carter kept a close eye on it and every time it threatened to get brighter he would halt their advance and they would go to ground once again.

Rising from another pause, Carter led the men across the grass to the hanger. He felt more comfortable, less exposed, in the deeper shadows.

The hammering was louder now and he could hear shouted conversations within the hanger. But despite their proximity he couldn't make out any actual words. The noise within helped to cover whatever small noises his men might make. They moved silently down the side of the hanger to the rear, around the corner and across the back to the far corner.

Taking a careful look, Carter could make out their objective. It was about a hundred yards away across a wide expanse of concrete hardstanding. Two aircraft were parked there, silent, but threatening in their power. They were of two different types, not that it mattered to Carter what they were. They were warplanes and therefore legitimate targets.

The moon slid behind another cloud bank. He checked it, to see how large it was. There was no sign of another imminent break. If they hurried, they could get across the hardstanding. The control tower was a squat square building with a glass encased greenhouse like affair on top, which gave a three hundred and sixty degree view. Dim lights could be seen behind the glass, shadows moving. That was good. With light on the inside it was unlikely that the occupants would be able to see past their own reflections to the darker world outside.

The men moved as one, thirty of them rushing across to the protective pools of darkness beneath the wings of the closest aircraft. Despite their numbers, their rubber soled boots made hardly any noise. They paused again, thirty pairs of ears straining to sense any sign of detection.

A figure came out onto the balcony that surrounded the glass enclosure. A match, or perhaps a lighter, flared then went out, leaving just the glowing tip of a cigarette. There was nothing they could do while the man was there, even though the flare of the lighter would have destroyed his night vision. He only had to glance in their direction to see them if they went out into the open again, their dark figures silhouetted against the paler concrete. His men crouched down beneath the low wings of the aircraft, the muscles in their legs screaming in protest after a few minutes.

The cigarette butt described a red arc as the smoker threw it over the balcony rail and, at last, the figure returned inside. Carter allowed another minute, just in case the smoker changed his mind, then he led his men across to the second aircraft. They were tantalisingly close now. Probably no more than thirty yards from their objective. One last rush would do it. Even if they were detected, at this stage it wouldn't matter. Nothing could stop them now.

The troop ran forward once again, surrounding the tower. Dropping into defensive positions, just as they were trained to do. Every action was a reflexive; no need for conscious thought after so much training and definitely no need for spoken orders. Carter located the entrance door. Beside it, at shoulder height, was what he needed. Grasping the end of the rope, he rang the fire bell, thrashing the bell rope from side to side to make as much noise as possible. To add to the effect, Sgt Chalk drew a Very Pistol and fired a flare into the darkness. It hung above them on its small parachute, illuminating a large section of the airfield.

It didn't take long for soldiers to arrive.

"You're all under arrest." An American voice shouted.

"Too late, I'm afraid." Carter shouted back. "Your men would have been cut to ribbons trying to rush us like that." He pointed to two commandos lying side by side in the grass, facing across the hardstanding in the direction from which the Americans had approached. "This is a Bren gun team and you ran straight through their field of fire."

In fact Carter's men were unarmed, a precaution against any of the Americans panicking when faced with armed intruders. But to say they were unarmed was like saying a tiger was unarmed. They weren't carrying any firearms, though all of them carried their commando daggers, their wicked eight inch spike bayonets and, Carter was sure, several of them had illicit sets of brass knuckles that could break a man's jaw with a single blow. Even against the rifles of the guard force, Carter would back his men to come out on top if it came to a fight.

There was a roar of a motor engine and a Jeep swung into view. They were becoming a more common sight on the roads in the area as the Americans built up their forces in Britain. It pulled up right next to Carter. The driver got out, fragments of light sparking from the badges on his uniform.

Carter sprang to attention and saluted. "Lt Carter, 15 Commando." He introduced himself.

"Well done, Lieutenant." He pronounced it Loo-tenant. "I had a bet with your commanding officer that you would be caught well before you got anywhere near the tower. It seems I have lost my bet. I am not used to losing bets, so you can imagine, I'm not too happy about it."

Carter knew of the bet, as did all of his men and probably most of the Colonel's men as well. It had started, as such things often do, with too much alcohol. The newly arrived Colonel Henry Shiner had invited the senior officers of neighbouring British units to dine with him in his newly established Officers' Club; an invitation the British were more than happy to accept, given the quality of the food the Yanks were bringing into the country with them.

Lt Col Vernon had been explaining the role of the commandos and their areas of expertise. "I reckon my men could get in here without your guards even knowing they were there." Vernon had boasted. Well, it wasn't so much a boast as a statement of fact. But the American CO couldn't let it pass unchallenged and the bet was made.

Unknown to the Colonel, Carter and his men had been there several times already, conducting reconnaissance patrols by both day and night. It had been apparent that the Americans had taken the bet seriously, with a flurry of patrol activity around the perimeter of the camp. But after a few days the flurry had dwindled to what Carter suspected was its normal level, with few foot patrols along the wire and only two motorised patrols each night; one at twenty one hundred and the other at oh one hundred.

It was Carter who had identified the blind spot, where the view from the control tower, the highest point of observation on the airfield, was obscured by the large aircraft hanger that the American engineers had constructed when they had arrived in late December of 1941. It coincided with a bend in the approach road that prevented a view along the road from the guardhouse, or Guard Room as the British would have called it.

The American officer turned to face the soldiers that had arrived, their rifles still levelled at the commandos. "Lieutenant Kasmire, what have your men been doing all night? While you've been sitting in the guardhouse drinking coffee, the British Army has been wandering all over my godammed airfield."

"Sir, I don't … that is we were …"

"You weren't doing your job, Kasmire. Do you know what this officer did just a few weeks ago?"

"N … no Sir."

"He led a team of men into occupied France and broke into a house there. A big house, full of Germans. Those Germans are all dead now. And if this hadn't been a drill, your fellow Americans up the top of the tower there…" he pointed upwards where three men were peering down from the balcony, " …would now all be dead. He was able to kill the Germans because they were sloppy and he was able to get in here tonight because you and your men were sloppy. Not only that, if they'd had explosives with them, two very expensive aircraft, the property of Uncle Sam, would now be just a heap of garbage."

"Sir, I'm sorry, Sir." Even in the darkness Carter thought he could see the young American officer turning red with embarrassment. A crowd had grown, with men running across from the aircraft hanger to see what was happening.

"Sorry won't cut it, Kasmire. Now, get back to the guardhouse before half the population of Scotland walks through the gates." He pronounced it as two words, Scot Land.

"Sir, yes Sir." The officer turned and chivvied his men back in the direction they had come.

"Thank you for demonstrating how poor our defences are, Lieutenant." The commanding officer of RAF Prestwick[1] said. "I'll see you in the morning."

"Yes, Sir." As part of the exercise, or drill as the Americans called it, Carter had agreed to return to brief the security personnel on the weaknesses he had discovered in their defences, both the ones he had exploited that night and also the others he had identified. "We'll go out the way we came in, if you don't mind, Sir. We have to repair the hole we made in your perimeter fence. By your swift arrival, I assume our CO told you we were coming tonight."

"He did. It was part of the agreement. I didn't want my men roughing you up." Carter refrained from suggesting that it if it had come to physical violence, it might well have been the Americans getting roughed up. "Are you marching back to Troon?" The American sounded shocked by the idea.

"No, we're running. It's only a couple of miles, Sir. It's the sort of distance we use for a warm up."

The Colonel looked astonished, quite sure that his own men would balk at being asked to run anywhere. "Well, thank you again. I'll arrange for a crate beer to be sent across for you and your men."

"Thank you, Sir. I'm sure the men will appreciate it. I believe your bet with Lt Col Vernon was for a bottle of whisky, which he promised to give me if we were successful."

"Well, you enjoy that. You've earned it." The Colonel climbed back into his Jeep and drove off, while Carter led his men through the crowd of curious mechanics and back to their entry point.

[1] RAF Prestwick – The majority of military airfields in the UK are managed by the RAF, so are referred to as "RAF" even when they are being operated by foreign air forces, such as the Americans. This convention continues to the present, with American bases such as RAF Mildenhall and RAF Lakenheath. The exceptions to the rule are Royal Naval Air Stations and Army Air Corps airfields. Prestwick airport was taken over by the United States Army Air Corps in 1942 as the UK end of the ferry route for large aircraft coming across the Atlantic Ocean from the USA. On arrival their extra large fuel tanks, needed to ferry them across the ocean, were removed and equipment that had been removed to make them lighter, such as machine guns and bomb racks, was replaced, From Prestwick the aircraft were collected by operational aircrews and taken to the airfields that operated them. The aircraft described as landing at Prestwick was a B-24 Liberator bomber, which was also used by the RAF, both as a bomber and as a transport aircraft.

* * *

Dawn was breaking as Carter cycled into the yard at Home Farm. Fiona must have heard the rattle of the bike, as she came to the door of the milking parlour to greet him. Carter took her in his arms and gave her a kiss. She smelt of a mixture of fresh milk and cow dung; a smell Carter was starting to get used to.

Carter felt a stiffness about her and pulled back to give her a long look. He noticed that she looked tired, her eyes red rimmed as though she had been crying.

"How did it go?" She asked, before Carter had time to say anything.

"Fine. I've a feeling we won't be getting a Christmas card from a Lt Kasmire this year. Have you been crying?"

"It's Daddy." She said, her voice breaking. She moved forward into Carter's embrace again, burying her face in his chest. He heard her sobbing. "He was taken to hospital last night."

"Is it bad?"

"I think he's dying. Damn those cigarettes. I hate them. They should be banned."

John Hamilton was suffering from emphysema, a disease of the lungs that the doctors blamed on him smoking. The commandos were the fittest soldiers in Europe, possibly the world, but Carter noticed that even amongst this elite, on stamina training exercises it was the non-smokers that were always the first to cross the finish line. He had always wondered if cigarettes were what was slowing the smokers down. Certainly John Hamilton's doctors were in no doubt about what had caused his illness.

"Is there nothing the doctors can do?" Carter asked.

"Nothing. They can give him pain killers to ease his suffering and oxygen to help him breath, but they told us that it's only a matter of time."

"I'm so sorry."

She looked up into his eyes. "I don't want this distracting you. You need your wits about you. I'll manage."

"Is there any way of getting some extra help?"

"Perhaps. Some Italian PoWs are being allowed out on licence to work, ones that were taken prisoner in Africa. I'll ask if there's one who knows about dairy farming who would like to come and work here. All it needs is someone who can do some heavy lifting, the sort of thing that me and the Land Girls struggle with."

"I'm not sure about letting an Italian on the farm." Carter said, concealing his smile in her hair. "Casanova was Italian, you know."

She thumped him on the chest with her fist, hurting herself more than him. "Gowk[1]! I only have eyes for you, my darling." She went up on tip-toes and kissed him. "Now, I've got fifty cows that need milking, so you go and get some sleep. What time do you want me to wake you?"

"I've got a car coming to take me back to Prestwick at ten."

"I'll wake you at nine thirty then. I assume you will want breakfast."

"Of course, nothing less than the full English."

"You'll get a full Scottish and like it!" She laughed as she went back through the door of the milking parlour.

[1] Gowk – Colloquial Scottish word for a fool.

3 – Fight Night

April drifted into May and the intensity of the training increased, as all the commandos knew it would. Speculation was rife about where they were going. Many of the practice landings took place along the Solway Firth, with its long sandy beaches and the tidal estuary. They were spending more time away than in Troon, much to Fiona and Carter's frustration.

"With beaches like that it must be Denmark, or maybe Holland." Carter heard one trooper say.

"Nah, I reckon it's the big one." His mate had replied. "The German mainland, somewhere around Wilhelmshaven."

Carter kept his own counsel. He had already worked it out. Not the fine detail, of course, nor the precise location. But he knew it would be Northern France. Vantage, the fake general that Warriner had dropped into the lap of the Germans, had let slip that there was to be a major raid which would support his lie about an invasion of France, aimed at drawing German troops away from Russia and Egypt. Carter felt sure that this operation was the one to which Vantage had referred when they went to Jersey to try to rescue him. Or at least, that was what Carter had thought they had been doing. It turned out that they were part of the same deception and the attempted rescue wasn't supposed to succeed.

Word had reached them that 3 Commando, based just along the coast at Largs, were also in intense training and if the rumours were true, other commandos were also working hard in preparation for a major raid. This was the big one, not some flea bite against Holland or Denmark. But Carter didn't care where it was. Nor did he share his opinion. They would be told where they were going when the time was right.

It was at the end of a tiring week of landing exercises along the Cumbrian coast that 15 Commando's commanding officer decided that his men needed some time off. He granted a twenty four hour break before the next series of landings, starting from eighteen hundred hours on the Saturday.

It seemed to Carter that he had only just closed his eyes when the telephone started to ring. At that time of night or, more accurately, the morning it was unlikely to be anyone ordering an extra pint of milk, so Carter climbed from his bed, rubbing his eyes. Out of deference to Mary Hamilton he pulled on his dressing gown and staggered down the stairs in the darkness.

Yawning mightily, he picked up the telephone handset and raised it to his ear. "Home Farm. Steven Carter speaking" He yawned again.

"Steven, is that you?"

Carter's sleep deprived brain decoded the question and the voice it was asked by. "Yes, Sir." He replied to his CO.

"My office. Soon as you can." He was ordered. The phone line went dead, not giving Carter any time to ask questions.

Suddenly he was fully awake. It had to be something important for the CO to be ringing at ... he checked his watch ... two o'clock in the morning. He ran up the stairs, taking them two at a time and began throwing his night clothes off and his uniform on.

"Wha ... What's going on?" Fiona asked, her voice muffled by pillows.

"CO wants me."

"At this time? I thought you were on a stand-down."

"So did I. It must be important or he wouldn't be calling."

"Well, don't wake the whole house on your way out. If I'm not up when you get back, you can make breakfast." She snuggled deeper into the blankets. Carter had a strong feeling that his wife would not only be up when he got back, but the cows would be milked and breakfast would already have been eaten. Besides, woe betide any man that attempted to cook anything in Mary Hamilton's kitchen.

As he cycled along the road to town in the darkness, Carter tried to imagine what might have happened to warrant this summons. Technically they were part of the force defending south west Scotland from invasion, but they weren't the first responders if such a thing were to occur; that duty fell to one of the infantry battalions stationed in the area. Besides, it seemed unlikely that the Germans could have managed to get an invasion fleet into the Firth of Clyde without someone noticing they were on their way. He ruled that out as a possibility.

Which meant it had to be something else. Perhaps one of his men had been injured; or worse. That would result in a phone call, to let him know. But it wouldn't warrant a summons to the CO's office. Which really only left one likely cause. One, or maybe more than one, of his men was in trouble with the police. In which case Carter would be summoned to the CO's office to be ordered to whichever police station the man was being held at, to sort out the mess. It also meant that the incident had to be more than a routine drunk and disorderly. If that were the case the man would be left to cool his heels in a police cell until morning and then Carter would get his orders over the phone.

He steeled himself for the worst.

Arriving outside the former sweet factory, Carter propped his bike against the wall. The sentries on either side of the door shouldered arms and slapped their right hands against their rifle butts in salute. Carter returned the curtesy as he hurried past.

There was very little lighting inside the building, just enough to allow Carter to see where he was going. There were certainly no signs of any sort of military preparations, which confirmed Carter's view that the Ayrshire coast wasn't under threat of imminent attack by the enemy.

The CO's office door stood open, a bright rectangle of light illuminating the corridor. Carter knocked and walked in, came to a halt and saluted as he did so.

It was only then that Carter realised that the CO wasn't alone. Stood to one side was one of the two Provost Sergeants[1], Bill Chitty. His powerful frame dominated any room in which he was present.

Chitty's presence told Carter that his conclusion about one or more of his men being in trouble was the correct one.

"Who is it?" he asked, without any preliminaries.

"Who are *they*, Steven. Three of your men have managed to get themselves arrested in Ayr, for fighting." The CO explained. Ayr was a seaside town popular with young ladies visiting for the weekend from Glasgow and therefore popular with the commandos when they had any time off. It wasn't the first time that a commando had found himself in trouble with the Ayrshire Constabulary while in the town.

"LCpl Green and Troopers Glass and O'Driscoll." Chitty elaborated. "O'Driscoll put a man in hospital."

"I want you to go with Sgt Chitty down to Ayr. Sgt Chitty can do the paperwork to get the three men handed over to us. Then you can take them back to their billets so they can pack their bags. They'll be on the first available train back to their units."

The set of Lt Col Vernon's jaw told Carter that it was pointless trying to argue with him on the issue. Better to wait for him to calm down, then see if he could do anything to save his three men. He doubted he would succeed; men had been RTU'd[2] for far lesser offences.

Carter saluted and marched out of the office, Bill Chitty following close behind.

"Was it a fair fight?" Carter asked as they walked along the corridor.

"Not really. According to the police there were at least six of them. They didn't stand a chance against our men." Carter suppressed a smile. It was an old joke that it needed at least three opponents to beat a commando in a fist fight.

The QM had managed to scrounge up an old Austin 'Tilly', a small utility truck built on a car chassis, that could be used to ferry a handful of troops or a small amount of cargo around the local area. Chitty had drawn the keys and now climbed into the driver's seat, struggling to get his large frame behind the steering wheel. Carter went around to the passenger side and climbed in.

"They probably would have got away with a ticking off and a bill for the damage to the pub. When the police arrived our lads backed off, but one of the Yanks saw a chance and took a cheap shot at

O'Driscoll. O'Driscoll retaliated with a haymaker and broke the man's jaw. There was nothing the police could do; they had to arrest him. Then Green ad Glass started arguing with the police and ended up getting arrested along with O'Driscoll."

"I didn't realise they were fighting the Yanks. I assumed it was a fight between our own blokes. I know that their rivalries can get out of hand sometimes and there's often the odd bit of aggravation that's been carried over from an exercise. And then there's the fights over girls, of course."

"That's the normal pattern of things, but there's been a lot more trouble since the Yanks have moved into Prestwick. Their dollars go a long way over here, they have access to stuff that our lads can only dream of and the girls think they're all Hollywood stars. Our lads don't go into Ayr much, so it hasn't been our problem. Not until tonight anyway. The Yanks usually clash with the Army and RAF based around Ayr. I may have to ask the CO to put the town out of bounds. If your men get RTU'd, some of their troop may decide to go and extract some revenge, which would only make matters worse."

They continued the drive in gloomy silence until they reached Ayr's police station.

Chitty stayed at the front desk and Carter was shown into an interview room. He was joined by his three men a short time later. They stood to attention in front of their officer and he didn't give them permission to stand at ease. They all carried some sort of memento of the fight, a bruise here or a cut there, but nothing serious. Carter glanced at their knuckles, clenched against the seams of their trousers. That was where most of the damage lay, where they had inflicted punishment on their opponents.

"What have you three idiots got yourself into?" Carter barked at them.

"It wasn't our fault, Sir." Green spoke for them, probably by arrangement. They'd had plenty of time to think about what they should say. "The Yanks started it."

"You should know better, Green. You're an NCO now. You should have ordered the other two out of the pub; gone somewhere else."

"It wasn't like that, Sorr. It was ..." O'Driscoll tried to speak.

"Quiet! When I want you to speak, I'll ask you a question." Carter shouted into his face. O'Driscoll visibly flinched under the verbal assault. This was a side of their officer that they had never had the misfortune to see before.

"Tell me what happened, Green."

"Like Paddy said, it was nothing, really. We were in this pub when the Yanks came in. They were friendly at first, we were chatting and getting on fine. Then one of them asked if we were part of the raid on Prestwick, back at the beginning of April. We said we were and we ribbed them a bit about how easy it was to get past their guards. That was when things started to turn a bit nasty. It turned out these particular Yanks had been part of the guard force that night. They'd got all sorts of heat off their CO because we got in. That just made us rib them a bit more. They didn't like that much. Then it started to get physical. Just a bit of pushing and shoving. Nothing serious, but then one of them swung a punch. One of us hit him, I can't remember who ..." Green was obviously lying about that.

"It was me, Sir." Glass owned up.

"OK, it was Danny." Green continued. "Anyway, the Yank went flying and knocked over a table, spilled some drinks, then the other five Yanks piled in. We were doing fine, then the police arrived. I guess the landlord must have called them. We knew we would be in trouble if we kept fighting, so we backed off. But one of them saw a chance and took a swing at Paddy ..."

"The gobshite." O'Driscoll growled. Carter glared at him.

"Paddy acted reflexively and knocked him cold. The police grabbed Paddy by the arm and we tried to tell them that we didn't start the fight, but they arrested us as well. So, we all ended up here."

"Were any Americans arrested?"

"Not by the police. Some of their own MPs turned up about then and I think they rounded the Yanks up and took them away."

"Well, I can tell you, the CO is fuming. You know what his rules are. Anyone who gets himself arrested is out of the commando. I've to take you back to Troon to pack your bags and put you on the next train back to your units, or wherever the hell we can send you that will take you." As they had come from the same unit, Carter knew Green couldn't go back to his battalion of the Huntingdonshire Regiment. They were all now either dead or prisoners of the Japanese. He would be sent to the regimental depot until they could find him a new unit. Given the disgrace of being RTU'd, the regiment would probably palm him off onto one of the reserve battalions, even one of the pioneer units that had been set up to build defensive installations.

All three of them stood ramrod straight, but Carter could tell by their expressions how hard this was hitting them. They were good soldiers and the shame of RTU was something that would be hard to accept. On the one hand he had to be the stern disciplinarian, but on the other he felt sorry for them. He also felt he owed them something. They had all shared adversity and been close to death as a result of operations he had got them into. They had gone to Jersey and then France because he had asked them to, not because the whole commando had been chosen for the raids.

He made up his mind; he would appeal to the CO, see if he could find some way out of this. They would still have to be punished for their transgression, of course, but he might be able to persuade the CO not to RTU them.

"Stand at ease." He said. Their left feet stamped into the hard concrete of the interview room floor. "Look, I'm making no promises, but I'll have a word with the CO. Maybe there's a way out of this."

A look of hope sprang to their faces. Carter had to manage their expectations. "I'll be straight with you. The way the Colonel was when I left him, I doubt very much he'll change his mind. You understand?"

"Yes, Sir." They chorused.

A police sergeant arrived in the interview room. "All done here, Sir. Your men can leave with you."

"There's a Tilly outside." Carter informed them. "Get in the back." Green called them to attention and they saluted, before marching out of the room. Carter turned his attention to the police officer.

"Will there be any charges?" He asked.

"No. The Yanks will deal with their men, which is normal and Sgt Chitty tells me that yours will probably be sent away, so the Inspector thinks that's probably punishment enough. There's a bill to pay for damages to the pub, though."

"Tell the landlord to send it to the CO of 15 Commando. The men will pay it off. It will probably take them till the end of the war." It had been noted before that bills submitted to the Commando for damage to property seemed to bear no relation to the actual amount of damage caused.

Carter apologised to the sergeant for the inconvenience that his men had caused, then went outside to the Tilly. Sgt Chitty was already sitting behind the steering wheel.

Carter sat silent during the return journey, deep in thought.

[1] Provost Sergeant – A Sgt drawn from within the unit to lead its internal police force. Not to be confused with the Royal Military Police. The Provost Sergeant is responsible to the Regimental Sergeant Major for the maintenance of discipline. He is usually assisted by a small force of Regimental Police (RPs) who are also drawn from the unit and who are selected mainly on the basis of their size.

[2] RTU – Returned to unit. The commandos didn't go in for formal disciplinary procedures. If a commando found himself in trouble he was sent back to his originating unit in disgrace. Formal disciplinary action, such as a Court Martial, might still follow if the offence was serious enough. As a threat it was effective. Such was the commandos' pride in their elite status that soldiers would do

anything rather than face such disgrace. It kept them on the straight and narrow. Once they had completed their training, only a handful ever suffered the penalty.

* * *

After breakfasting at Home Farm, Carter cycled back into Troon to talk to the CO. He found Vernon in his office with the Second in Command, Maj Couples, discussing the training plan for the forthcoming week. The CO hardly ever seemed to take any time off, even when he had granted leave to everyone else in the Commando.

"Ah, Steven. Come in." Vernon invited. "I take it your three are on the train back to their units. You'll need to send signals warning them that they're on the way. You'll also need to tell the Adjutant so he can …" Vernon saw that Carter was trying to get a word in, but was too polite to interrupt his CO. He turned to the 2IC. "Could you let me have a few minutes please, Teddy."

"Of course, Sir." He shot Carter a glance that said 'warning', but left the room. The sound of his feet could be heard echoing along the empty corridor.

"I'm not going to change my mind, Steven." The CO said before Carter had time to launch into his appeal. "You know the rules and your men know the rules."

"Sir, I know how you feel about these sorts of incidents, but in this case I think there are extenuating circumstances. My men didn't go looking for trouble."

"Yet it found them anyway."

"I know, Sir, but they were set upon by six American soldiers. It seemed they took exception to the way we bested them by getting into Prestwick so easily. The Americans were embarrassed, but my men weren't the ones that set the challenge."

"Are you saying it's my fault that your men got into trouble?" Vernon sounded incredulous.

"Of course not, Sir. But it's a matter of cause and effect. If we hadn't been sent to test the defences at Prestwick airfield, the Americans wouldn't have felt embarrassed about their failure and my men wouldn't have fallen victim to what amounted to a revenge attack. If anyone was at fault it was me, for coming up with a plan that was good enough for us to succeed. They were a victim of my success."

"Our success." Vernon said.

Yes, thought Carter. Success has a hundred fathers, but failure is always an orphan[1]. Carter thought he saw a twitch of a smile but couldn't be sure. The CO was immensely proud of his unit and had taken great pleasure in getting one over on their American neighbours. Carter saw his chance and took it.

"I was thinking, Sir. If I go and have a chat with the Base Commander at Prestwick, Colonel Shiner, maybe I could find some form of punishment that will satisfy him for the injury suffered by his soldier. At the same time it will make it clear to our own men that bad behaviour won't be tolerated."

"What sort of thing did you have in mind?"

"I don't know yet. It would have to be something fairly public. What's the old saying? 'Not only must Justice be done, it must be seen to done?[2]'"

"I certainly support that view, Steven. So, first of all Green will lose his Lance Corporal's stripe. I expect my NCOs to set an example of good behaviour and Green failed to do that. As for the rest, if you can come up with a proposal that satisfies the Y... the Americans, I'll give it due consideration. But if I don't like it, your men are out."

---

[1] Pedants may think that it is unlikely that Carter would have known this saying, as it was supposedly used for the first time in April 1942 by Count Galeazzo Ciano, Mussolini's son in law. It was popularised by President John F Kennedy when he used it in a speech in 1961 in relation to the Bay of Pigs fiasco. The original may have been said by the Roman writer Tacitus as early as 98 AD, so it is possible that a well-educated man such as Carter might have come across it.

[2] Attributed to Lord Chief Justice Howert who used a similar turn of phrase during an Appeal Court hearing in 1923. His actual words were "justice should not only be done, but should manifestly and undoubtedly be seen to be done." The verdict in the original case was quashed by Lord Howert on the grounds that one of the officials at the court, a Clerk to the Justices, had a connection to the case that could be interpreted as bringing bias to the court, regardless of whether or not it actually had. It was a ground-breaking decision and had far reaching implications for the judicial system with regard to the selection of court officials, magistrates, judges and jurors.

* * *

With three Americans in the office, Carter was feeling decidedly outnumbered when he visited RAF Prestwick the next day. As well as Colonel Shiner there was the unfortunate Lieutenant Kasmire, his face set in a mask of anger. The third officer was introduced as Captain Philo Walton, the officer commanding the security platoon at the airfield.

"Thank you for agreeing to see me, Colonel." Carter opened. "I have come to apologise for my men's behaviour and to see if we can find some way of making recompense for the injury to your man."

"I'm seeing you against my better judgement." Shiner replied. "Not only have I got a man in hospital, but I've got another five under arrest in the guardhouse, all claiming they didn't start the fight."

Carter had decided not to debate the issue of blame with the Americans. If you were to believe the criminals, prisons only contained innocent people, despite the opinions of judges and juries up and down the land. Maybe the Americans had started the fight, but maybe Carter's men had. After all, Green, Glass and O'Driscoll weren't the sort of men who backed away from confrontation; that wasn't the commando way. It was far easier just to accept the blame and try to move on.

"Yes, Sir. I'm not here to make excuses for my men. I'm here to see if we can find some way to make amends."

"What do you have in mind, Lieutenant?"

As Carter had been talking, he had been taking in the décor of the Colonel's office. It was heavy on photographs showing the Colonel as a young man, holding trophies and lined up with team mates. There were several gaudy trophies standing on the top of a book case, not prominent, but, at the same time, hard to miss. An idea struck him.

"Do you have any boxers in your unit, Sir?"

"I guess so. Do you know of any, Philo?" Shiner redirected the question to his subordinate.

"Well, there's Johanson, Sir."

"Oh, yes; Johanson. Any others?"

"There is a boxing club on base. I could have a look and see if any of them are any good."

"What are you thinking, Carter?" The Colonel returned his attention to the British officer.

"Sir, your men seem a bit raw about my me and my men having managed to break in to your base a few weeks ago. If we were to organise a boxing match, it would give your men a chance to get their own back, but under controlled conditions. We would put up Green, Glass and O'Driscoll, the three men that got into the fight on Saturday night. You put up your best three men against them."

A smile spread across Shiner's face. The idea appealed to him. "Well, I have to say I'm a sports fan myself. I played some college football when I was younger. I even played at The Point[1]" He waved his hand nonchalantly towards the photographs, but just managed to avoid pointing at the trophies. "What do you two think, Philo?"

"Well, I'm sure Johanson would fancy the prospect."

"I have to warn you that Johanson was an up and coming boxer before the war. He had a couple of pro fights and won them. Would your men want to risk the sort of beating they might get from someone like him?"

"My men have little choice in the matter. If they want to avoid being kicked out of the commandos, they'll have to go along with anything my CO and I come up with."

"You intend doing that? Kicking them out of the commandos?"

"That's normal for us, for this sort of indiscipline."

"That would be a terrible waste of trained manpower, but that's your call, not mine. What do you think, Kasmire?"

"I like the idea. I can think of a couple of men who would fancy their chances one on one with the Limeys. But I'd like to suggest something else." A wolfish smile spread across his face.

"Go ahead." Shiner gave his permission.

"The big fight is me against Lt Carter here."

"I don't know about that." Shiner could see some of the issues it might raise. "Do officers' normally go in for that sort of thing in the British Army?"

"I can't say I've heard of it happening before. But the commandos are different. We never ask our men to do something we're not prepared to do ourselves. We certainly boxed during our training at Achnacarry. If Lt Kasmire wants to try himself out against me, I'll be happy to give him his chance."

Carter took a better look at Kasmire. He was young and had an athletic look about him. His height and build were similar to Carter's, but he knew he had the edge when it came to fitness. But they would be fighting under amateur rules, which meant only three rounds, so fitness might not play such a big part in the contest. Kasmire looked as though he might be useful in a fight.

But this wasn't just a fight. One on one Carter was pretty sure he could take Kasmire using the unarmed combat techniques he had been taught. But this was a boxing match and required particular skills. He had boxed a little at school but had never been good at it. He had also boxed a few rounds at Achnacarry; all the commandos had, but he'd had no formal training there. But he could stand in a boxing ring and take a punch. If Kasmire beat him then so be it. It might actually be diplomatic of him to allow Kasmire the victory. It would be meaningless in real terms and might serve to reduce the tensions between the two units.

There was no doubt there were tensions and it wasn't just about Carter's test of the defences at the airfield. The Americans were having to suffer unfair comments about being late into the war 'just like last time'. The soldiers weren't responsible for their government's foreign policy and there were many who had enlisted in the Canadian armed forces so that they could get into the war. There were three entire RAF squadrons, the Eagle squadrons, made up of Americans who had claimed British or Canadian citizenship so that they could fight, though many were transferring back to American command now that their country had entered the war.

There was also a lot of friction between British servicemen and the Americans, who the British saw as trying to take 'their' women, using nylons, chocolate and good dentistry to attract them.

"It has to be approved by my CO, though Sir." Carter added. "He might not want to risk my health so close to an operation. But I'm up for it if he approves the fight."

"Very good. In that case I agree. Philo here will act as your contact for our end of things. We'll also claim home advantage. We can use our big hanger to stage the fight. I'm sure all my men will want to see it, so we'll need somewhere big."

[1] The Point – West Point. Its official title is the United Sates Military Academy, the training school for professional officers in the United States Army. It is the equivalent of the Sandhurst Military Academy in Britain. It is located on the Hudson River, north of the city of New York, adjacent to the small town of Highland Falls.

* * *

Much to Carter's surprise Lt Col Vernon was very much in favour of the idea; excluding Carter's part in it. "So you think they'll win?" He asked.

"They seem quite confidant about their man Johanson, who's an ex-pro. As for the others, it depends who they find. Normally I'd back our men against anyone other than another commando, but this isn't a fight, it's a boxing match. Besides, the object isn't for our men to win. It's about the Americans getting a chance to see our boys being knocked around the boxing ring, so they'll feel better and leave our men alone when they're out and about."

"You'd order them to lose?"

"I couldn't do that, Sir. But I'd make it clear that I wouldn't be unhappy if they did lose."

"I don't think I could let you fight though, Steven."

"Why not, Sir? I know it doesn't quite fit with the 'officer and a gentleman' image, but we're at war and in war strange things happen."

"What happens if you get seriously injured? I can afford to lose a couple of troopers in a good cause, but not an officer."

"If I lose, you could always offer Lt Kasmire my post."

Vernon laughed and Carter knew he had won the argument. The CO was always the first to see the bright side of any situation, which was probably why he had been given his command in the first place. "OK, Steven. Make the arrangements. Sgt Chitty used to be a boxer, so he can manage our team. Actually, it's an opportunity to build bridges with the local dignitaries as well. We'll invite some of them along to watch."

With that the matter was closed and they got back to training again. The 2IC provided them with a date when the event could take place, but Carter noticed that he didn't look any further through his diary than the end of May.

Carter decided that Fiona didn't need to know that he would be taking an active part in the boxing. He didn't want to deceive his new wife, but he knew what her reaction was likely to be.

The discussion with Green, Glass and O'Driscoll was a short one. Box against the Americans or go back to your billets and collect your kit and be on the next train out of Troon. Just as Carter had anticipated, they didn't argue.

* * *

The big aircraft hanger had been converted into a boxing arena for the evening. In the centre was a regulation sized ring borrowed from a boxing club in Glasgow that had produced quite a few champions.

The judges for the night were all coaches at the same club. Arranged around the three sides of the central ring were long benches on which the soldiers from the base were sat. On the remaining side were chairs for the officers and dignitaries; the mayors of local towns, the aldermen, the business men and officers from other units. Vernon had decided that it probably wasn't a good idea for his men to attend, just in case things got heated. No one below the rank of Sergeant would be present from the commando.

Before the match the Americans had hosted a dinner for the commando officers and their guests. Carter had to decline the hospitality. He wasn't certain, but he was pretty sure that fighting on a full stomach wasn't a good idea; or was that just swimming? Mary Hamilton had made him up some sandwiches 'for the road' as she put it when Carter had explained he wouldn't be getting anything to eat during the 'training exercise' in which he was participating.

There were no formal changing rooms available in the hanger, but there was a locker room where the mechanics kept their personal possessions. With a couple of blankets hung on a rope along the middle to partition it, it served both of the four man teams. Bill Chitty went from one to the next binding their hands with bandages before putting on their gloves and tying them securely, These were also borrowed from the Glasgow boxing club. The Americans had made their own arrangements. The men bounced up and down on their toes, shadow boxing, trying to keep their nervousness hidden.

In between their training for their operation, Chitty had given all of them some lessons in the fundamentals of protecting themselves and throwing punches, but Carter was under no illusions about how low his skill levels were. He wondered if Kasmire had ever fought before, or if their former pro, Johanson, had provided any lessons.

The Master of Ceremonies for the evening was Philo Walters and he came in to see if they were ready. From the hanger they could hear the sound of an electronically amplified voice, though not the words. Every few seconds there would be laughter and applause.

"One of our guys used to be a comedian in vaudeville." Walton explained. "He's doing his act for the men, just to get them in the mood. He wanted us to hire some dancing girls as well, but the Base Commander wasn't too keen on that idea. He thought it would send out the wrong message about British women."

He led the way into the hanger, where space had been left for the boxers to stand behind the officers. They positioned themselves in their teams, on opposite sides of the locker room door. Carter took the opportunity to eye up the opposition.

There was no missing Johanson. He wasn't big, probably no more than a middleweight, but he had an aura of power about him. He was wearing proper boxing shorts with a broad band around the waist, whereas everyone else was wearing ordinary sports shorts; Carter's happened to be his rugby shorts. They also all wore PT vests, with their feet clad in plimsoles. Again, Johanson was different. He wore proper boxer's ankle length boots. He was also bare chested, marking him out as a professional amongst amateurs. The Americans were muscular, but Carter knew that didn't mean anything. All three of his men, and Carter himself for that matter, could carry an eighty pound pack for ten miles and still be fresh enough to tackle an assault course at the end of it.

The comedian did a couple more jokes in the vein of 'my wife's so ugly' and then brought his act to an end to raucous applause. Although the Americans rationed alcohol on their bases, Carter suspected that illicit supplies had been circulating. Climbing out of the ring the comedian was replaced by Capt Walton, who picked up the microphone to make the announcements.

"Ladies and gentlemen." He called, extending the vowels in 'ladies' for several seconds. There were some hoots and cat calls as there were no women present, but that didn't deter Philo Walton.

"We have on the bill tonight four rounds of boxing. The finest boxers in the American armed forces will take on four boxers from the British commandos." There was booing in response to that, but it was good natured.

"Each bout will consist of three rounds, with three minutes each round. The contest will be settled on a knock out, a judges' decision or the referee may stop the fight. Your judges for tonight are Tam

Bonner." He paused and Mr Bonner got to his feet and took a short bow. "Eric Stewart" pause for another bow "and Callum Reilly."

"They're all Limeys." A voice protested from the crowd. "They'll be biased against our guys." This brought boos from the crowd.

Tam Bonner got to his feet and shouted back. "All the commandos are Sassenachs[1] and if y' ken anything aboot the Scots and the English, y'll ken that we'll never favour the English over anyone else. They'd have a better chance if they were German."

This brought some uncertain laughs from the British officers and NCOs and more cheers from the Americans. So much for neutral judges, Carter thought.

"Your referee for tonight is a former Scottish champion boxer, Sandy Hunter." This brought some cheers from the local dignitaries. Hunter had been a prominent professional boxer in the 1920s, but judging from the silence from the American benches, his fame had never spread beyond the shores of Scotland.

"Your first contest tonight will be between, in the blue corner, Sgt Hank Langdon, fighting out of St Louis, Missouri, weighing in at one hundred and forty five pounds." There was lengthy applause, whistling and the stamping of feet as Langdon made his way down to centre of the hanger and climbed into the ring. He shadow boxed for a few seconds, until the applause started to fade, then retired to his corner where his seconds were waiting to pour water into his mouth and flap a towel in front of his face, even though he hadn't done anything to get himself overheated.

"And in the red corner, Trooper Danny Glass, fighting out of Acton, London, England, weighing in at one hundred and two pounds."

The weight difference was stark, a featherweight fighting a lightweight[2], but it didn't stop the Americans booing Glass for several seconds, despite him being the underdog.

Glass looked as if he didn't have a care in the world. He had been no stranger to fights in his youth and was confident that he could hold his own. At Achnacarry he had a been a regular in the ad hoc matches that were arranged to keep the men occupied at the weekends and other breaks in training. He may not have had any formal training, other than that recently provided by Bill Chitty, but he had some raw talent. His opponent was well muscled, but the muscles looked as though they were the product of gym training rather than hard work; but strength was strength, even if it didn't provide stamina.

The referee called the two boxers into the centre of the ring and had the traditional words with them about their conduct during the fight. They touched gloves and retired into their corners, waiting for the bell.

With the sound of the bell, the noise levels rose dramatically, the Americans cheering of their champion drowning out the much smaller British contingent. Langdon may have been strong, but he wasn't a skilful boxer. Glass was able to keep him at bay while landing the odd blow. The first two rounds were lacking in major incident, Glass keeping his guard up and taking advantage of the openings offered by the American's wilder attempts to land a punch.

By half way through the third round it was evident that the American was tiring. His guard was getting lower and lower, leaving openings that Glass was able to attack. Following a series of rapid lefts and rights from Glass, Langdon went down and it took a count of eight from the referee before he was back on his feet. The Americans booed and some got their feet, gesticulating wildly. Whether they were booing their own man or Glass, Carter couldn't tell.

Time was running out and it was clear that Glass would get a points decision. Surely even the most biased judge couldn't award the fight to the American. Then the unlikely happened. Glass dropped his guard a fraction and the American launched a left jab directly at his head. Glass went down and stayed down. As the referee shouted "ten", the bell rang and the occupants of the hanger went wild with delight.

Carter was dumbfounded. He was sure that the punch had barely touched Glass; it had been a glancing blow at best.

After the bell Glass got groggily to his feet, aided by Bill Chitty and his cornerman, another commando from 4 Troop. Glass remained in the ring until the result had been officially announced by Philo Walton, then was helped through the ropes and down the aisle towards the locker room. As he passed Carter he turned to look at him and gave a broad smile and a slow wink.

When calm had been restored, Walton introduced the second bout. "In the blue corner, fighting out of Omaha, Nebraska, weighing in at one hundred and forty nine and one half pounds, Corporal "Dutch" van der Fleet.

The American was tall and skinny, his arms and legs seemingly sticking out at odd angles. But his height and the length of his limbs would give him a formidable reach. The only hope for his opponent would be to get inside his guard and attack his body. His height also gave him additional weight, which would help him in the clinches.

The way that the American capered around the ring showed that he thought himself to be a bit of a funny man. He held his hands above his head in a classic boxer's clinch and danced around, shuffling his feet rapidly back and forth in a parody of speedy footwork. The crowd loved it and it only encouraged Van Der Fleet to greater efforts. Walton had to grab his arm and send him to his corner before he would stop and even there he continued to wave his arms around.

"And in the red corner, fighting out of Deptford, London, England, weighing in at one hundred and forty one pounds, Trooper Archibald "The Prof" Green."

Green looked tiny alongside his opponent, but the power in his body was noticeable. While the American was bony, Green had solid slabs of muscle visible, even through his army issue PT vest.

The bell rang on what would turn out to be the shortest bout of the evening. As Carter had suspected, the American was content to keep his distance and aim jabs with his long arms. Green had no problem blocking them, the distance from which they were launched provided time for them to be anticipated, but Green was struggling to get any blows of his own on target.

Playing to the crowd, the American dropped his guard and beckoned Green forward. It was the wrong thing to do. Green stepped forward, getting inside the American's arms and started pummelling his body. The American had no option but to retreat. He found himself against the ropes and it was only the intervention of the referee that stopped Green from landing a match finishing blow. Green backed off at the referee's insistence. The American used his long legs to press himself hard back against the ropes, increasing their tension and using them to launch himself back into the centre of the ring where Green was waiting. Whether the American tripped over his own feet of whether he had a loose shoelace, Carter never discovered. The American fell forward and the point of his chin landed forcefully on the top of Green's glove.

As a child Carter had been told that there was a nerve that ran through the cleft of the chin that, if hit exactly in the right place, could render a person unconscious immediately. He had never believed it, until that moment. Van Der Fleet fell to the floor with a sickening thud and lay still, his arms and legs sprawled out around him. It didn't take a count of ten for the crowd to know that he wouldn't be getting up.

The mood of the crowd turned ugly and Green had to be escorted from the hanger by a bodyguard of American troops in order to avoid being set upon by the crowd. It was unjust, as the knock-out blow hadn't been Green's fault.

One bout each, but Carter was up next. It had been decided that the fight with the former professional, Johanson, should be top of the bill. Carter was happy to form part of the under card.

He and Kasmire stood side by side, half way along the aisle, waiting for their introductions. As with the others, the American would be introduced first.

"In the blue corner, fighting out of Attica, New York state, weighing in at one hindred and forty four pounds, Lieutenant Kas, "The Killer" Kasmire." The crowd went wild and Carter suspected that it was partly at the prospect of seeing one of their officers getting hit. Carter had had time to take a good look at his opponent.

He was solid looking but didn't look particularly strong. The smell of tobacco smoke from him also told Carter that his stamina levels might be affected. Whether or not he had any skill as a boxer, Carter had no idea. But it was Kasmire that had issued the challenge and Carter doubted he would have done that unless he had thought he could win.

"And in the red corner, fighting out of Spalding, Lincolnshire, England, weighing in at one hundred and forty nine pounds, Lieutenant Steven "Lucky" Carter."

Carter wondered who had told Walton about his nickname. It wasn't in the information that he had provided Walton with before that evening. Carter climbed into the ring and took the few short steps to the centre, to stand to Walton's left. The MC left and was replaced by the referee. They turned to face him, Carter fixing his opponent with his eyes, as he had seen the professionals doing in films. "Establish mental dominance" Chitty had advised him. Carter hoped that it would be enough, because if he had to win this fight with his boxing skill, it probably wouldn't go well for him.

But he wasn't there to win. He was there to put on a good show, that was all. If Kasmire won, it wouldn't count for anything meaningful. He had considered throwing the fight completely, as Glass seemed to have done, but couldn't bring himself to do it. he was a commando and they never gave in on anything. It was in their blood to win.

"Right, lads." The referee was speaking. "I wan' a good clean fight. Protect yoursel's at all times. No hittin' below the belt, no gougin' and no hittin' your opponent when he's down. Obey my instructions and stop fightin' when the bell sounds. OK?"

Carter nodded, as did Kasmire. "Now, touch gloves and go back to your corner, come out fighting when the bell rings."

They touched gloves, Kasmire breaking eye contact before Carter. Carter turned and walked back to his corner.

"You ready for this, Sir?" Chitty asked.

"As ready as I'll ever be."

"Remember, keep your guard up and don't get lured into clinches."

The bell sounded and Carter turned. Kasmire was already skipping into the centre of the ring. Carter raised his guard, the smell of leather and stale liniment strong in his nostrils. Carter went up onto his toes and bounced forward to meet his opponent.

Deciding that attack was the best form of defence, Kasmire came at Carter with a flurry of jabs and hooks. Carter fended them off, taking the blows on his wrists and upper arms. The solid mass of his bicep muscles must have jarred Kasmire's fists, because he backed off with a puzzled look on his face. Carter took the opportunity to launch a left jab at Kasmire's face, but he was quick enough to get his guard back up and the other boxer's gloves absorbed the blow.

Kasmire went at Carter again but the commando officer was content to let the American tire himself against his solid defence. In the background Carter started to sense that the crowd were getting restless, this wasn't what they wanted nor expected. They wanted to see the two officers slug it out, trading blows to the head and body. Neither boxer was about to let that happen.

By the end of the first round Carter had some pain in his upper arms, partly from the blows that had landed on them but mainly from the effort of keeping his guard up. Of the two, Kasmire was breathing more heavily as he returned to his corner. Carter's plan to tire him out seemed to be working.

"That was good, Sir." Chitty said pouring water into Carter's mouth as the other cornerman flapped a towel in front of the officer's face. "Just keep your guard up and you'll get home to your wife without so much as a bruise. Now, this round he'll start to get tired. His guard will drop and that's when you strike. Got it?"

It was no more than Carter already knew, but the Sergeant was just trying to be helpful. Carter nodded his head. The bell rang and Carter got to his feet, returning to the centre of the ring as he put his guard up.

Kasmire tried his flurry of combination punches again but got no better result than in the first round. Carter held the centre, taking the blows on his upper arms once again. As he withdrew, Kasmire let his guard down a fraction and Carter swung a right hook at the side of his head. The blow was poorly aimed and skimmed off across his short cut hair, deflecting harmlessly upwards, but it gave Kasmire a warning. He took a step backwards, yielding the centre ground to his opponent. Dodging left and right Kasmire looked for an opening in Carter's guard. Realising that he wasn't going to find one, he ducked his head down behind his gloves and sought to get under Carter's guard instead. He loosed a couple of jabs at Carter's stomach, then a hook to his ribs.

Carter felt the blows land, but they didn't cause him any real injury. Coming in from short range they had little power when they hit and Carter's stomach was protected by layers of muscle that were hidden by his vest.

But in lowering his head, Kasmire had exposed the sides and Carter was able to get a couple of hooks to land, but like Kasmire's offensive, the short range robbed them of their potency.

The two boxers drew apart, Kasmire almost against the ropes while Carter still held the centre of the ring. Carter looked into the eyes of his opponent. There was no fear there, but there was a degree of cunning. Kasmire was about to try something; but what?

It didn't take long to find out. Kasmire's hands dropped away from his face, inviting Carter to strike him. Carter accepted the invite, but when his jab reached the place where the American's head had been, it only found empty space. Kasmire had leaned back against the ropes, letting them support him as Carter's left fist flew past his head. It created an opening for Kasmire's right and he swung a hook into the side of Carter's head.

Lights exploded behind Carter's eyes as the punch landed with some force. Carter staggered away, vaguely recognising the sound of cheering as his befuddled brain fought to recover. Two more blows landed, one on the left of Carter's head and then a second in the middle of his face. Carter tasted blood as it trickled down his throat from his nose. Struggling to get his guard back up, Carter retreated as more blows reigned in at him. They were wild, Kasmire was getting carried away by his success and not taking proper aim.

Carter's vision cleared and he saw Kasmire's big gloved fist coming at the side of his head again. He leant away from it and jabbed with his own left, the two arms sliding past each other. With Carter's on the inside he made contact with Kasmire's face, while the American's own glove slid past Carter's head. Carter's blow must have made a solid contact, because he staggered away. Carter followed the jab with a right hook and felt that connect as well. Kasmire dropped to one knee, shaking his head, trying to clear his senses. The referee's arm went out to prevent Carter from attacking again and he was ordered into a neutral corner as the referee began to count.

The count reached five before Kasmire struggled to his feet and the referee continued as far as eight before he signalled that the boxers could close on each other again.

Carter could see that Kasmire's knees were still wobbly. This was the time to go in and finish the American off.

But it was also the time for the bell to ring and it was with some relief that Kasmire lurched back to his corner.

"You Ok, Sir?" Chitty's face was full of concern. "He got you a couple of good ones there."

"Yeah, I think so. I tasted blood. Am I bleeding?"

"A small trickle, Sir. Nothing to worry about." To confirm his diagnosis, Chitty dabbed at Carter's nose and top lip with a towel and showed him the result. Just a smear of blood was visible. He poured water into Carter's mouth and the officer swilled it round his mouth before directing a red tinged stream into the bucket on the floor.

"OK, Sir. He's almost out on his feet. Time to put him on his arse." Chitty said as the bell sounded to signal the start of the final round.

If he had been hurt in the previous round, Kasmire showed no sign of it now. He was bouncing on the balls of his feet in the centre of the ring as Carter returned to the fight. But Kasmire's fatigue was obvious. The blows that he launched on Carter lacked power and were easily fended off. As he withdrew after his initial attack Carter saw that the American's hands were lower, exposing the upper half of his face. Carter jabbed, his fist skimming over the top of the American's glove. It was enough to deflect the jab upwards, allowing it to slide over the top of Kasmire's head. But it also warned the American to restore his guard.

They circled each other, each seeking a fresh opening. Carter let fly with a couple of ineffectual hooks at Kasmire's upper body, which landed on the American's arms, doing no real damage. Kasmire retaliated with a couple of jabs that bounced off Carter's gloves. But the American was tiring. His feet were leaden, hardly lifting off the canvass as the two of them paced around each other. Kasmire's next punch was so slow that Carter had time not only to dodge it, but also to return a jab through the open guard to strike Kasmire on the face. It wasn't a hard blow, but it sent the American back a step. Carter saw his opening and slammed a jab-hook combination into the American's head.

Kasmire went down on his knees again and Carter backed off without being told. In terms of points, Carter knew he had just won the round. He heard the sound of booing from the crowd. They knew the American had probably just lost the fight.

As Kasmire got to his feet once again, after a count of seven, the bell sounded the end of the fight. Carter returned to his corner to receive hearty slaps on his back from his corner team. "Well done Sir. You got him in the end."

"It depends on the judges." Carter responded, as Chitty wiped sweat from his face.

"Yeah, well, if the judges are honest you'll be awarded the win."

Walton was back in the centre of the ring, microphone in hand. The bell clattered and the two boxers returned to the centre to stand either side of the referee. Carter felt the man take his right wrist in a firm grip, ready to raise it aloft when the result was announced.

"Ladies and gentlemen." Walton shouted, once again elongating the a and the e in ladies. "The judges have made their decision.

Judge number one awards two rounds to Lieutenant Kasmire and one round to Lieutenant Carter." Walton paused to wait while the cheering died down. That would be Tam Bonner, who had made his dislike of the English clear at the start of the evening. "Judge two awards one round to Lieutenant Kasmire and two rounds to Lieutenant Carter." This time Walton had to wait for the booing to subside. "Judge three awards one round to "Lieutenant Kasmire, one round to Lieutenant Carter and one round tied." The crowd couldn't make up its mind about that one. Half of them cheered while the other half booed. "With the judges decision tied, that leaves the final decision in the hands of your referee, Sandy Hunter."

Carter felt his wrist jerk as the referee started to lift his arm. But Hunter must have realised where he was and how unpopular his decision might be and the wrist was lowered back down before it had barely even moved. Instead Carter saw Kasmire's hand raised aloft as the crowd started cheering once again.

Feeling cheated, Carter was about to protest the result, then changed his mind. The objective of the evening wasn't for the British boxers to win. It was to make the Americans feel better about having lost to the commandos on their previous meeting. His personal result didn't matter, there would be no reports of the contests in the national press and in a few weeks he might be dead anyway. There were more important things in life than the outcome of this match. Things like how he was going to explain to his wife how he had got the swelling that he could feel on the side of his face.

Carter climbed out of the ring and headed back towards the locker room to get changed. That was where he was when Kasmire returned after taking his plaudits from the delighted Americans.

The American appeared between two of the blankets, his right hand extended. "No hard feelings?" Kasmire said.

Carter took the hand and shook it. "No hard feelings. You fought well."

"Look, I know the result wasn't the right one. I was pretty much done in when the final bell went. I reckon you could have knocked me over with a feather if there had been enough time left."

"It doesn't matter. You boxed well. The result's been announced, so that's what the men out there will take back to their barracks with them tonight."

"I've got a bottle of good Scotch whisky back in my room. Fancy a shot when this is over?"

"That would be nice, thank you."

The American's words had sounded sincere. Whatever had been itching at Kasmire to make him want to fight Carter, it had obviously been cured by his experience in the ring.

As Carter left the locker room he was approached by a diminutive soldier wearing the single stripe of a Private First Class. "Permission to speak, Sir." The soldier said as he saluted.

"Certainly." Carter replied.

"I was in the pub that night. The one when the fight happened."

"So you saw what happened."

"Yeah, it was my buddies who started it. I just wanted you to know that."

"What actually happened?"

"My buddies were still sore about that raid. Well, I call them my buddies, but I don't work with them. They've sort of taken me under their wing. Anyhow, they thought that Lt Kasmire hadn't done a very good job. They couldn't do anything about the Lieutenant being wrong, but when they saw your men in the pub, they thought they could get some satisfaction that way. I don't think they intended to start a fight, but they did anyway. It was certainly one of our guys that threw the first punch. I think that if the police hadn't turned up, your guys would have fought ours to a standstill. Your boys certainly wouldn't have lost the fight. Hanratty was an idiot, trying to get one final punch in. He deserved what he got."

"Well, thank you for telling me all that."

"I told you because I was hoping you could get this last fight stopped. It doesn't seem fair that your man is going to take one hell of a beating from Johanson."

"You're sure of that?"

"Oh yeah. I'm sure. On the ship coming over, Johanson took on one of the sailors. He was a big guy, much bigger than your man, also an ex-pro boxer. Johanson put him in the sick bay with multiple bones broken. OK, it was bare knuckle, not like tonight, but Johanson is an animal, Sir. He'll hurt your man for the fun of it and he doesn't deserve it."

"Thank you for your concern, but I think it's too late to get the fight stopped, even if I wanted to. I made a deal with your Base Commander and I don't think he's going to want to disappoint all those men out there by cancelling the big fight of the night."

"But your man …"

"Will have to take his chances. Thank you for trying though, Private. When your base doctor has finished patching O'Driscoll up after the fight, you can take him some grapes."

"I think the only thing he'll be able to eat is soup, sucked through a straw, Sir."

Carter chuckled. "OK. You go back and enjoy the fight now. By the way, did you get involved in the fight?"

"Look at the size of me, Sir. I'm not exactly built for fighting. I found the biggest thing I could hide behind and stayed there till the cops arrived."

"What happens if you ever have to face the Germans?"

"I'm an aircraft mechanic, Sir. The day America declared war I volunteered for the Air Corps so that I wouldn't ever have to face the Germans or the Japanese. I'm happy to let the fly boys do that. Let's just hope the Krauts never turn up in this neck of the woods. We all fight the war in our own way, Sir."

The PFC saluted again and went ahead of Carter back into the hanger where there was an expectant buzz of conversation as the audience waited for the start of the final bout. A soldier in uniform was making a good effort at singing one of the dance numbers that were popular with the Americans and were starting to gain in popularity with the British. As the song came to an end Captain Walton climbed through the ropes and took the microphone from him.

"Let's hear it one more time for Corporal Randy Buchanan." He gestured towards the place in the audience where the singer was just reclaiming his seat. The soldier stood and waved, then sat down as Walton started to talk once again.

"Now we come to the final bout of the evening."

There was a huge outbreak of cheering. "In the blue corner, fighting out of Chicago, Illinois, weighing in at one hundred and eighty two pounds, it's Jurgen, the Blond Bombshell, Johanson." The boxer climbed through the ropes and took centre stage, shadow boxing as the crowd stood, whooping and cheering their champion. His chest was bare above the broad waistband of his boxing shorts, revealing waves of muscle like the ribs of a washboard. His broad chest was covered in solid slabs of muscle and his bulging biceps moved like a couple of cars trying to reverse around each other. Carter tried to identify a single part of the man that wasn't covered in a thick layer of muscle, but failed. His head was square in shape, handsome, but the good looks were marred by a broken nose. There was also scar tissue across his brow. He hadn't had it all his own way in previous fights, Carter thought. As well as his muscled body, the boxer was also tall. He would dwarf O'Driscoll.

"In the red corner, fighting out of Westport, County Mayo, Ireland, weighing in at one hundred and fifty two pounds, it's Padraigh, Paddy O'Driscoll[3]."

The difference in their size wasn't quite in the same class as David and Goliath, but it was significant. On every dimension Johanson was bigger than O'Driscoll. The Irishman didn't seem at all bothered and bounced around the ring, shadow boxing as though he was in a gymnasium.

The referee called the two boxers together. Johanson glowered at O'Driscoll in a way that Carter thought might cause O'Driscoll to melt under the fury, but again he seemed unaffected, his habitual good natured grin on his face.

Carter crept forward to grab Chitty's arm. "If it looks like he's taking too much punishment, throw in the towel quickly."

"No problem, Sir. I even brought a special towel for the job." Chitty grinned, pointing to a clean unused one laying on top of his cornerman's kit.

The two boxers were sent back to their corners to wait for the bell. The noise rose to fever pitch as the mainly American audience bayed for O'Driscoll's blood.

The bell sounded and Johanson was quickly into the centre of the ring, his guard high but loose. O'Driscoll didn't bother to face off with him, instead he danced around the American forcing him to turn and change direction in seemingly random patterns. It was O'Driscoll who attempted the first blow, landing a jab on the American's gloves. He retreated quickly, anticipating the counter attack that followed. He wasn't disappointed, the Americans fists blurred into action, fast combinations of lefts and rights. But hardly any landed and those that did lacked enough power to break through O'Driscoll guard.

It couldn't last, of course. Carter knew that; the whole crowd knew that. Johanson was big, but he wasn't stupid. He watched O'Driscoll, taking note of the pattern of his attacks and retreats, which way he skipped after throwing a punch. A right hook from O'Driscoll opened up a gap in his armour, he skipped to the right as he had when throwing other right handed punches and Johanson sent a massive left hook through the gap in O'Driscoll's guard to land on the right hand side of the Irishman's head.

O'Driscoll immediately recoiled from the pain of the blow. His legs looked a bit wobbly and he had to place both his hands in front of his face to fend off the follow-up blows that Johanson rained down on him. He eventually retreated so far that he was leaning against the ropes and the referee stepped in to prevent him from being tipped over the top rope and into the crowd.

The respite was short lived. As O'Driscoll levered himself off the ropes Johanson was on him again, letting left and right hands fly. The bell sounded the end of the round, but still Johnason continued to pour the punches in against O'Driscoll's head and arms. Only the referee's intervention stopped the attack.

As Johanson returned to his corner the referee followed and issued a warning about obeying the bell and threatened to disqualify the American if he contravened again. Johanson gave a knowing smile. He had done what he had set out to do, so he didn't need to do it again.

But his actions seemed to have turned some of the crowd against Johanson. The cheers weren't as loud as they had been and some of the audience were standing up, conducting a heated debate with neighbours over what had just happened. Everyone loves a winner, or so it is said, but the Americans had a sense of fair play as well and some in the audience considered Johanson's actions to have crossed the line.

In his corner, Carter could see that O'Driscoll was bleeding from a cut above his eye, which Chitty was trying to stem. There was also visible bruising starting to show on O'Driscoll left cheek, the only one that Carter could see from his seat. If he took a similar beating in the second round, Carter doubted that there would be a third.

The opening of the second round was similar to the first, with O'Driscoll dancing around his heavier opponent, looking for an opening once again. Johanson dropped his guard, shouting at his opponent to stop fooling around. O'Driscoll did as he was bid, launching a jab from distance to land in the middle of Johanson's face. It sent the big man staggering back a couple of paces, but he recovered quickly. The successful punch angered the big man and he launched a frenzied attack on O'Driscoll, beating him back onto the ropes once again. As the referee tried to intervene Johanson dropped his right hand and threw a punch into O'Driscoll groin. The crowd gasped in horror. It was the worst possible offence for a boxer to commit. The cat-calling against Johanson increased, with his supporters falling silent.

The referee sent Johanson to a neutral corner while he checked that O'Driscoll wasn't too injured to continue, but he didn't start a count. Happy that no serious damage had been done, Sandy Hunter crossed the ring and gave Johanson another stern warning. It was obvious to all that the big American was ignoring the telling off. He didn't take his eyes off O'Driscoll for a second.

Once again, the respite gave O'Driscoll the chance to recover, the clock hadn't even been stopped while the referee had dealt with the incident. Once again O'Driscoll bounced around his bigger opponent, seeking an opening, jabbing at the least hint of a gap, but the bigger boxer wasn't being punished in the slightest and when the bell went he ambled back to his corner as fresh as he had been at the start of the round.

In O'Driscoll's corner an argument seemed to develop as Chitty advised O'Driscoll and the Irishman disputed the instructions he was receiving. Carter suspected that Chitty wanted to stop the fight before any real damage was done, but O'Driscoll wasn't having it. So much time was spent that there was barely enough left to treat O'Driscoll's new injuries before the bell sounded once again.

As O'Driscoll went to start his circular dance once again, Johanson pre-empted it by cutting his opponent off and trapping him a neutral corner. Carefully, the American made sure not push the Irishman too far in, which might lead to the referee coming to his assistance, but there was no escape. Every time O'Driscoll tried to escape to his left, a right hook sent him staggering back into the corner; an attempt to go right resulted in the same treatment from Johanson's left hand.

Bobbing to either side, O'Driscoll was able to prevent many of the direct punches from making a solid connection, but they were sliding off his ribs, arms and head. Then Johanson played his sucker move. He took two steps backwards, at the same time dropping his guard as though offering O'Driscoll a way out. O'Driscoll fell for it. he dropped his own guard momentarily and Johanson launched a right uppercut that seemed to lift O'Driscoll off his feet. If it had, he didn't stay airborne for long. He crashed to the canvass and lay still.

Johanson danced into the neutral corner on the opposite side of the ring, clasping his hands above his head, sure that the fight was his.

The referee started his count, making it a slow one, giving O'Driscoll every chance to regain his feet. At six O'Driscoll sat up. At seven he was on one knee. At eight he levered himself upright. The referee went on to nine as O'Driscoll took his guard in the centre of the ring.

But Chitty had seen enough. A pristine white towel flew over the ropes from the red corner and landed half way between it and O'Driscoll. The referee was just about to react to end the fight, when O'Driscoll quickly bent over, pinned the towel between his gloved hands and picked it up. He took it to the side ropes, furthest away from the still capering Johanson and dropped it over the side. The crowd went wild, cheering and whistling this act of defiance.

As O'Driscoll returned to the centre of the ring once again, the referee crossed to him and they had a brief conversation. Even at the ringside no one would have been able to hear what was said, the noise from the crowd was so loud. But the referee was asking questions and O'Driscoll was answering, nodding his head vigorously in reply.

The referee decided that the fight could go on, much to the delight of the audience. Johanson was summoned back to the centre of the ring. His premature celebrations had affected his concentration as was soon demonstrated as O'Driscoll threw some quick combinations, some of which managed to break through and strike Johanson on the face or head. As before, that only served to make Johanson angrier. But his punches were wild and the referee twice had to step in and warn the big American about low blows and illegal punches to the back of the head.

The outcome of the fight was inevitable and the crowd new it in their heart. After the final bell sounded Johanson was awarded the fight on a unanimous decision from the judges.

But it was O'Driscoll that was cheered. When the American raised his hands in victory, by far the majority of the crowd booed him, while O'Driscoll was applauded from the ring.

It seemed that the Americans loved a plucky loser almost as much as the British.

[1] Sassenach – A Gaelic word meaning 'Saxon', referring to the Anglo-Saxon origins of the English and used in a derogatory sense.

[2] These were the weight divisions as they existed in 1942 and had been in use since the late 19th and early 20th centuries. Additional weight divisions, known as 'super' divisions, were introduced in between the main weight divisions from the 1950s onward.

[3] Padraigh is the Gaelic rendition of the name of Ireland's patron saint; Patrick is the anglicised version. Many men given the name Padraigh will be called by the nickname Paddy. While it is offensive to refer to all Irishmen as Paddy, O'Driscoll grew up being called by that name, even by his mother.

* * *

After seeing that Paddy O'Driscoll was OK, Carter went to meet up with Kasmire.

"If you think I look bad, you should see the other guy." O'Driscoll had said.

"I did." Carter replied. "He's totally unmarked."

"If you'd given me another round, I'd have had the big bollix."

"If we'd given you another round we'd be arranging your funeral." Carter said. "Now, get changed. There's money behind the bar at McNeil's for the three of you to have a drink, but you'll have to get a move on if you want to get there before closing time."

Outside the side entrance to the hanger, Carter found a Jeep waiting, a driver sat behind the wheel. "I've to take you to the BOQ." The driver said. Carter had no idea what a BOQ was, but it turned out to be the bachelor officers' quarters. The rather grand name covered up the fact that it was just three large wooden huts, separated down into single rooms with an additional hut serving as a combined dining room and bar.

"Welcome to my humble abode." Kasmire said as he showed Carter into the small room. It was sparsely furnished, just a bed, a couple of lockers and a small desk with a chair. Kasmire had made it a bit more homely with the addition of some family photographs and some sporting memorabilia.

Carter's eye lit on a particular photograph, Kasmire with a young woman, smiling at the camera.

"Your wife?" he asked, pointing at the picture.

"I hope she will be, one day. Right now we're just sweet-hearts. How do you want your whisky?" he asked, showing Carter a bottle of Talisker.

"Just as it comes."

"I'd offer you some ice, but they haven't gotten around to providing us with ice machines yet."

"You have machines just for making ice?" Carter couldn't hide his incredulity.

"Sure. Don't you?"

"I'm afraid not. We may have some somewhere, but I've never come across them."

"Don't you even have refrigerators[1] in your homes?"

"I've heard of them. I was studying engineering and we discussed the theory of their operation, but I doubt if I would know where to go to look at one."

"So how do you Limeys keep food cold."

"It's not a problem in the winter, not with our climate. We have a cold cupboard in most houses, with a marble slab that stays cool. In summer we just buy food fresh and cook it as soon as possible after we get it home."

Kasmire shook his head, not able to comprehend the backwardness of the country he was helping to defend.

"Cheers, Lucky." Kasmire offered his glass for Carter to clink. "Is that really your name?"

"It seems to be, now. My men gave it to me after a hair brained plan that should have failed actually worked. You can use it if you like, or call me Steven. What about you? Are you really known as Kas?"

"Since I was able to persuade others to call me that. My Mom and Pop called me Cecil." He pronounced it the American way: See-sill.

"I didn't like it much. The 'The Killer' part was made up by Philo Walton, though. I think he has a hankering to become a boxing promoter."

"Well, here's to you, Kas."

"Cheers. But I didn't ask you here to discuss nicknames or modern kitchen appliances." He settled on the bed and offered the chair to Carter. "I'm looking for a bit of advice."

"If I can help, I'd be happy to."

"After we met with Colonel Shiner, to talk about the fights tonight, he kept me back afterwards. He asked me what my problem was with you. I told him I thought you commandos were over rated. I told him you'd got lucky," he grinned to acknowledge Carter's nickname, "finding the only blind spot where you could get into the airfield and then across all that open area to the air traffic control tower. Scuttlebutt has it that I didn't have any patrols out that night, but I did. There were three foot patrols. None of them saw any sign of you. The Colonel pointed that out. He also pointed out that you'd led several reconnaissance patrols here to watch what we were doing and we hadn't spotted a single one of them, either.

Anyway, the Colonel sent me up to that Achnacarry place where you do your training. We have a lot of our boys up there right now, doing your course, which I didn't know. Apparently we're going to be setting up our own units soon. We're going to be calling them Ranger battalions[2].

I was shown around by one of your Sergeant instructors, Harkness. He remembers you well; told me all about you and that stunt you pulled that nearly got you kicked out of training. I also got to talk to a whole load of our guys. What I saw and heard really opened my eyes."

"But you decided to fight me tonight anyway."

"By that time news of the fights was all over the base. If I pulled out it would make it look like I was scared of you. I didn't want my men thinking that."

"So what advice do you want from me?"

"I'm thinking of applying to be a Ranger. I wondered if you thought I could make it."

"We don't take Air Force people as commandos. They don't have the right military background. Is it different in the American army?"

"I'm not Air Corps. I'm infantry. I think that rankled with me a bit as well. Being up here guarding a bunch of grease monkeys and fly boys. I want to be where the fighting is. So what do you think?"

Looking deep into the amber of the whisky, Carter considered the question. It was one he had wrestled with himself only a year before. There was no right or wrong answer, but there was an honest one.

"No one can say with certainty if they've got what it takes. You have to be physically fit, of course. More men are kicked out of training for lack of fitness than for any other reason. If you can run nonstop for ten miles, up it to fifteen. If you can do fifteen, up it to twenty. There's no such things as being *fit enough* for the commandos.

But there's more to it than that. It's about the quality of the individual. I could take ten of your men and in a couple of weeks I could have them trained to get into this base just the way we did, get to the tower, kill the guards with their bare hands and blow the whole place to Kingdom Come. But there's more to being a commando than that. We aren't braver than any other soldiers, not really. We're just better at overcoming our fear. When other soldiers are diving for cover, we're getting up and charging." Carter remembered the attack on the machine gun nests at Kirkesfjord and how terrified he had been. "We train and we train and we train and when we've done enough training we train some more. The training gives us confidence and it is that confidence that allows us to conquer our fear. We just can't imagine failing.

I'll tell you what I told my own CO when he interviewed me last year and he asked me if I had what it took to be a commando. I said 'I won't know until I try.' The same applies to you. You won't know until you try."

Kasmire topped up Carter's glass and they chatted some more; Kasmire asking about the operations Carter had been on and Carter trying to sound modest when he answered and almost succeeding. Eventually Carter looked at his watch. "It's late. I have to get home to my wife."

"Your wife is up here with you?"

"I married a local girl; a farmer's daughter. And she is going to kill me when she see's this." Carter pointed to the bruise on his cheek.

"All those Germans you've fought and you're scared of your wife?"

"I most certainly am. So I'd better get going or I'll be in her bad books for two reasons."

"The driver who brought you here will take you back to Troon. Just give him directions. I'll just go and give the Motor Pool a call."

[1] By 1939 only about 2 million American homes boasted a refrigerator (the total population was about 134 million). It would still have been a luxury item, giving some clue as to what sort of family Kasmire came from. The Electrolux brand dominated the market. In the UK, refrigerators were almost unheard of. They wouldn't become a common item in UK homes until the late 1950s. A heat wave in 1959 provided a major stimulus for sales as large amounts of food was spoiled in the 34° heat.

[2] There had been Ranger units in the US Army as far back as 1775, during the American War of Independence, when they were formed as specialist sharpshooter regiments using the first rifled weapons. They were later replaced by regular infantry, though the name was revived during the American Civil War. The first modern United States Ranger battalion was established at Carrickfergus, Northern Ireland, on 19th June 1942 under the command of Major (later Brigadier) William O Darby. His men had all been trained at the Commando Training Centre, Achnacarry. The first domestic training school for Rangers was established at Fort Benning, Georgia, in 1950.

4 – Bishopstone

With the sun bright in his eyes, Carter had to squint to read the dial of his watch; six thirty. Plenty of time. The day's training for his troop was a map reading exercise and wasn't scheduled to start until eight. Plenty of time for breakfast. He stretched his arm out to his wife's side of the bed. The bed was empty and the sheets cold. Milking was a seven day a week task and the cows couldn't be kept waiting.

Struggling out of bed, Carter rubbed at his eyes as he made his way along the corridor to the bathroom. The side of his face throbbed where he had been hit by Kasmire. Oh, yes, he remembered. He needed to think of something credible to explain that.

Ten minutes later he walked into the kitchen to be greeted by the mouth-watering smell of frying food. Mary Hamilton, his mother-in-law, turned around from the cooker at the sound of his footsteps.

"Good morning, Steven. That's some bruise y've got there. Hoo did ye come aboot that?"

"Oh," He grimaced in mock embarrassment. "Silly of me. I ran into a tree in the dark."

Two eggs were cracked into the frying pan before Mary spoke again. "D'ye ken Archie Munroe?"

"Archie? Of course." Archie arrived most mornings driving the lorry that collected the filled milk churns for his father's dairy business. He had been turned down for military service on medical grounds and never missed an opportunity to tell Carter how much he wanted to be a soldier but wasn't allowed. Carter had once suggested that he volunteer for the merchant navy instead, because they didn't conduct such stringent medicals; Archie had avoided his company for weeks afterwards.

"Well, he was up here this morning. Y' ken his father's an Alderman[1]?"

"I didn't know that." Carter didn't like the sound of where this was going.

"Aye. Apparently, last night Jim Munroe was invited to a boxing tournament between your commandos and the American sodjers at Prestwick. Were y'no there yersel?"

"Er …" Carter didn't like the idea of lying to his mother-in-law. Especially as she clearly knew the answer to her own question. Mary Hamilton let him off the hook.

"Apparently, one of the fights involved a commando by the name of Carter. He gave a good account of himself, or so Jim Munroe told Archie."

Damn small-town gossip, Carter thought. "There's a couple of Carters in the commando, apart from me, of course."

"Ah, well, it might have been one of them, I suppose." She laid an enormous plate of food in front of him. Apart from Fiona, it was one of the major benefits of living at Home Farm. "Anyway, I saw him in the yard a little while ago, talking to Fiona. Thye were at school together, y'ken. She didnae look happy, for some reason. She'll be in for her breakfast in a few minutes. Y'can ask her aboot it then."

Carter broke all records for eating his breakfast, grabbed his webbing and pack from behind the door and almost ran across the yard to his bicycle. He was rattling out of the yard when he heard Fiona's voice call after him. He decided it would be better, for him at least, if he didn't hear it.

[1] In Scotland, a local councillor is sometimes still referred to as Alderman, as had been the practice during the Middle Ages in England. Originally Aldermen were selected by their colleagues rather than being elected, but that is no longer the case. It is from the Anglo-Saxon ǽldorman, meaning, literally, an elder man – someone to be respected.

* * *

Arriving at the sweet factory Carter at once recognised that something out of the ordinary was happening. NCOs hurried around with clipboards and every troop office was crowded with bodies as ad hoc meetings were held.

The Troop Commander, Martin Turner, spotted Carter as he pressed his way into the room. "Ah, Steven, glad you're here. Your training for this morning is cancelled. We're on the move, apparently. A bit of a surprise, the CO didn't expect the orders until next week. Something to do with the availability of trains apparently. He'll give us a full briefing at ten hundred hours, but in the meantime we can get ahead of the game by doing some of the ground work."

"Any idea where we're going?"

"Not yet, but it's close to where our flotilla of landing craft is being assembled. The op itself isn't for a few more weeks, but they want us wherever it is so that we can train with the other units that are participating."

"What do you want me to do."

Turner thrust a clipboard in Carter's direction. "Go and sort out our equipment table[1]. Make sure we've got everything on it, then move the kit into here. We don't want any of those robbers from the other troops nicking all the lavatory paper. Ask Sgt Chalk to detail four men to do the carrying."

The list ran to four pages and covered everything from socks to bombs for the two inch mortars. "Will we be coming back here after the op?" Already Carter's mind was working on what he would tell Fiona."

"No Idea, Steven. Now, there's a million things to do and not much time to do them. Officer's to be back here at ten hundred for the CO's briefing. The men can keep on working. Troop commanders will brief them later."

Considering himself to be dismissed, Carter went off in search of his Sergeant. As every good officer knew, if something needed doing, the first thing to do was to find a sergeant and ask him how it should be done.

As always when the commando assembled for a briefing, the atmosphere was tense with expectation. Although the officers were to be briefed first on this occasion, that hadn't changed. The officers stood in their groups of three for each troop, occasionally merging into neighbouring groups to exchange rumours before separating again.

The Second in Command, Maj Teddy Couples, called the room to attention as the CO strode in, a wad of papers in his hand.

"At ease, gentlemen." He drawled. On this occasion he didn't waste any time building up expectation, as he had done on the first briefing for Operation Absalom. "We've been caught a little on the hop this time. I was expecting orders to move, but not this soon. That can't be helped. We're in the hands of the Ministry of Transport at the moment, rather than those of Combined Ops[1] or the War Office.

Now, as you know, we have been in training for several months in readiness for our next operation. I can't go into details of that at the moment, that will be briefed later, but in readiness for that operation we are to move into a concentration area where we will start to train alongside the other units that will be participating.

So, our mission, is to move the commando from Troon to our concentration area.

---

[1] Equipment table – to save time having to work out what equipment will be needed when crises arise, all military units have pre-prepared equipment tables that tell them what equipment they should take and in what quantities. As with the one described for Carter's troop, this can cover everything from utility items such as lavatory paper, to items of uniform, through to armaments. Nowadays, military units have such complex needs that a lot of the equipment listed on their equipment table may be held at logistics depots, to be called forward when units are notified that they are to be deployed on operations. Rapid response forces, however, will hold most of their equipment on base so that they can move quickly when ordered to.

To do this we will be en-training[2] at Troon station at oh six hundred hours tomorrow morning. That means that we and all our equipment will be on board and ready to go. It doesn't mean that we will be standing around on the platform drinking tea and smoking fags."

The remark brought a chuckle, but they could see from Vernon's face that he hadn't been joking.

"I know that most of you have been busy organising your men and equipment. I'll be having a review meeting with Troop Commanders at fifteen hundred hours to see how you are progressing and to find out if there's anything that we should have but haven't yet got, but the purpose of this briefing is to make sure you all know what is happening.

Now, the Quarter Master has already left with the Adjutant and half a dozen men to try to sort out accommodation for us at the other end. However, the whisper from Combined Ops is that there isn't a lot and we may have to rough it for a while. I know the men won't mind that too much, they're used to it after all, but I can only hope that it will be a short-term thing.

We will also be leaving a rear party here with the QMS and half a dozen men under the command of the 2IC to close down this HQ."

Carter put his hand up.

"I was going to leave questions to the end, Steven, but I think I can guess what yours is, so you may as well ask it."

There were a few suppressed chuckles at Carter's embarrassment.

"Er, yes, Sir. You make it sound as though we won't be returning to Troon after the op."

"We're not sure what is going to happen after the op, but I have been advised by HQ South West Scotland that this building is to be taken over by the RAF as the HQ for a flying boat squadron. That is why we are closing it down completely. We won't be leaving so much as a paper clip behind. If we do return to Scotland, we will have to find a new operating base."

"Thank you, Sir." It was a blow to Carter and he knew it would be a blow to his wife. Despite the dangers of his job, they had both assumed that the commando would remain in Troon when not on operations. This news threw that into doubt.

Returning to his prepared script, Vernon continued with his briefing and Carter struggled to concentrate as he wrote the relevant information into his note book.

[1] Combined Ops – HQ Combined Operations. This was the overarching organisation that identified targets for commando operations and carried out the high-level planning for them, drawing resources from the three arms of Britain's armed forces to ensure that the operations had what it needed. The Chief of Combined Operations was, at this stage of the war, answerable directly to the Cabinet Office.

[2] En-training – The army created its own jargon for many routine activities. It therefore refers to embussing and debussing for the acts of getting on and off of lorries. For rail travel this was adapted to en-training and de-training, for air travel it became en-planing and de-planing. For seaborne travel they adopted the naval terminology of embarkation and disembarkation.

* * *

The long May evening had disguised the length of his working day as Carter propped his bicycle against the wall. He must remember to find somewhere in the barn to store it, he reminded himself. It would be a long time before he needed it again. The tantalising smell of food drifted out of the kitchen window. The Hamiltons would have eaten and retired to the parlour to listen to the radio by now. Fiona may already be in bed, but Carter doubted that she would have gone up without welcoming him home. Mind you, it might not be the sort of welcome that he might hope for. Not only did he still have to explain the boxing match, but he now had to tell her he was leaving in the morning.

He found her sitting at the kitchen table, mending an item of clothing. She looked up and gave him a big smile. A good start, Carter decided.

"I heard the bike rattling." She said. "Your dinner's keeping warm." She rose and opened her arms to embrace him. Carter dropped his webbing by the door and made his way across the big farmhouse kitchen to wrap his wife in his arms.

As they broke apart they both spoke at the same time.

"Darling, I have some news …" They laughed.

"You first." Carter insisted.

"I was at the doctor's today." Fiona said.

"I didn't know you had been feeling ill."

"Not exactly ill, Darling. We're going to have a baby."

Carter's jaw dropped open. "Erm …"

Her face fell. "Don't tell me you're not pleased."

"No Darling, it's not that." He took her in his arms again and gave her a reassuring hug. "It's just that … well, I knew one day I'd marry and have a family, but I didn't expect it to be …" His voice tailed off.

"This soon." Fiona finished the sentence for him. "Well, we haven't exactly been careful, you must admit that."

"No, I suppose we haven't. I didn't know how to … approach the subject, I suppose."

"I'm a farmer, Steven." She gave him a look that told him that he should have known better. "Since I was a wee lassie I've known that if you put a bull in with a heifer you're probably going to end up with a calf at some time in the future."

"Yes, I suppose … OK, I take your point. You took me by surprise, that's all. I am really happy." He gave her another hug, then a long kiss. "Do your parents know yet?"

"No. I wanted to tell you first. I think my mother might suspect, it's difficult to hide something like that from her, but I doubt she's said anything to my father. We'll tell them together after you've had your dinner."

"We have two things to tell them. There's my news as well."

A dark cloud seemed to pass across Fiona's face, her happiness wiped away like a drop of spilled milk. "I know. You're leaving in the morning. When I was in the doctor's, everyone was talking about it."

It was the curse of living in a small town, with over three hundred soldiers billeted on the local population. It only needed one soldier to tell his landlady that they were on the move and the news would be around the town within the hour. No doubt several of the commandos had said as much. The soldiers and their hosts got on well, had almost become family. It would be natural to announce their departure. Carter could only hope that the news didn't reach the wrong ears. If a spy network decided to keep track of their movements to find out where they were going, it wouldn't be difficult. Once they turned up on the south coast, as Carter knew they would even if Vernon hadn't said as much, it wouldn't take a genius to work out that they were preparing for a raid.

"It's worse than that. We've pretty much been told that we won't be coming back to Troon."

"Oh, I hadn't realised …"

"No. No one had. I think we all took it for granted that Troon would be our home for the duration. You're getting some RAF sea planes in exchange for us." He paused, taking her in his arms again. "Look, it won't be that bad. We get leave after every operation and there will be other times when we can get together. You can come and visit me as well. Bring the baby when he arrives."

"You seem sure it will be a boy." She gave a wry smile.

"Well, if it's a girl you can bring her as well. One day the war will be over and I'll come back up here and we can be a family. We're no worse off than thousands of other married couples, hundreds of thousands probably."

"You're right. I've been spoilt having you here for these past few weeks." She went to the cooker and took his dinner from the oven, placing it on the table as he took a seat.

"Ah, this is what I'm going to miss the most." He said, tucking into the baked ham that Mary Hamilton had prepared.

"Thanks." Fiona said, throwing a tea towel at him. "Now, one other little thing we need to talk about. How did you get that great big bruise on your face?"

* * *

The railway company seemed to have found the most dilapidated rolling stock in which to transport the commando. Hardly one carriage was in the same livery as the next, the paint was chipped and peeling and steam leaked from broken linkages in long hissing plumes. Most of the carriages had been used for commuter trains, so they were made up of individual compartments with no corridor to allow people to move around. The only way in and out was through the doors onto the platform. They had been told that there would be regular stops for comfort breaks and food, but that didn't put Carter in a better frame of mind as he approached the train. He suspected that the carriages had been sitting in sidings for years before being brought back into service to carry troops.

"Well, what did you expect?" Sgt Chalk bellowed as the commandos gave the train disgusted looks. "The fucking Orient Express? Now, get that kit loaded and let's not hear any moaning."

At the rear of the train there were two baggage cars into which the soldiers loaded their equipment from the lorries and stowed it away, before walking along the platform to the carriages that had been allocated to their troop.

The interiors of the carriages weren't any better than the exteriors. Most seemed to lack any light bulbs, the upholstery was worn, with splits where the horsehair stuffing sprouted like grass between paving slabs.

Each compartment was supposed to hold eight people for a short journey. Someone had counted very carefully because there was almost exactly the right number of seats for the commando.

Only the carriage for the officers offered any sort of comfort. It was an old First Class pullman car, also fairly dilapidated, but at least it offered space and a corridor leading to a toilet cubicle.

"I'll stay with my men, if you don't mind Martin." Carter informed his Troop Commander.

Turner nodded approvingly. "I'll be doing the same. Save me a seat. I'll join you just as soon as I've got the rest of the troop settled."

Oh six hundred hours arrived and Carter expected the train to pull out of the station. He was disappointed. That may have been the time that they had told to be on board, but no one seemed to have told the driver, or perhaps the signalman. The train sat in the siding, the engine chuffing noisily as the driver waited for permission to set off. A commuter train bound for Glasgow drew into the station, took on the waiting civilian passengers and drew out again. That was what they had been waiting for, the commandos decided, they would be off in a minute.

Again they were disappointed. Two more trains came and went before theirs was finally allowed to leave. Carter looked at his watch; oh six forty five. Forty five minutes that he had been deprived of sharing with his wife.

Fiona had driven him to the station that morning but hadn't stayed to see him off. "It's not fair for me to be standing waving my hanky when so many of your men have no one to see them on their way." Carter suspected that she just couldn't bear the pain of their parting. It was better for her to go straight home.

Not all the population of Troon had seen things that way. Landladies, sweet hearts and wives had watched them march into the station but hadn't been allowed to follow. The train had been sitting in a siding along the track and it was deemed unsafe for the civilians to cross the lines. It hadn't prevented others from going to the far side of the station and lining the flimsy fence to send their friends and loved ones on their way. A hundred shouted conversations must have taken place from the windows and doorways of the carriages.

Now, to the accompaniment of an ironic cheer from its passnegers, the train lurched across the points and headed north, towards Glasgow. It would be redirected across to the main Glasgow to London line, stopping at frequent intervals to allow the regular, timetabled trains to speed past in both directions.

It was nearly midday when the train finally drew to a clattering stop at Carlisle station. A journey that shouldn't have taken no more than three hours had taken almost six. More than one trail of urine had streaked the windows of the carriage windows in the train's slipstream as the commandos had been forced to relieve themselves through the only means available.

The soldiers were told that there were sandwiches and mugs of tea available from canteen trucks that had been set up alongside the train, but that they weren't allowed to leave the platform. To reinforce the order there were Redcaps[1] posted at the foot of the stairs that connected to the bridge above the platforms. The busiest direction of travel, however, was towards the toilets. Howls of protest were soon heard when the soldiers found they would still have to spend a literal penny to use the facilities.

A harassed looking RTO[2] hurried along the train looking for the CO. "Where have you been, we were expecting you hours ago."

Carter could see the amount of patience the CO was using as he explained to the junior officer that they were only passengers; they weren't actually driving the train.

The sandwiches were bully beef and there weren't any cups for the tea, so the soldiers had to return to their compartments to collect their mess tins from their webbing, but the break after sitting for so long in such camped conditions was a relief. There was a lot of cat calling and booing when the RTO ordered the men back onto the train after half an hour.

Soldiers with time on their hand rarely became bored. Apart from the odd twenty four hour pass, it had been weeks since the commandos had any time off and they weren't about to waste what they had now been given. Games of cards were started and paperback books and magazines passed from hand to eager hand. Even sitting upright, most of the soldiers were able to snatch an hour or two of sleep to help pass the time. The RTOs had been careful to prevent any alcohol from being smuggled aboard, though the resourceful commandos had made sure they brought their own supplies, with bottles and half bottles being passed around in the compartments where there were no officers. Carter, Turner and Gilfoyle, the other junior officer in 4 Troop, made sure they moved around between compartments, turning a blind eye so that no group was deprived of access to their contraband for more than one leg of the journey.

The rest of the journey went no more quickly. There were stops at Crewe and Rugby for more of the ubiquitous tea and bully beef sandwiches and comfort breaks and it was late at night when the train made its final stop at Clapham Junction.

"'Ave I got time to nip 'ome and see me Mum?" A voice with a distinctly London accent called out, which resulted in an outbreak of laughter.

"I wouldn't punish an innocent old woman by letting you visit." A sergeant replied, to more laughter.

"You can visit your Dad, though. He's in Brixton[3] and we pass quite close to there." Another wag joined in.

[1] Redcap – slang name for Royal Military Police, because of the red covering to their peaked caps. RAF Police are nicknamed "snowdrops" for similar reasons.

[2] RTO – Rail Transport Officer. Officers, usually from the Royal Army Service Corps, appointed to manage the smooth transit of huge numbers of troops travelling through the rail network during World War 2. With most of the station signs removed as a precaution against spies, soldiers frequently became lost and missed trains. The use of RTOs was supposed to alleviate the problems, though most of them were swamped by the amount of work. London rail terminals and major rail hubs such as Crewe and York had RTOs stationed on them for quite a long time after the war.

[3] In 1942 this would have been understood as a reference to Brixton prison.

* * *

The train clattered and banged its way into Bishopstone station in the early hours of the morning, the noise probably waking half the village. The darkness hid any clue as to their whereabouts and, as with all railway stations, the signage had all been removed as a precaution against spies.

The troops de-trained, yawning and stretching, looking around them for some clue as to their location. They knew they were south of London, but that was about all. The tang of salt in the air might have given a clue that they might be by the sea but having lived for so long in Troon they hardly noticed the scent anymore.

Sergeants started shouting, organising working parties to unload the equipment stored in the baggage trucks at the rear of the train, while corporals chivvied the remainder of the men into ranks along the platform. The officers congregated near the Station Master's office, waiting for orders.

The QM emerged, looking as tired as any of the travellers. He sought out the CO, his face sombre.

"Sorry, Colonel." He started. Carter knew it was never a good sign when an officer started a conversation with an apology. "There's nowhere in the local area for the men to sleep. The Canadians have occupied the hotels, guest houses, B&Bs and the civilian billets and what the Canadians haven't occupied the commandos that got here before us have monopolised, as well as the TA[1] drill hall and all the empty buildings. No one seems to know who is in charge, so we're in the hands of South East Command and they don't seem to know what's going on either."

"So, what are we supposed to do?" Vernon's voice was steady, controlled, but it was obvious that he wasn't happy.

"Stay here, I guess Sir. There's nowhere else to go. The men can bed down on the platforms and we can store the equipment in the waiting rooms and offices."

"Has the Station Master agreed to that?"

"There hasn't been a Station Master since Adam was a lad, Sir. This is barely a 'halt', let alone a station. It's managed by Newhaven. But possession is nine points of the law, as they say. If we haven't got anywhere else to go they'll have to lump it. I've told Command that we'll stay here until someone provides us with accommodation, so it's their problem to deal with the railway company now."

"OK. I'll go up to HQ in the morning and shake a few trees, see what falls out. Have you got a vehicle I can use?"

"No, Sir. The Tilly only made it as far as Bedford. I doubt we'll ever see it again. I had to take trains from there. I'll scrounge around in the morning, see what I can lay my hands on."

"Thank you, Alex. I'm sure you did your best. We'll call it part of the training for the moment."

"I've managed to get you a room in a guest house if you want it, Sir."

"No, I'll stay with the men for now, but I may take you up on it if we don't find somewhere soon. What about food?"

"In the short term we have the training stocks we brought down with us. The Commos[2] have promised us rations as soon as I give them a nominal role. It will be compo[3] I'm afraid, but at least we won't have to worry about setting up a field kitchens to cook it. The men can do that for themselves."

"OK, get onto that straight away. The men last ate a couple of hours ago, but they'll need breakfast as soon as they're up and about and there aren't enough training packs to feed everyone more than once. How did you get into the Station Master's office, by the way?"

"I used my key, Sir." The QM gave a grim smile and pointed to his booted foot.

"I'll use it as my office until further notice." Vernon said. "OK, gentlemen." He addressed his officers. "You all heard what the QM had to report. Spread your men across both platforms, use whatever rooms you can gain access to. Let the men get their heads down as best they can. I'm sure we'll get orders in the morning, but in the meantime, we assume that this is our home."

[1] TA – Territorial Army, Britain's part time reserve army, now called the Army Reserve. Most towns had a "drill hall" where the local TA unit would meet and train.

[2] Commos – nickname for the Royal Army Service Corps, one of whose responsibilities was the provision of rations. The newly established Army catering Corps was only responsible for cooking food, not supplying it. Both their functions are now carried out by the Royal Logistics Corps.

[3] Compo – Composite rations. Tinned and dried food issued to soldiers in the field. One pack provides 5,000 calories and makes up 3 full meals plus snacks, tea and coffee. Also comes in a pack big enough to feed 8 men (a "section") for a day. All the food is easy to heat in mess tins on a small portable stove fuelled by a hexamine block (similar to a fire lighter), but in an emergency the food can all be eaten cold.

* * *

Although it was now almost June, it was still quite chilly in the early morning at Bishopstone station. Carter watched as the Troop Sergeant Major, Keith Mahony, marched the men off the station forecourt for their day's training. The army hates having soldiers sitting around doing nothing so until the 2IC could co-ordinate a training plan with the other units, 15 Commando would find its own ways to keep the soldiers occupied. Today would be a route march, so that they could familiarise themselves with the layout of the area.

The officers, on the other hand, were being sent off in different directions to look for specific places for the different types of training they would do. They needed places where they could mount ambushes, attack buildings, defend buildings, search buildings, beaches for landings and a dozen other different types of war games. Carter had been singled out to try to find cliffs that could be climbed.

"You've been there so you know what sort of cliffs they have across the water." The 2IC had said. "The CO has told me we will have to do some climbing, so we had better get some practice in."

"We're in the right sort of place if we're going straight across." Carter had replied. "The cliffs on the other side are very similar to what we have here. The main problem will be getting to the base of them. Even at low tide some of them can't be reached from the sea, let alone from the land."

"Spread your net wide, then. If we need transport to get there, we'll sort it out."

Faced with exploring a coastline with which he was unfamiliar, Carter decided his best bet would be to find someone who was familiar with the local area. He marched off towards Newhaven in search of the person he needed.

The estuary of the River Ouse was packed with landing craft of various sizes. It was far busier than the last time Carter had visited. The lifeboat station was not far up river from where Carter had boarded the MTB that took him to France on his previous visit to the town. The landward door was open, so Carter walked in.

"Hello" he shouted, peering around the bulk of the lifeboat that filled the interior of the building, which was no more than a very large shed.

Footsteps sounded from the other end of the building, followed by the person making them.

"And what can I do for you, Sir?" The man said. His face was weather beaten, a pipe clamped between his teeth. He wore a thick woollen jumper, despite the fact that the day was getting warmer.

"I'm looking for the Coxwain." Carter said.

"Well, you've found him. Len Peddlesden." He offered his hand for Carter to shake. "How can I help?"

"Steven Carter." Carter shook his hand. "Your knowledge of the coast would be helpful. My men need to practice their climbing skills and I was wondering if you could point me in the direction of some suitable cliffs. Ideally we should be able to get to them by land, if possible, but if not, at least we must be able to get ashore beneath them, from a boat."

The Coxswain took in the commando and combined operations badges on the sleeves of Carter's battledress. "So, you're one of them lot. Well I won't ask you why you want to go doing dangerous things like climbing cliffs. I'm sure you have your reasons. Come into the office and we'll take a look at the chart."

He led the way. One wall was dominated by a map of the coastline from Beachy Head to Brighton. "This is the area we're responsible for. Would you like a cup of tea?" Peddlesden asked.

"That would be nice." Carter accepted.

"You study that while I go and make it. Milk and sugar?"

"Yes, two spoons please."

As well as the roads, the map was of a large enough scale to show footpaths, some of which went right down to the sea's edge. The contour lines told Carter a lot about the layout of the cliffs.

"I reckon your best bet would be Cuckmere Haven." Peddlesden said, returning and handing Carter a steaming tin mug. He pointed to a point on the map to the east of Seaford. "It's at the mouth of the Cuckmere river. When the tide's low you can walk along the bottom of the cliffs there. Even at high tide you can still get to the nearest end of the cliffs."

"How can I get there?"

"You got a car?"

"No, I'm afraid not. Could I get a bus?"

"Probably, but I've got a better idea." He lifted the handset from the telephone and dialled a number.

"Hello, is that Arthur?" There was a pause while the other party answered. "Len Peddlesden here, at the lifeboat station. I've got a soldier here, a hofficer, wants to go and have a look at the cliffs at Cuckmere. Would you fancy giving him a lift?"

There was another pause as the person at the other end answered. "OK, see you in a few minutes."

"Mate of mine, Arthur will take you. You finish your tea while you wait."

"Has the war been keeping you busy?" Carter asked, just to make conversation."

"It certainly has. Not as busy as the summer of 1940, mind. We were out almost every day then, pulling fighter pilots out of the sea; ours and theirs. But we still get called out quite a lot even these days."

"That's an impressive looking boat you have. I've never seen one close up before."

"Yeah, the old Lily ain't a bad old tub. We've had her since 1930."

"Lily, is that her name?"

"That's what we calls her. Her full name is the CECIL AND LILIAN PHILPOTT, BUT THAT'S A BIT OF A MOUTHFUL, SO WE CALLS HER LILY FOR SHORT. THE KING HIMSELF CAME AND LAUNCHED HER. COURSE HE WAS STILL ONLY THE DUKE OF YORK BACK THEN."

THEY WERE INTERRUPTED BY THE SOUND OF A STEAM WHISTLE. "THAT'LL BE ARTHUR. COME WITH ME, STEVEN."

PEDDLESDEN LED THE WAY ALONG THE SIDE OF THE LIFEBOAT AND TO THE TOP OF THE LONG RAMP THAT LED DOWN TO THE WATER. AT THE BOTTOM SAT A LITTLE STEAM POWERED LAUNCH, A MAN STANDING ON THE BOW HOLDING IT AGAINST THE FOOT OF THE RAMP WITH A BOAT HOOK.

"ARTHUR, THIS IS LT STEVEN CARTER. HE'S ONE O' THEY COMMANDOS THAT'S FILLING THE TOWN THESE DAYS. HE WANTS TO GO AND TAKE A LOOK AT CUCKMERE HAVEN."

"WELL 'EE BETTER GET ON BOARD THEN, 'ADN'T 'EE." ARTHUR LAUGHED.

"YOU GO ALONG WITH ARTHUR, NOW. HE'LL TAKE CARE OF YOU."

"IS THAT THING SAFE?" CARTER ASKED, GIVING THE LITTLE BOAT A DUBIOUS LOOK.

PEDDLESDEN LAUGHED. "HE WANTS TO KNOW IF YOUR BOAT'S SAFE, ARTHUR."

"IT WAS SAFE ENOUGH TO BRING TEN MEN BACK FROM DUNKIRK, YOUNG MAN." ARTHUR SOUNDED OFFENDED.

CARTER DECIDED TO SAY NO MORE. HE WISHED PEDDLESDEN A GOOD DAY, WALKED DOWN THE RAMP AND CLAMBERED ONTO THE LAUNCH.

"SAFE INDEED." HUFFED ARTHUR, LETTING GO WITH THE BOAT HOOK AND SITTING AT THE WHEEL, POSITIONED JUST IN FRONT OF THE WHITE PAINTED FUNNEL, WHICH WAS BELCHING SMOKE.

THE LITTLE LAUNCH WASN'T REALLY SUITED TO BEING OUT ON THE SEA, SO CARTER WAS GLAD THE WEATHER WAS FINE. A GENTLE SWELL WAS RUNNING, WHICH CAUSED THE OCCASIONAL WAVE TO BREAK OVER THE PROW OF THE BOAT, SHOWERING HIM WITH SPRAY, BUT GENERALLY THE RIDE WAS A SMOOTH ONE. ARTHUR WASN'T THE CHATTY TYPE, ANSWERING CARTER'S CONVERSATIONAL SALLIES WITH MONOSYLLABLES. IN THE END CARTER GAVE

UP. THEY PASSED SEAFORD ABOUT A HUNDRED YARDS OFF SHORE, BEFORE THE CLIFFS STARTED TO DESCEND IN EASY SLOPES INTO A BROAD ESTUARY. "THAT'S CUCKMERE." ARTHUR SAID.

"CAN YOU GET ME IN CLOSE ENOUGH FOR ME TO GET ASHORE?"

"SO LONG AS YOU DON'T MIND GETTING YOUR FEET WET."

"THAT WILL BE FINE." CARTER REPLIED. HE REACHED DOWN AND STARTED TO UNBUCKLE HIS GAITERS[1], THEN UNLACED HIS BOOTS. "WHAT'S THE STATE OF THE TIDE RIGHT NOW?"

"ABOUT AN HOUR OFF FULL FLOOD. IT WON'T GET RIGHT IN TO THE BASE OF THOSE CLIFFS. AT LEAST, NOT HERE. A BIT FURTHER THAT WAY ..." HE POINTED TOWARDS BEACHY HEAD "... AND IT WILL THOUGH."

Arthur nudged the little launch into the shingle and Carter stepped off the bow into knee deep water. The smooth stones weren't comfortable to walk on in bare feet, but they didn't hurt too much and it didn't take long for Carter to cross the broad strip to the base of the cliffs.

From the broad flood plain of the Cuckmere estuary, the cliffs rose gently towards the heights further along, separating them from Eastbourne, which lay on the other side of Beachy Head. Carter's father had taken him climbing as a child, even though Carter junior was scared of heights. His protests had been ignored and he had to endure the terror of being suspended from ropes and forced to either climb up or down perilous slopes. So, although he was experienced, he wasn't an expert and knew his limitations as a climber. But it had been his idea that the commando undertake rock climbing training, so they could infiltrate sections of coastline where they would be least expected and which would only be weakly defended.

But this place looked promising as a training area for the commando. On the west side of the estuary lay a row of cottages, but there was no clue as to who the occupants might be; fishermen, perhaps, or maybe they belonged to the Coastguard. Nestled into the grass on the tops of the cliffs, Carter could make out concrete defensive positions, no doubt built in 1940 when the threat of invasion from across the English Channel had been very real. They, too, would be useful, providing realistic targets for the commandos to assault.

From his brief study of the map at the lifeboat station, Carter knew that a lane ran behind the cliffs, close enough for the commandos to be able to walk along the banks of the river to reach the shore. And, of course, there was also the option of using landing craft for the journey. In fact that would be far more realistic, given the operation for which they were training.

Having seen enough, Carter headed back to the launch. Arthur had taken the little craft a few yards out from the shore to prevent it being damaged or run aground by the constant driving force of the waves, but seeing Carter returning he brought it close inshore once again. Carter clambered aboard and walked along the varnished decking to the cockpit at the rear.

"Whose are those cottages?" Carter asked as he reached for his boots and gaiters.

"Coastguard." Arthur grunted. "Cuckmere used to be pop'lar with smugglers, couple o' hundred years back. Simplest thing to do was put the Coastguard 'ere and that stopped 'em."

Carter nodded his understanding, then took another look at the tiny launch. "Did you really bring ten men all the way back from France in this?"

"Well, not all the way and not all together. I picked up five from the beach and took 'em out to a navy ship lying offshore. Then I went back for another five. I woulda gone back for more but the Navy wouldn't let me. Thought it was too dangerous. I was going to go, but they tricked me.

One o' the soldiers I'd picked up was wounded, so they sent a couple of sailors down the scramble net to help him. Only that were just a trick. They grabbed me and tied me up, then had my little boat winched on board the destroyer. Bastards."

"What's she called?" Carter couldn't recall having seen the little boat's name. It was probably painted across the stern, as was traditional.

"Steamy Sal." Arthur chuckled.

"Steamy because she's steam powered?"

"No, Steamy because I named her after my wife and she was hot stuff." Arthur laughed. "I bought her back in the thirties, just to take people for rides up and down the river at Newhaven. Made a nice little living in the summer months, but the war's put paid to that."

Carter took what he imagined to be a hint. "How much do I owe you for this trip?"

Arthur waved dismissively. "Call it my contribution to the war effort. What are you gonna be doing at they cliffs anyway?"

"Climbing them. It's something that the commandos have had to learn."

"Makes sense. Don't want to go ashore where the Jerries put their machine guns. It was the same in the last lot. The Generals always seemed to want us to attack where the enemy had the most machine guns."

"You were in the last war?"

"I was. I joined up in 1912. I was in the Orange Lilies." Seeing Carter's puzzled expression he explained. "That's' the Royal Sussex Regiment to you. They called us that because back in the days of the old red coats, we had orange facings on our lapels. They say William of Orange granted us the right to wear the colour. They also called us the Haddocks, but we didn't like that much."

"Did you see much action?"

"All of it lad. I was there at Mons in August of 14 and still there at Arras in August 18. I was wounded there and got sent home."

"So, you're one of the Old Contemptibles[2]."

"I was that, son. I was that." Arthur seemed to go into a bit of a reverie at that point, perhaps remembering his war. Carter let him have his peace and just enjoyed the ride back to Newhaven.

[1] Gaiters – These were thick webbing wrappings worn around the ankles that held the trouser cuffs in place, preventing them from snagging on barbed wire and other sharp objects. They also concealed any actual damage that might occur. The bottom of the gaiter went over the neck of the boot, preventing the ingress of stones etc. They replaced the long puttees (from the Hindi word *patti*, meaning bandage) that had been worn during the First World War and which were wound around the legs from knee to ankle.

Gaiters went out of use in 1960 and were replaced by ankle length puttees until the 1980s, when high topped combat boots were introduced after the Falklands War.

[2] The Old Contemptibles – When Kaiser Wilhelm heard the size of the British Expeditionary Force (BEF), sent to France at the outbreak of the First World War, he referred to it as a "contemptible little army" as it numbered barely a hundred thousand men compared to Germany's two million. The BEF fought the Germans to a stand still in southern Belgium, threatening the Germans Army's right flank and preventing them from completing their advance on Paris and bringing Germany an early victory. Those soldiers of the BEF that survived the war became known as the Old Contemptibles and bore the name with pride.

* * *

The situation at the railway station hadn't improved while Carter had been gone. Sentries patrolled the small station forecourt and strolled along the platforms, making sure that the Commando's equipment and personal belongings didn't fall victim to casual theft. Not that Bishopstone was the sort of place that might attract casual thieves. It was a small place, barely two hundred houses. How it had even warranted the existence of a railway station was a mystery. Perhaps an executive of the company that had built the line had lived close by.

None of the troops were yet back from their route march. Carter sought out the 2IC and reported his findings, then went in search of some lunch. The rations had yet to arrive so there was nothing to be had at the station. He should have stopped at one of the cafés in Newhaven, Carter realised. He retraced his steps and found one that had cheese sandwiches on offer.

He was munching his way through his snack when a platoon of Canadians marched past the café, rifles sloped on their shoulders. They looked smart enough, but Carter knew that they'd had no active role in the war up to that point. Experience counted for a lot these days. He had heard the QM mention Canadians the night before and wondered what their role in the operation was to be. If they had been brought into the concentration area they must be involved in some way. He would find out in due course, he supposed.

The café gave a view over the river and the mass of landing craft that were moored there. His eyes followed the Canadian platoon as they wound their way down the hill to the river side. Coming to a halt on the quayside an officer started to address them, his voice not carrying as far as Carter. He was pointing to the craft, gesticulating, then pointing out to sea. One of the craft broke away from the mass on the distant bank and powered its way to the quayside where the Canadians were assembled. The crew seemed to know what they were about as they swung it in alongside the harbour wall and brought it to a halt, rocking on its own wash. The infantrymen crowded forward to get a closer look as the officer pointed to various features of the craft.

Carter was taken back to Achnacarry and his first introduction to landing craft. They were pretty basic. Just a long marine plywood box with a wheelhouse at one end, the sides just high enough to provide protection against the sea for the troops that would be squeezed into the confined space of the hull. Armour was minimal, just a little bit on the bulkheads of the wheelhouse and the two machinegun cockpits.

The one the Canadians were examining must have been one of the early models, as it didn't have a drop down ramp at the front, which had only been added to the design the previous year. Instead, wooden ramps were lashed to the inside of the hull, to be lowered over the blunt bow when the craft grounded on the beach. The commandos tended to jump down into the water, to reduce the amount of time taken to get ashore, reducing their exposure to enemy fire. Carter wondered if anyone had mentioned that to the Canadians.

Finishing his tea, Carter returned to the railway station once again.

* * *

The short line of four landing craft raced in towards the shore. "Get your head down!" Sgt Chalk bellowed at one of the troopers towards the rear of the craft. "Do you want it shot off by a fucking Jerry sniper?"

There was no chance of that happening this time, Carter knew. But it was best to keep things as real as possible, even for what was just a demonstration. It seemed that someone had thought that it would be a good idea for the Canadian troops to witness the landing craft in use before they tried it for themselves. 1 and 4 troops of 15 Commando were selected for the task, for no other reason than that Martin Turner and Roger Dixon-Jones, the officers commanding the two troops, were the first to cross the CO's path after he received the order to conduct the demonstration.

There had been some grumbling when the commandos saw that they were using the older boats. They had been training and operating with the newer ones since before the Kirkesfjord raid. With no proper drying facilities it would be difficult to get their boots and clothes dry again. With landing craft with drop down ramps there had been at least some chance of keeping their feet dry.

"Fifty yards to go." The tinny sound of the speaker mounted at the front of the wheelhouse announced. The men braced themselves as the pitch of the craft's motor changed and it slowed down to avoid jamming itself into the shingle.

"Stand bye" Carter yelled, bracing himself to leap onto the bow as soon as the craft hit the beach.

The craft was still going too hard when the bows crunched against the gravel and the weight of men was pushed hard against Carter, preventing him from moving. As the momentum was eased he felt the weight being removed as everyone swayed rearward again and he was able to grab hold of the plywood of the narrow foredeck and pull himself upwards. A second figure was doing the same on the other side; Cpl Franklyn of Easy Section.

Carter teetered on the top of the bow for a second then leapt forward, landing with a great splash, the water rising around his knees and thighs as a wave rushed passed him. Use the forward force, he told himself. If he waited until the wave passed, he would be held back by the undertow as it receded once more.

The shingle beneath his boots shifted as he drove himself forward, slowing him down. It was much harder to move than on the sandy beaches they had been practicing on. He was nearly bowled over as a man landed behind him. Keep moving he told himself, or you'll get buried under your own men. He drove his boots into the shingle, forcing himself past the front edge of the waves and onto dryer terrain. It made no difference, the shingle slid from beneath his feet, robbing him of power, slowing him down. Figures fanned out on either side of him, almost as far as the first figures from the next landing craft, where Carter could see the tall figure of Martin Turner waving his men forward.

Yes, encourage the others, he reminded himself. He turned, but found he had no need. Not only were his men clambering over the bows of the landing craft, they were throwing themselves over the sides as well, knowing that every second wasted was a second longer that the enemy had to line up a machine gun on the flimsy wooden structure.

Carter threw himself up onto the top level of the wave washed shingle, where it started to flatten. He dived down, crawled forward a few feet then took aim with his rifle. They had no ammunition, it wasn't that sort of exercise. Along the top of the beach they could see the lines of Canadians, drawn up and watching proceedings. Had they impressed them? Perhaps. Had they learnt anything? That was impossible to say until they tried it for themselves.

Which they were about to do.

The two captains put whistles to their lips, blowing long blasts and calling the exercise to a halt. The men climbed to their feet and made their way to the concrete path that marked the landward edge of the beach. Beyond were the houses of the local population. Housewives stood in gardens, arms crossed over their chests as they watched what was going on, curious after years of only reading about the war or seeing it on the cinema newsreels and hearing about it on the radio.

Corporals started forming the men into ranks as Sgt Chalk arrived at Carter's elbow. One section from each troop would remain where they were to act as an "enemy" for the Canadian's first assault, while the officers would act as observers, reporting to the Canadians on their performances.

"Thank you, Sgt Chalk. Take your four sections back to Bishopstone. Get them dried off as best they can."

The sergeant saluted and headed off to take charge of his men. Only Able section from 4 Troop would remain behind. Seven men, six with rifles and one with a Bren gun. Already the first platoons of the Canadians were filing down the shingle to board the four landing craft. They would be taken about half a mile out to sea before the craft would turn and run back into the beach, just as they had done with the commandos.

A commando started to pass along the line of soldiers, handing out clips of blank ammunition. The men had been briefed. One shot for each Canadian that shows himself on the bows for too long. Each shot would tell the officers that their men were too slow. It provided a clear signal of where improvements needed to be made.

"You guys made it look easy." An officer said, approaching the two troops.

"We've practiced it often enough. If we can't do it by now we'll never get it right." Carter replied.

"How was it for your guys, the first time?"

"The first time I did it, I slipped as I went over and nearly drowned under the weight of my own equipment." Carter responded with a wry smile. "I suggest you have a few men on stand by just in case anyone struggles. The sea isn't too heavy today, but that doesn't mean a man can't drown."

"Thanks for the tip."

"Have you heard what the operation will be?" Carter asked. He didn't expect an answer, but the Canadian might know something.

"Only rumours. Everything from recapturing the Channel Islands to liberating Paris. It will be good to get into the war, though. We've been here two years and the closest we've come to fighting is in a pub on a Saturday night."

"Be careful what you wish for." Carter advised. "I've lost men already and come close to getting killed myself. This isn't a game."

"We know that, but all this sitting around isn't doing much for the morale of our men. They need action."

"Let's see how they get on, then we can tell you if they're up to it."

The Canadian laughed but didn't rise to the bait. He gave Carter a brief wave that might have passed for a salute and sauntered back to his own men, still standing in lines along the path.

The landing craft had turned and were now on their run in to the beach. Carter could see a body hanging over the side of one of the little craft, vomiting into the sea. God help him when he gets into really rough water, Carter thought. One of Able section had seen him as well and a single shot rang out. Carter took out his notebook and opened it at a blank page. Writing the date, time and place at the top he wrote underneath *'Don't lean overboard when you feel sick. Keep your head inside the craft.'*

Bouncing on the increasing swell, the craft completed their run into shore, where the fun and games really started. There were different approaches to getting ashore, some more successful than others. In one craft whoever was in charge thought that using the ramps was a good idea and Able section's troopers let them know how bad it was with a steady fusillade of blank shots and an extended burst from the Bren gun. As Canadians struggled to get the ramps outboard and each soldier climbed precariously along the rungs to the beach, the other section, the one from 1 Troop, also joined in.

In another of the craft the men seemed reluctant to disembark at all. They each climbed onto the bows of the little craft, took a look then looked back to exchange words with the men behind. This indecision gave the commandos plenty of opportunities to fire their rifles. In the end it was probably only the steady banging of the weapons that told the Canadians that they were in danger and they started to leap into the shallows. Some made dryer landings than others.

Carter filled the page of his notebook and started a second as a figure squelched up the beach towards him, soaked from head to toe. "Not as easy as it looked, is it?" he said as he passed.

After each assault Carter and the other commando officers debriefed the ones that had just come ashore, with the officers of the remaining platoons within earshot so they could learn from the efforts of those who had gone before. Casualty numbers were provided, based on the number of rounds fired.

"You can't be sure all those shots would have hit." One Canadian officer complained.

"You can't be sure that they wouldn't." Martin Turner had replied. "Besides, the Germans would be using machine guns, sited in well dug in defences. Those landing craft are made of wood. The longer it takes to get out, the greater the chance of getting hit and the longer the machine guns will keep murdering your men." The word 'murder' provoked some thoughtful looks in both officers and men.

The Canadians were quick enough to learn. The next company to try it did better, then the next. The final company were sufficiently improved for the two commando troops to still have ammunition left over by the time the Canadians simulated their final assault.

At the end of the day Carter and the other commando officers were invited to the hotel that the Canadians had adopted as their unofficial Officer's Mess, much as 15 Commando had done with The Clansman in Troon.

As the officers drank Canadian whisky and exchanged small talk, there was more speculation about the possible targets for the upcoming operation. The commandos, more used to Scotch, wrinkled their noses at the Canadian brew, but with nothing else on offer they tolerated the drink out of politeness to their hosts.

The half-drowned Lieutenant had changed his uniform and joined the gathering. "Have the Canadians ever thought of forming commando units?" Carter asked him.

"There's been some talk." He replied, taking a long pull at his whiskey. "I think there have been some observers who went up to Scotland to have a look at your training, but nothing seems to have come of it.[1] We find that mixing some ginger with the whiskey makes it taste better." He smiled as he saw Carter's grimace as he took another sip.

"Thanks for the tip."

"So, how do you think we did this afternoon?"

"No worse than anyone else when they try landings for the first time. We start off on a lake in Scotland where there usually aren't any waves, so when we try it at sea for the first time, we usually get quite wet as well. I'm sure you'll get plenty of practice before the operation."

"Well, well." A voice came from behind Carter. "If it isn't the Great White Hope[2] himself, Lucky Carter."

He knew that voice, but what was its owner doing here? He swung round and there, behind him, stood Kas Kasmire.

"What ... erm I'm ..."

"I think the words you're looking for are 'Hi Kas, great to see you.'"

"Yes, of course. Hi Kas. But what ..; why ..."

The American laughed. "Remember that conversation we had a few weeks back, the one about the Rangers?"

"Yes, I remember it well. We were drinking a rather nice Scotch."

"Well, I did volunteer and they sent me up to Achnacarry. But there are no training places at the moment. They're putting so many men through there right now, Army, Marines, Rangers, it will be weeks before they can fit me onto a course. So they sent me down here as an observer, to see what you guys are doing right now. There's another fifty with 3 and 4 commandos, but they're fully trained. My understanding is they're going on whatever it is this little jaunt is about."

"I hadn't heard that, but it makes sense. Let them see first hand what it's all about."

"I'm hoping that your CO will let me tag along as well. That's why I'm here. I wondered if you might introduce me."

"Of course I will, but I'm not sure he'll approve. I don't think he would want to take an untrained man along with us."

"Maybe if I do all the training you guys are doing, he'll change his mind."

"What about your own command? Won't they have something to say?"

"My orders are to watch and learn. No one said I had to stay on English soil while I did it."

"OK, well, the CO is over there." Carter pointed across to where Vernon was in conversation with the commander of the Canadian battalion. He excused himself from his Canadian host and escorted Kasmire across the room.

"Excuse me, Sir. Sorry to interrupt."

"Ah, Steven." Vernon smiled. He turned back to his Canadian counterpart. "Col Hawkes, allow me to introduce Steven Carter. One of my most experienced officers."

"Pleased to meet you, son." The Canadian extended his hand to be shaken. "You guys are doing a great job keeping the Krauts awake at night."

"We do our best, Sir." He turned his attention back to Vernon. "May I be allowed to introduce Lt Kasmire. You may remember, Sir, I met him in the boxing ring back at Prestwick."

"How could I possibly forget."

"Kas, here is waiting for a place on a course at Achnacarry so he can join the Rangers. I understand that some of their number are with 3 and 4 commandos at the moment, getting some hands-on experience. Which is why Kas is here. He wants to join us for our training for whatever we have ahead."

"More than that, Sir." Kasmire interjected. "I'd like to go on the operation with you, if you will allow it."

"Joining us for training isn't a problem. I assume you have the necessary authority to be here. But going on the raid … I'm not so sure about that."

"My orders are quite open to interpretation, Sir."

"That's as may be, but you aren't trained. I can't take anyone who could turn out to be a liability. I'd leave some of my own men behind if I thought they weren't up to the job."

"I understand that, Sir. I wouldn't want to get in the way. Perhaps if you'd allow me to prove myself, then maybe I could convince you that I'm up to it."

"Putting it that way, I suppose I could at least give you a chance. But I'm warning you, if I suspect for a moment that you could put the lives of my men in danger, you won't get within a hundred miles of the target."

Carter suppressed a smile. Given where they were, geographically, it was already likely that they were well within a hundred miles, but he refrained from mentioning it.

"Looks like you've got a new recruit there, Bob." The Canadian Colonel chuckled at Vernon.

"And I hope he doesn't make me regret it." Vernon gave Kasmire a grim look.

[1] A joint US-Canadian commando, called the 1st Special Service Force, was founded on 2nd July 1942 and trained in Montana, USA. It's first operation was supposed to have been against the Japanese in 1943, on the Aleutian Islands, but when they arrived at their objective they found the Japanese had left. They later served in Italy and were part of Operation Dragoon, the invasion of Southern France. They were disbanded on 5th December 1944. One of their nicknames was "The Devil's Brigade", which became the title of a not very accurate film about them.

[2] The Great White Hope – A term originating in the USA before the First World War to describe the search for a white boxer capable of beating Jack Johnson, a black boxer who was beating all the white

fighters of the day. The term was used as the title of a play by Howard Sackler, with fictional fighter Jack Jefferson having to combat racism in the sport as well as the boxers in the ring. The play was based loosely on Jack Johnson's real-life story. It was turned into a film in 1970 starring James Earl Jones as Jefferson.

5 – Briefing

The officers squeezed into the Station Master's office at the station. In the days since their arrival little had changed in terms of accommodation. The soldiers still slept on the platforms, cooked their compo rations on hexamine stoves and made the best they could of a bad job. As always with the commandos, there was very little grumbling. To live in harsh conditions was a badge of honour for the men and most of them had experienced worse than Bishopstone railway station in high summer. They smiled at the insulting comments of the other British troops in the two neighbouring towns, the jibes of "gypsy" and worse.

The presence of concealed maps and a large covered model table told the officers why they were there. This was to be the first briefing for the operation. Conversation was muted as they waited expectantly. The men of the commando had been dispatched to the beach at Seaford for swimming, so that there would be no eavesdropping on the session, which would only lead to rumours flying through the ranks.

Promptly at oh nine hundred hours the CO entered the room. "As you were, gentlemen." He commanded, forestalling the stamping of feet on the wooden blocks of the parquet floor as they were about to come to attention. He started off with a comment about their accommodation.

"I would like to be able to tell you that we can expect to move to somewhere more comfortable, but I'm afraid I can't. Neither Combined Ops nor HQ South East Command can find anywhere for us to live that isn't miles away. It has even been suggested we move as far inland as Crawley, but I vetoed that idea. Given our need to train in this area, it seems sensible to remain here, despite the discomfort. I have asked for tents to be provided, so that we might move into the fields, but I doubt they'll arrive before our departure date. Which brings me to the main reason for today's gathering, the initial briefing for our operation."

He pulled the blanket off one of the blackboards to reveal a map of northern France, a section of coastline that stretched from Calais to Cherbourg. Two large paper arrows pointed to specific locations, the tip of the first rested on the town of Dieppe and the second pointed at the estuary of the River Seine.

"There will be two operations running concurrently, both designed to test the German defences in Normandy. I will concentrate on our part of the operations, naturally, but first I'll tell you a little about what will be happening elsewhere." Vernon used a pointer to indicate Dieppe.

"Dieppe is the objective for Operation Jubilee, which will involve an assault by a brigade of the Second Canadian Infantry Division, supported by three full commandos. Two of those commandos will be used to neutralise shore batteries a couple of miles to either side of the town, while the third commando, one of the new Royal Marine units, will go ashore with the main force.

Meanwhile, we will be involved in Operation Percival. The objective is the town of Honfleur." Vernon moved his pointer until the tip rested on a town on the western bank of the Seine estuary. "If you are unfamiliar with the town, I'm not surprised; it is quite small. However, when Shakespeare's Henry V exhorted his men once more into the breach, it was the siege of Honfleur to which he was referring. Between it and Paris lies the battlefield of Agincourt. But enough of history. We are interested only in the present." There was a polite chuckle from the officers.

"This operation involves another assault by a second brigade of Canadians. Ourselves and 16 Cdo will be supporting them. 16 Cdo will go in with the main force, then punch their way through the town to take control of the road that leads to the bridge across the River Seine, which lies a few Kilometres inland. Their job is to prevent German forces arriving to reinforce the town.

Our role is to capture an artillery battery that sits on the cliffs to the west of the town close to the village of Villerville. It has been given the nickname of the 'Himmler' battery and capturing it has been designated Operation Dagger. Once we have captured the battery, we will leave one troop to hold it, while the other four move inland to set up defences on the roads that lead to Honfleur from the west, to prevent reinforcements from arriving from that direction. Any questions so far?"

Andrew Fraser, Carter's roommate at Achnacarry, raised his hand. "Why Honfleur, Sir? Surely Le Havre, on the other side of the estuary, would be a more important objective in military terms."

Vernon gave an indulgent smile. "I think the answer is actually in the question, Andrew. Yes, in military terms Le Havre is more significant, but the Germans know that and it's heavily defended. Far more heavily than we could hope to overcome with anything less than a full division."

But there was more to it than that, Carter thought. By landing on the west bank of the estuary it would force the Germans to ask why. With an assault on Dieppe at the same time, the Germans might conclude that the intention was for the Canadians at Dieppe to attack inland until they reached the Seine, linking up with their colleagues who would advance inland along the other bank from Honfleur. Le Havre risked being cut off, surrounding the garrison there and also splitting the German forces in northern France in half. It would look like the aim was for the two forces to advance along both sides of the river until they reached Paris. More importantly, it would look like the invasion, which a man called Warriner had spent a lot of time and effort trying to convince the Germans was imminent. That deception had nearly cost Carter his life the previous January.

Of course, it wasn't an invasion, it was only a raid. A big raid, but still a raid. But it would probably help to sell the story to the Germans and make them think that an invasion was imminent, and that the Allies were testing their defences ahead of that. Most of all, it might make the Germans think about bolstering their defences by withdrawing troops from Russia and easing the pressure on Stalin's armies. But, of course, Carter was the only one in the room that knew of Warriner's plan.

The Colonel had started talking again. He uncovered a second blackboard to reveal a larger scale map, showing the beaches to be assaulted by the main force and the objectives once the landing had been completed. There was no point in just getting off the beach and standing around. Damage had to be done to the German defences, weapons and installations destroyed, prisoners taken and French men recruited to return to England and join De Gaulle's Free French Army.

There was a pause while the CO then revealed the model on the table that occupied a lot of the available floor space. It showed a length of shoreline dominated by cliffs, on top of which sat an artillery battery comprising six French guns, captured when France fell. Beyond that lay the coast road and then the interior of France and more narrow country roads.

"We'll be crossing in landing craft, departing from Newhaven a couple of hours before the main assault force, so that we land while it's still dark." The CO continued. "There are sufficient landing craft for five of our troops. Six Troop will be a floating reserve. They'll cross in a thing called a 'landing craft anti-aircraft', that's LC Ack-ack for short. It's big and, as may be guessed from the name, very well armed. Part of its purpose is to protect the right flank of the assault against air attack. Once the first five troops have landed, two landing craft will return to collect 6 Troop, who will then secure the beaches for the commandos' withdrawal."

Another hand shot up; Capt "Dickie" Bird. "If we're attacking the battery ahead of the main assault, Sir, won't that wake up the German defences along that stretch of coast, letting them know we're coming."

Carter may have been mistaken, but he thought he saw a frustrated look cross Vernon's face before he regained his composure. "Yes, Dickie, that is a possibility. That's why we will have to make the best attempt we can to capture the battery without making any noise. I fear it is a faint hope, but we'll have to try." A sad smile played around his lips, as though he had already had the same argument and lost.

Vernon paused to take a breath and a sip of water. "The reason we have been chosen for this particular part of the operation is our rock-climbing skills. A number of men from each troop will scale the cliffs and anchor ropes at the top, which the rest of the troop will climb. There's probably an optimum number of ropes to have, so we'll decide how many when we do our rehearsals. Yes, Steven." Vernon acknowledged Carter's raised arm.

"I told you about the way we got ropes to the top of the cliffs when we took part in Operation Tightrope. Could we not use the same method here?" For that operation the Navy had adapted mortar bombs for Carter's small force, firing grapnels over the tops of the cliffs to dig in and anchor climbing ropes.

"Not this time, Steven. With the climb being where it is, so close to the battery, the mortars and grapnels would make too much noise and possibly alert the sentries above our heads, so we're taking a more traditional approach."

Not as much noise as three hundred commandos trying to haul themselves up ropes, Carter thought, but the decision had been made. His job was to support and implement it, despite any reservations that he might have.

The briefing continued as the CO described how they would capture the battery and then move inland to set up defensive positions along the roads to prevent the enemy reinforcing Honfleur from the west.

"1 Troop will have the longest hike, moving inland about two kilometres. We can't go any further inland because it would spread our line too thinly. Even as we are, we will have our left flank exposed. But we're not there to hold that line all day, just long enough for the Canadians to do their thing in the town, then we can withdraw, blow up the guns and get out the way we went in. Any questions?"

There was a forest of raised hands as every officer tried to identify things that would affect their own part of the operation. Carter filled several pages of his notebook before he was done and the briefing came to a close. A rota was posted that would allow each Troop Commander to use the maps and the model to brief his own men during the course of the rest of the day.

"Tomorrow," Vernon announced before they left, "we start our climbing practice. It's the most important part of the operation for us. If we can't get to the tops of those cliffs, the whole raiding force will be exposed to the firepower from that battery."

* * *

The darkness was almost complete. On the beach two troops of commandos crowded into the narrow gap between the waves and the cliffs. They shivered in wet uniforms, soaked by spray and waves as they had stumbled ashore from the landing craft that were already drawing back from the beach and turning to head back to Newhaven.

It was just another of the climbing exercises that had dominated their training. They had started on the lower cliffs nearest to the Cuckmere estuary, climbing in daylight under the supervision of instructors. When they had first started their practice, there had been men at the top with safety ropes, held taught around their bodies as the men below them climbed upwards. But soon they had discarded the safety ropes and they hadn't been used for a couple of weeks. The men had to have confidence that they could make the climb without them. Not every man would climb, of course. The best were chosen and they would carry ropes with them, coiled around their bodies. These would be anchored to the top of the cliff and then lowered back down, where the men below would attach the heavier equipment and allow it to be hauled upwards.

Then the men themselves would use the ropes to pull themselves upwards, hand over hand, their feet searching out very nook and cranny in order to give themselves some extra leverage.

Having mastered the techniques in daylight they had then practised at night, before taking it to the next level and making an assault from the sea. Tonight, it was the turn of 4 and 5 Troops.

Stationed at the top of the cliffs were listeners. 3 Troop, old rivals of Carter's, lay in three extended rows, starting at the top of the cliff, then fifty yards inland, with the third and final row a hundred yards inland. Their job was to report on every noise that the commandos made, from the rattle of poorly secured equipment, to whispered commands and even the sound of falling rocks.

If the most distant row of listeners heard anything, the climb would be regarded as a failure for having alerted enemy sentries. If the middle row heard anything it would be regarded as a need to improve and if the front rank didn't hear anything the climb would be considered a complete success.

Commandos from each troop squatted half in and half out of the water, their rifles pointed towards the top of the cliffs where a curious sentry might appear at any moment. Four men from each troop stepped forward and started to climb. They appeared as black shadows against the mottled paleness of the chalk. From a distance it appeared white, but closer up it was more of a grey. This section of cliff was between eighty and a hundred feet in height, the estimate for the cliffs that they would have to ascend in France.

They climbed slowly, testing each hand and foothold before applying their full weight. The chalk was soft and sometimes broke under their hands, so it was important to make sure that each bit was solid before moving.

Some climbers were faster than others and one from 5 Troop was soon higher than the rest, moving quickly from handhold to handhold, scrambling up the cliff space like a large spider on a white wall.

His speed worried Carter. It looked like he wasn't testing each handhold or foothold properly. He knew that mountaineers would drive pitons into cracks and thread safety ropes through carabiners which they attached to the pitons, so that if they slipped the rope would go taught and prevent them from falling to the bottom. But the commandos couldn't do that. The hammering of the pitons would make too much noise, as would the rattle of the spare carabiners. It was risky, there had already been falls that had resulted in broken bones. But risk was part of a commando's life.

But the trooper, whoever he was, had almost reached the top. Then disaster struck. His hand came away from the rock and there was the rattle of falling rock, if the soft chalk could be given such a solid sounding description. The man's body swayed outwards as he flailed to try and regain his handhold. It was a fight with gravity that only gravity could win. The man's own bodyweight pulled him further outwards until his straining fingers were unable to retain their grip on his remaining handhold. His fingers gave up the unequal straggly and the man seemed to fall in slow motion, his upper body going horizontal, then vertical as his feet stayed in place on the cliff face until they, too, parted company with the cliff. He plummeted headfirst down the face, bouncing once to arc out and land at the feet of the men waiting below.

They clustered around the inert body, its arms and legs sticking out at impossible angles.

An officer forced his way through the crowd, then spread his arms to usher then men back from the dead man, giving himself some space in which to look for any signs of life, though they all knew that there would be none.

"Keep climbing!" Another officer called. It might have been Martin Turner, but Carter couldn't be sure. Despite the tragedy, the exercise had to continue. If it were to happen in France they would have to carry on, so they had to carry on here as well.

In terms of stealth the exercise was compromised, of course. But the value of it now was that they learn the lesson that had cost a man his life. Don't rush things. Take your time and test your hand and foot holds and, even if a man falls, don't start shouting orders.

The trooper who was killed was Thomas Yardley of 5 Troop. At his funeral his comrades remarked in hushed tones how he hadn't uttered a sound as he fell. "That's commando training for you." They muttered with pride in their voices.

Yardley's family would never know how he died. In his letter to them, Lt Col Vernon would just say that he died on active service, upholding the finest traditions of the commandos. It would be something for them to cling onto as they mourned. They wouldn't be told where he was buried until after Operation Dagger was complete and the commandos had moved on to pastures new. Even the death of a loved one couldn't be allowed to compromise security.

After the 2IC and the CO were satisfied that the commandos had mastered the necessary climbing skills, a Royal Artillery battery was set up on the cliff tops, dug in much the same as aerial photographs showed the German guns to be sited. Night after night the commandos climbed the cliffs to attack the gunners, who got heartily sick of the whole thing.

But by the end of July the CO declared himself satisfied that the commandos were skilled enough to carry out the first phase of Operation Dagger no matter what they might have to face. The artillery battery returned to their barracks and the commandos started rehearsing the defensive tactics they would use to prevent the Germans from reinforcing Honfleur.

From night-time cliff assaults the exercises extended to include the daylight hours. A Light Infantry battalion was drafted in to provide enemy reinforcements and some of the ambushes were decided by punches being thrown. The green jackets[1] decided that it wasn't wise to dispute the commando's claims of victory..

It was exhausting, but it prepared the commandos for what they would have to face when they went ashore for the real thing.

[1] Green jackets – a nickname applied during the Napoleonic wars when light infantry regiments were first formed and used. Their founder, General Sir John Moore, had served during the American War of Independence and encountered the first United States Marines. He noted that, compared to the British Redcoats, their dark green uniforms made them difficult to see in the thick forests of Massachusetts and decided that such an advantage would be considerable for the role of scouting and reconnaissance that the light infantry would provide. In 1958 the Oxfordshire and Buckinghamshire Light Infantry, the Kings Royal Rifle Corps and the Rifle Brigade all merged to form the Green Jackets regiment, who were granted the title "Royal" in 1966. In 2007 the Royal Green Jackets merged with three other infantry and light infantry regiments to form The Rifles.

* * *

The commandos shuffled along the quayside, organised into their troops so that they didn't become separated during the boarding process. They moved quietly, keeping commands to a minimum. While police patrolled the neighbouring streets to keep casual observers away, there was no point in attracting attention by making excessive noise. It was hoped that the first the population of Newhaven would know about the raid was when they looked over the harbour and saw the absence of the shipping that had been crowded in over the previous weeks. However, as they were boarding in daylight it was a slim hope. Perhaps the people would think they were just embarking for another training exercise.

Carter climbed down the ladder and took his place at the front of the landing craft. It was his job to be first out, first onto the beach, setting an example for his men to follow. He would be useless once he got there, because he wasn't one of the men selected to make the climb up the cliffs, but it was important to be seen leading from the front. It was the commando way.

Behind him another twenty one men climbed down the ladder until it was finally removed and the cox'n powered the craft out into the middle of the estuary to tag onto the flotilla that was forming there. In the evening light the craft were clearly visible, low on the water, waves lapping around them.

Landing craft normally held thirty men at a time but given the ten hour duration of the crossing it had been decided to reduce this to twenty one plus officers or senior NCOs, giving the men space to be able to sit on the bottom boards. But that meant they needed more landing craft, which were in short supply because of the sheer number of troops involved in the various operations. There had also been drop-outs due to mechanical failure, but that was to be expected as well.

Instead, they had been provided with a Landing Craft Ack-Ack, or anti-aircraft. It was a much bigger boat, well-armed with pom-pom guns and heavy calibre machine guns. Crammed in below its deck was 6 Troop, who would be the floating reserve. The boat would stand off shore until the initial wave of commandos were ashore, when some of their landing craft would return and collect 6 Troop and ferry them to the beach.

The Canadians would have it easier. They would be transported across the English Channel aboard landing ships, only transferring to landing craft about an hour before they were due to attack.

At a signal from the quay, the landing craft started to move. The vibrations beneath Carter's backside increased as power was applied to the single propeller. As they cleared the harbour wall the swell hit them and the first sounds of retching could be heard from the commandos. At this distance from France it was OK for the men to be sick over the side. The craft wallowed as they started to form up into a flotilla, five craft abreast, one from each troop, followed by two more rows of five behind; fifteen in all. To their right, the western side, the Landing Craft Ack-Ack took station, It's anti-aircraft guns sweeping the skies, searching for threats. Beyond that a Royal Navy destroyer, HMS Tyndal, acted as guard ship to deter any seaborne threat.

On the left a steam gunboat from the 1st Steam Gunboat Flotilla belched black smoke. Lt Col Vernon had made it his floating HQ. Using its Royal Navy radio he could maintain contact with the operational commanders, both land and sea, as well as keeping in touch with his own troops using their Type 18 radio sets until he, too, stepped ashore in France.

Looking at the small fleet, Carter was impressed with the fighting capability they represented.

6 – The Channel

The course they would take wasn't a direct line. They would first steam down the Channel towards the Isle of Wight before turning south east to approach the French coast at an angle, keeping a safe distance from the defences of Le Havre. It added time to their journey, but it was better than running into any shipping that might be patrolling the harbour mouth. The Canadian's landing ships would take a similar route.

High above them, Carter could make out the tiny cruciform shapes of fighter aircraft, shepherding them from above, keeping the airborne threat at bay. They would shadow the small fleet until darkness fell.

The swell grew heavier as the land fell away behind them, making the flat bottomed landing craft buck and roll. Most of the commandos were used to the motion, but some of the newer recruits were suffering badly.

Gradually the summer sun began to sink in the north west, turning the sky golden, then gradually deeper shades of blue and pink until, at last, darkness fell. The commandos breathed a collective sigh of relief that they had managed to get that far without discovery. It would only require one German aircraft to get a sighting of them to raise the alarm. But the *Luftwaffe* hadn't ventured out that evening. Once it was dark it didn't matter. They would simply be some black shapes against a blacker sea when viewed from above. The phosphorescence of their bow waves and wakes the only sign of their passing.

This was the worst part for all of the commandos, the waiting. There was nothing in their training that could prepare them for the tedium of the sea crossing and the way it played on their minds. Inside the blacked out hull of a landing ship they had enough light to play cards, read books or tend to their kit, but in a landing craft in the dark all they could do was hold muted conversations, or commune with their own thoughts.

Trouble, when it came, was as swift as it was unexpected. They were probably no more than an hour from their destination, the shoreline of France invisible ahead of them in the darkness. From in front and to the east there was a bang and a whoosh, before a star shell lit up the night.

Shouts of alarm went up from the commandos, before the bellow of Cpl Franklyn's voice ordered the men to be silent again. He was the ranking NCO because Sgt Chalk was in the landing craft that carried How section.

Carter raised his head carefully and peered over the side of the landing craft. Strung out ahead of them was a small convoy of merchant ships, three in all. Ahead of them, setting the pace, was what appeared to be a trawler and probably was. Both sides used armed trawlers for convoy escort work. Damn and blast, Carter thought. Both the British and Germans used the darkness to cover the movement of merchant ships along their respective coastlines. Somehow their flotilla had run into one. The possibility of a meeting at sea should have been considered. Already radio signals would be sending the news of their presence back to France.

But it wasn't the armed trawler that was the real danger, it was the pair of E-Boats that had swung away from the convoy's flank and were now bearing down on the landing craft at speed. Carter estimated their angle of approach and realised that they would pass behind his own craft, probably going between the front and the second rank of boats. The second E-Boat increased its speed and formed line abreast with its partner. It looked to be heading for the gap between the second and third ranks of landing craft.

Although the E-Boats were armed with torpedoes, they weren't a threat. The landing craft had a very shallow draft and a torpedo would be bound to pass underneath them, doing no damage. No, it was the 20 mm machine guns that would inflict the damage; one mounted in front of the bridge and another pair mounted aft.

The lead boat started firing its forward machine gun, aiming towards the landing craft that was on the eastern end of the flotilla in the second rank. The thin marine plywood wouldn't offer the commandos any protection from the large calibre rounds. Once between the two ranks, the E-Boats would be able to bring their aft guns to bear as well, pouring machine gun fire into both flanks.

The gunboat opened fire with its Oerlikon cannons. Its 3 inch gun would be useless at such close range. The E-Boats turned the attention of their aft guns on that, spraying it with heavy calibre rounds. Somewhere on board the gunboat a steam pipe was severed, sending gouts of white vapour into the night air.

Lewis guns began to answer back from the landing craft, but they were far smaller calibre and would be unlikely to do any serious damage to the E-Boats. Their only hope was to hit members of the crew.

Where was the Navy? Carter wondered. HMS Tyndall was with them specifically to counter this sort of threat. But the whereabouts of the destroyer was unknown. The darkness seemed to have swallowed it up.

There was only one way of escaping from the assault. If they stayed where they were it was only a matter of time before the E-Boats chopped them into mincemeat.

"Pass the order back to the cox'n." Carter instructed the man nearest to him. "Tell him to increase speed to maximum. Head for the landing beaches as fast as he can get this tub to go."

At last some answering gunfire could be heard. The Landing Craft Ack-Ack had opened up with its pom-pom guns and heavy machine guns. But it had to be careful. With the landing craft and the E-Boats so close together it was as easy to hit a friend as an enemy.

The vibrations beneath Carter's feet increased as the Cox'n obeyed the order to increase speed. Looking aft, in the dying light of the star shell, Carter could see the rest of the flotilla starting to fall astern. One landing craft was wallowing, dead in the water, it's nose starting to droop as the sea began to claim it. Small arms fire twinkled along the flanks of some of the landing craft as the commandos tried to fight back, but they might as well have been using pea shooters. The E-boats had broken through on the far side of the line and were starting to turn back for a second pass, zigzagging to confuse the aim of the gunners on the Ack-Ack boat.

"Lucky escape, Sir." Cpl Franklyn said, from his position beside Carter at the front of the boat.

"Not for the guys still back there." Carter said, keeping his voice low.

"Perhaps a word for the men, Sir. Keep their spirits up, sort of thing."

"Of course." Carter coughed, attracting the attention of those closest to him, who passed the word back that the officer had something to say.

"Men, it's unfortunate that we ran into that trouble. But nothing changes. The operation goes ahead. There are thousands of Canadians who are relying on us to silence the Himmler battery. If we fail, then what we have just witnessed will look like a Sunday afternoon in the park by comparison. I'm sure other landing craft will get through, so between us, we'll have enough firepower to sort out the battery and then hang onto it until it's time to withdraw."

"What about defending the roads, Sir?" A voice called from the darkness.

"That will depend on how many of us get through. We'll certainly put patrols out, but beyond that, I can't say just yet. But the first part of the plan remains the same. We climb the cliffs and take the battery."

Their rehearsals had prepared them for all eventualities. Although it was 5 Troop's responsibility to capture the battery, all the troops had practiced doing it, so the men knew what was expected of them. Was it the right decision? Carter wondered. There were so few of them. Was he now leading a suicide mission?

But they had no choice. What he had told his men was the truth. If that gun battery was still operational when the Canadians started their run into the beaches at Honfleur, they would be blown to pieces. It was his job to stop that, even if it meant certain death for himself and his men.

He peered into the darkness on both sides of the boat. He was sure he could make out the bow waves of other landing craft, at least one on either side. Perhaps they weren't alone.

He raised himself up on tip toes and stared aft. Tracer still arced across the night sky as the E-Boats continued their deadly attack and the Ack-Ack boat and the gunboat replied. But there was a boat burning there as well. From what Carter could make out it was either one of the merchant ships, or perhaps the trawler. If so, the E-Boats would be forced to break off the attack in order to protect their charges. Carter doubted that the *Kriegsmarine* would be very forgiving if the merchant ships were sunk because the E-Boats had neglected them.

A voice spoke immediately behind Carter. "Cox'n says to stand by for landing." No 'Sir' was attached, not now they were in the field. The cox'n, as instructed, hadn't used the loudspeaker system to give the warning. Technically they were still trying to make a silent approach, though the carnage behind them made a mockery of that.

"Stand by men." Carter said, keeping his voice low. The instruction was relayed back from man to man.

Carter's head was filled with thoughts. He could imagine the radio transmissions made by the Germans when they discovered the flotilla of landing craft.

"Enemy landing craft, course south south east, estimated speed ten knots. I am engaging."

Then the answering message. "Please confirm course, speed and numbers."

Then the radio transmission being repeated. Somewhere in France, probably Le Havre, the duty *Kriegsmarine* operations officer reaching for a telephone to report to his superiors, the message being relayed through each level of the command structure until it reached the *Hôtel de La Marine* on the *Place de la Concorde* in Paris then, eventually, Berlin. At the same time more telephone calls would alert the *Wehrmacht* and *Luftwaffe* commands in northern France, giving a warning of an impending attack. Pre-prepared plans would be implemented. Soldiers, sailors and aircrew would be dragged from their beds. The garrison commander at Honfleur being woken by the duty officer and told that something was happening out at sea.

How quickly would word spread? Carter wondered. Was the guard already being turned out at the Himmler battery, still concealed by the darkness ahead of them? Were they now expected but very unwelcome guests?

7 – The Himmler Battery

The craft had hardly grounded itself on the beach when Carter was up onto the prow and jumping down into shallow water. Despite it being the middle of August, the water was cold enough to shock his system. A wave surged passed his knees and he used its power to hasten him forward onto the chalky sand.

There were splashes as his men followed, no commands were necessary, not for these men. If they didn't know what to do by now, they were in the wrong unit. Carter crouched at the base of the cliff and let his men come to him, spreading out along the junction between chalk and sand. One man started to climb, a heavy coil of climbing rope adding to his already heavy burden. A second man started, further along the beach. That was all for this craft, just two climbers.

The cliffs weren't vertical here, not like those at Cuckmere Haven. Aerial photographs had shown that. No more than eighty degrees from the horizontal, less in places. Steep enough to require skill to climb them, shallow enough to be able to stop yourself from falling if a hand hold gave way.

In places enough soil had settled for grass to grow, even the odd hardy shrub, especially close to the tops where the slope was even shallower.

Carter turned as he heard the sound of another landing craft grounding. A dark wave of men streamed over its bows, racing the short distance to the base of the cliffs. Carter turned back to locate Cpl Franklyn. "Keep the men going, as per the plan. I'm going to consult with whoever is in charge that of that LC." He trotted off along the beach until he found a commando who could direct him towards his officer. It turned out to be the Adjutant, Dickie Bird.

"Dickie. Glad to see you." It was bizarre, chatting like they had just met on the boundary of the village cricket ground.

"And you, Steven. I see you've got your men started already."

"As the old saying goes, the show must go on."

"Indeed. Ah, more reinforcements." Bird pointed along the beach, past Carter's landing craft to where another was just disgorging it passengers. As they watched, another grounded on the shoreline beyond.

"Runner!" Bird called in a hoarse whisper. A commando appeared at his side. "Get along and find the officers in those two LCs." He ordered. "Ask them to join me here, then guide them back."

"Don't you have radio contact?" Carter asked.

By way of reply, Bird turned to the commando that was squatting behind him, the bulk of a Type 18 radio set weighing him down. The man was speaking into his handset. "Well, Collins. Any contact yet."

"No sir. Not a cheap."

"There's your answer. Nothing from the CO and nothing from any of the other troops, either. Where's your set?"

"With Martin Turner in the second landing craft, wherever they are."

"I think the same applies to all the troops. The only reason I was in the leading craft is because young Wilkie twisted his ankle this morning. Who knows what's happening back there. If they had to bail out, they'll have ditched all their equipment to stop them from drowning."

"So, you seem to be the ranking officer. What do we do now?"

A line of four men jogged towards them from along the beach. The first was the runner that Bird had sent. The second two were commando officers, Andrew Fraser from 3 Troop and Ian Motson from 5 Troop. The last in line was distinguishable by his very un-British style of steel helmet; Kas Kasmire, who had finally persuaded Lt Col Vernon to allow him to accompany 15 Cdo on the raid. As they clustered around Bird, another figure appeared from the direction of the nearest landing craft.

"Mind if I sit in, chaps?" It was Lt Buxton, the Naval officer commanding the flotilla of landing craft.

"Welcome to France, gentlemen. Does anyone know if there are any other LCs coming?"

Andrew Fraser shook his head. "I doubt it, Dickie. I saw 1 Troop's leading LC with its bow down, as though it was sinking. Those behind were being shot up by those E-Boats. I doubt any will get through and even if they did, they'll be full of the dead and wounded."

"Yes, if they survive at all they'll have had to turn back, I think." Motson added.

"The Navy have been ordered to maintain radio silence." Buxton informed them. "I've been listening in, but there has been nothing on the network. I didn't want to break silence myself. We'd be bound to give away our presence if I did."

"I think the E-Boats have done that for us, but you're right, it's best for you to follow your orders. In that case it's just us. Eighty men to do the work of three hundred."

"We carry on?" Kasmire sounded incredulous.

"Of course we carry on. Lives are at risk if we don't. I won't have it said that 15 Cdo were found wanting. Does anyone disagree?" As the ranking officer, it wasn't necessary that his subordinates agree with him, but Bird wasn't about to force them into doing anything that they didn't wholeheartedly support.

The other three commando officers confirmed their agreement. Only Kasmire stayed silent. But he wasn't a commando. He wasn't even a Ranger.

Carter became aware that there weren't many commandos still in their vicinity. So many had now managed to reach the cliff tops that the officers and a few stragglers were all that was left. Further along the beach the later arrivals were still ascending, but even their numbers were starting to dwindle.

Once the initial climbers reached the top, they had lowered their climbing ropes to allow the rest of the commandos to follow. First to grab the ropes were the men with the wire cutters, necessary to breach the first line of defence at the top of the cliffs. Next to go were the scouts, specially selected for their skills at moving silently through the countryside at night, creeping close to the enemy defences to assess their strength and state of readiness. The rest of the men then followed, spreading out along the cliff top in preparation for the attack on the battery.

"OK. We didn't come ashore in the right order, but I'm not going to try to reorganise us now. That means 3 and 4 troops will make the assault on the battery. Between you there should be enough men. while 2 and 5 troops cover the flanks. Steven, I'm putting you in charge of the two assault troops. You'll lead the attack. No offence, Andrew, but Steven was here first." Fraser grunted an acknowledgement, not totally happy to have to concede the leadership to his old friend and rival.

"When we've captured the battery, the other two troops will pass through and spread out on the other side to prevent any counter-attack. Once we've done that, I'll convene an O-Group[1] and we can discuss what we do next, other than hang on to the battery, of course."

"What about communications?" Fraser asked.

"We'll have to rely on runners, just the way they did in the last war." Bird replied. "But keep your troops close enough to allow the last man of each troop to be able to speak to the first man in the next. We can relay simple messages by word of mouth that way. Within your troops stick to hand signals if you can. There's just about enough light to see them." As if looking for confirmation, he glanced skywards where the occasional star could be glimpsed through the broken cloud.

The officers muttered their understanding.

"What do you want me to do?" Buxton asked.

"Be here when we get back. But if you have to leave to save your men, do so."

"The Navy will be here." Was Buxton's grim reply.

"Now, gentlemen, I think our men are waiting for us to give them orders, so I suggest we join them."

The five officers split up and returned along the beach to where a single commando stood, holding on to the end of each of the climbing ropes.

Carter slung his Tommy gun across his back to get it out of the way. At Kirkesfjord he had gone ashore with only a Webley revolver with which to defend himself and soon found out how inadequate it was. He'd had to take a rifle from a dead German. For his other two missions he had been issued with Sterling sub-machine guns, but the commandos preferred the Thompson, an import from the USA. It was far less prone to jamming than the Sterling.

Carter pulled on the rope to make sure that it was properly anchored. A dozen men had already climbed it, but there was no harm in making sure. Reaching upwards he heaved with his arms while planting his feet firmly onto the chalky soil of the cliff face. Hand over hand, foot over foot, he pulled himself up the cliff, glad of the darkness to conceal the increasing drop below him. As he neared the top, hands reached down to drag him the last few feet onto firmer ground. The first thing Carter saw was the thin pale line on the eastern horizon, heralding the approaching dawn.

They had to get a move on, before it became light enough for the sentries at the gun battery to see them.

Cpl Franklyn arrived next to him. "Everyone's ready, Lucky." Carter insisted that the men use his nickname when out in the field. There was no place for salutes and 'Sirs' when enemy snipers were looking for targets.

"OK, are the scouts back?"

"Yes. Danny Glass is here." The corporal waved Glass over to join them.

"What did you see?" Carter asked the scout. They'd worked together on two previous operations and Carter knew that Glass could be trusted not to exaggerate his report.

"The defensive positions aren't manned. If the alarm's been raised then they're keeping it a secret. I could hear voices from close to the guns. That will be the sentries, but otherwise it was all quiet."

Perhaps the sentries had assumed that the fireworks out at sea were just a naval conflict of some sort. Such night-time encounters weren't common, but they also weren't unknown. "OK, Danny. Re-join your section. I'll need you to guide us, so we don't fall into any weapons pits."

If the alarm had been raised, then the defences would be manned and ready. It was taking the Germans longer than he had expected to react to whatever they'd been told about the contact between the landing craft and the E-Boats. But dawn was approaching and armies across the world always 'stand-to' just before dawn, manning their defences just in case of a surprise attack; an attack just like the one he was about to launch. He doubted that the Germans, perched above the English Channel, would do anything different.

Carter checked his watch. "Pass the word.along the line." He instructed in a whisper. "We advance at oh four thirty exactly." Just two minutes away. He paused to gather his thoughts. What else did he need to do? He needed to keep the enemy's heads down. That was important. "Get a Bren gun out on each flank of the troop." He ordered Franklyn. "If the Germans start shooting, they're to keep up covering fire as we attack. There'll be no messing. When I give the word to charge, then everyone charges."

Franklyn nodded his head in understanding. It was the way it had been rehearsed. He hurried off to detail two Bren gun teams to their task.

Carter stared at his watch as the second hand edged around the face to the appointed time. As it hit the twelve mark he held his hand to his side and waved it forward; advance. To reinforce his words, he stepped forward. But Glass was already ahead of him, weaving a path through the gorse bushes that topped the cliffs. They passed through the gaps cut in the barbed wire. It wasn't the vicious entanglements that he had met on his previous visit to France, just a few strands supported by rusting posts, enough to prevent someone from getting too close to the cliff edge. Whoever had set up the defences on this section of the coast hadn't considered the risk of anyone climbing the cliffs in the dark. But then again, the commandos were still a very novel weapon of war.

With the black of the night behind them they would still have the advantage of concealment, but the darkness couldn't stop a noise from being heard. The downside was that when the sun rose, it would be directly in their eyes, making it difficult to see the enemy. It was better that they attacked in the dark. Had he ordered the men to fix bayonets? He glanced to his side, towards the nearest commando. The eight inch steel spike was just visible on the end of the man's rifle. Good for Cpl Franklyn. He'd remembered, even though Carter hadn't. 'Old', he thought wryly. The corporal was younger than Carter by at least a year.

He felt the tension building in his stomach, his heart starting to pound in his ears. At any minute a gunshot could split the night and leave him wounded or dying on the ground. What was he doing here? He asked himself, not for the first time. He was here because he had wanted adventure and excitement, he reminded himself. Well, he had both now. Today could be the last day of his life; he might as well do his best to enjoy it.

He fought down the fear and concentrated on his training. Mind where you put your feet. Take each step slowly so that you don't step on a loose stone or a twig that might snap. Put your weight on the outside edge of the boot to minimise contact with the ground, then roll inwards to get a firm footing before moving your other leg. Peer ahead into the darkness, looking for danger. But above all, listen. In the darkness the first sign of danger will almost certainly come in the form of a sound.

Ahead of him, Glass came to a halt and raised his hand; not high, just to shoulder height. Carter obeyed the signal, coming to a halt himself. The men beside and behind him did the same. They sank to the ground, turning to face in different directions, alert for any sign of trouble.

Glass took a few steps backwards until he was almost beside Carter. He leant in close so he could whisper. "We're just about to go through the first line of defences. Best get the men in single file, so no one stumbles into a trench." It was just a suggestion, but not one a wise commander would ignore.

Carter raised his hand above his head. The nearest man saw and moved in behind him, the rest responding as the signal was relayed through the sections. 3 Troop would be advancing on a parallel course, about a thirty yards to their right, where they would be doing the same.

Glass took the lead again and Carter gave the signal to advance once more. He was amazed that twenty men could move without making any noise worth talking about. They had practised it enough times, of course, but it was unbelievable that they could do it across unfamiliar ground while under such stress.

As he passed through the line of slit trenches and gun pits Carter paused so he could wave the men behind him back into line abreast on either side of him as they, too, cleared the obstacles. As they passed him Carter placed his hand against the stock of his weapon and lifted it off, replacing it and lifting it again: Keep spaced out. The worst thing they could do was to bunch up, making a single large target for a machine gun, mortar or grenade. They kept going and when the last man was through, Carter rushed to catch up with Glass again.

The defence line had been a hundred yards behind the cliff edge, but fifty yards in front of the gun battery, arranged around it in a circle, but with more slit trenches facing the sea; the direction from which an enemy would come. They were so close that even a deaf sentry would soon be able to hear their footsteps.

The thought had hardly crossed his mind when a loud clanging broke out ahead of them. Metal striking metal, repeatedly and very loudly. If that wasn't an alarm signal, then Carter had never heard one. Had they been detected, or had the alert message finally reached the battery? No challenge had been issued; no German shout of '*Halt! Wer geht dahin?* Halt! Who goes there?' It must be the alert signal finally reaching the battery, Carter concluded. It meant they still had the element of surprise, but only for a few minutes, seconds even.

Soon the guard force would be flooding out of their hut to take up their stand-to positions, followed soon after by the rest of the battery's personnel, who would even now be falling out of bed, reaching for trousers and boots, rifles and sub-machine guns.

There was no longer anything to be gained by sneaking around.

"Charge!" Carter yelled, adding to the message by firing a short burst from his Tommy gun into the darkness. He doubted if he had hit anything, but that wasn't the point. Bren guns opened fire on either flank, their bullets forming two converging lines on the dark shapes in front of them.

Carter tried to visualise the layout of the camp that he had worked so hard to memorise. Almost directly in front of them were the guns, each one dug in behind protective earthworks. They were on 3 Troop's line of advance, so he would leave them for Fraser's men to tackle. Behind them were earthen bunkers where the 'ready use' ammunition was held. Just enough to keep the guns firing for the first few minutes, while soldiers brought more shells up from the larger ammunition bunker set back at a distance of about a hundred yards. Between the ready use bunkers and the main ammunition dump were three large huts and a smaller ablutions block. Two of the huts provided eating and living space for the battery personnel, about sixty men in all, while the third hut acted as a combined headquarters and guard room. The officers probably lived in there as well.

A vertical rectangle of light appeared diagonally to one side of him. It must be the guardroom door. Black shadows flitted through it as the guard turned out. Carter sent short bursts of Tommy gun fire towards them. The right hand Bren gun shifted its aim to focus on the threat.

Shots were returned as the guards retaliated and the men on either side of Carter raised their weapons to their shoulders and fired towards the twinkling muzzle flashes.

A second rectangle of light appeared from another hut but was quickly extinguished as someone within realised that it created an ideal aiming point. A short burst of sub-machine gun fire ripped from the entrance, sending bullets crackling past Carter's head.

Don't take it personally, Steven, he told himself. He's just shooting into the dark and you happen to be in the direction he's facing. But he returned with a long burst of fire of his own, emptying the Tommy gun's magazine.

He pressed the release lever and felt the magazine drop to the floor. Reaching into his ammunition pouch he withdrew a replacement and slid it home before cocking the weapon to make it ready to fire again.

He heard shouts from his men as they drove forward in the attack.

"Over here!"

"Cover me!"

"Get that bastard!"

"Fuck, I'm hit!"

Carter realised that he wasn't really leading his men, he was just another gun firing in the darkness. If he didn't do something the attack would break down into a series of individual combats and that would result in chaos.

"Easy and Fox sections, on me!" he shouted.

"Right here, Lucky." He heard Cpl Porter's voice from a few feet away.

"And me." Cpl Franklyn echoed from the other side.

"OK, we're going for the right-hand hut. When we get within a few yards we'll open up with everything we've got." He turned to his right. "George section, cover our right flank! He bellowed above the crack and rattle of small arms fire.

He didn't wait for a reply. He just ran forward and hoped for the best that he would be followed. The hut loomed out of the darkness. The door was shut, but Carter could hear shouts from inside. No doubt an NCO trying to get his men out and into a position to defend the battery.

Carter dropped into a kneeling position, one knee of the ground and the other bent so that he could rest his left elbow on it and steady his weapon as he fired. The men on either side either knelt, like him, or fell onto their bellies, whichever was their personal preference.

"Fire!" Carter commanded. Ten rifles, two Bren guns and three Tommy guns opened up on the hut, raking it with fire. Light appeared as bullets penetrated the wood, which made it easier for the commandos to focus on their target. Then the light went out, whether someone had switched it off or whether the bulb had been hit by a stray bullet it wasn't possible to tell. The fusillade became more ragged as each commando stopped and reloaded, before firing again.

"Cease fire!" Carter shouted. When the weapons had fallen silent he ran forward, reaching for a grenade dangling from his webbing harness. Letting his Tommy gun hang on its strap he pulled the pin of the grenade and then felt for the door handle. Finding it, he levered it downwards. The door swung outwards, away from him and he lobbed the grenade through before throwing himself to the ground, shouting "Grenade!" as a warning to his men as he did so.

The few seconds it took for the grenade to explode seemed endless to Carter, but finally explode it did. Splinters of wood and glass flew outwards. It was followed by an eerie silence, broken only by someone screaming in pain.

Carter's men didn't need an invitation. They threw themselves into the hut, the corporals leading the way with their Tommy guns, firing all around them. The other commandos fired their rifles from the hip, not looking for targets, just keeping the enemy pinned to the floor under their onslaught. Someone screamed and this was followed by shouts of '*Kamerad*!' and "'cease fire'. A few seconds later silence fell again, at least in the space in and around the hut. Elsewhere the noise of combat continued as Carter's other section and Fraser's 3 Troop continued the assault.

Corporal Franklyn appeared in the doorway. "Three dead, half a dozen wounded and the rest have surrendered, Lucky." He reported.

"What about your men?"

"All fine and dandy, same for Fox section."

"OK, round up the prisoners and keep them under guard at the back of the hut. Tell Porter to set up a perimeter around the outside of the hut. I'll go and see what's going on."

In the gathering light, Carter could now make out distinct shapes. There were heads wearing the soup bowl shaped helmets of the British moving among the guns, now behind Carter. To his right the Germans had managed to set up a defensive line, but they had no cover. It wasn't a matter of if they would surrender, only a matter of when. George section was trying to engage the left flank of that line but were poorly positioned. Carter could see a solution for that which would distract the Germans and allow 3 Troop to roll them up from the other flank. Carter scurried across until he found Cpl MacMillan of George section.

"Get a Bren gun on top of that bunker there." He pointed back towards the grass covered mound that lay between them and the artillery positions. MacMillan at once issued the order to his Bren gun team and they set off at a crouching run. Carter followed behind. As they squirmed to the top, Carter pointed out their target. From this elevated position the left flank of the German line was wide open. They would have to turn and engage the commandos or retreat to somewhere safer, which meant leaving the battery behind and taking to the open ground that separated the battery from the fields beyond.

The Bren started firing, short, controlled bursts, raking its way along the German line. Two men fell before the Germans were able to react. They tried to wriggle backwards, out of the line of the Bren gun's deadly assault, but that just took them closer to 3 Troop, who were occupying the gun sites. A second Bren gun opened up from there, pinning the Germans down. One, at the end closest to Carter, threw his rifle away and raised his hands, clambering to his knees as he did so. Carter ordered the Bren to fire to his right, where a German was taking aim with his rifle.

The first surrender started a chain reaction. All along the skirmish line the German gunners threw down their weapons and raised their hands. An officer berated them, gesticulating with his machine pistol, threatening them. But he knew that his men no longer had any fight left in them. He released his grip on his weapon, letting it hang by its sling and raised his hands.

Silence fell as the British ceased firing. A section of commandos ran forward from the battery and started kicking weapons away from the Germans. A second section appeared, and started frisking the prisoners, looking for concealed weapons.

Carter shouted across to where Cpl McMillan was still watching the flanks. "MacMillan, send a runner to 5 Troop and tell them to advance on the left flank and take up a position at the rear of the huts."

The corporal started issuing orders. As if by magic, Cpl Franklyn appeared at Carter's elbow. "How's it looking, Lucky?"

"Pretty good. Carry out a roll call, see what casualties we may have suffered, treat any German wounded as well. Then get a search of the huts under way. I want any documents, maps, books etc brought to me. They may have some intelligence value. I'm going to find Capt Bird and he'll decide what we do after that."

"Very good, Lucky. What will we do with the prisoners? We haven't really got the men to guard them, not if we're going to have to defend the battery as well."

"I know. It's one of the thing's we're going to have to decide. The original plan was for them to be taken down to the beach, put in a landing craft and ferried out to the Tyndal, but as we have no idea where the Tyndal is and we can't spare the men for an escort, that plan won't work anymore."

"Well, I'll keep them under guard in that hut we captured. It will do the for the moment."

"Yes, do that. As soon as I get new orders, I'll let you know."

Carter headed for right flank of the gun battery, where 2 Troop would be moving around to set up a defence, linking up with 5 Troop who would be circling around the other side. The light was now good enough for him to be able to make out the features of individual commandos. 2 Troop, or those of the troop that had made it ashore at least, were filing down the side of the battery, spreading out. A Sergeant pointed and a Bren gun team split off, dropped their equipment on the ground and started to work with trenching tools to improve the height of the gun pit. Not nearly as much care had been put into their construction on the landward side of the battery.

Carter recognised Dickie Bird strolling towards him, his redundant radio operator close behind. "Well done Steven."

"I didn't actually do very much Dickie. We were almost into the battery when the alarm was sounded, so we caught the Jerries napping. We captured a whole hut full before they could even get their boots on."

"Doesn't matter how you did it, it only matters that it was done. What's the butcher's bill?"

"Roll call is still in progress, but I've had no reports of deaths. I heard one man shout that he'd been hit, there may be others, but I think we got off lightly."

"The element of surprise always helps. But now we have to decide what we do next."

"I've got a search of the huts going on, looking for intelligence."

"That's fine, but it isn't our highest priority. Tell me, if you were defending this battery, how many men would you want to do it."

"Depends what we could expect from the enemy. If he has armour, then all eighty of us won't be enough. But if it's just infantry then I could hold him off for several hours with thirty men, if we can get them dug in well enough.

"That's about what I was thinking. We can put the remainder out in front of the battery, watching the roads, mounting delaying actions, that sort of thing."

"According to the map there's small hill about half a mile inland. If we could get a section on top of that, they'll be able to see further and direct troops to intercept an advance."

"That would work. The road is only a couple of hundred yards beyond that. We can put a Troop there and another troop between the hill and the battery."

"We'll need to cover the approach from Honfleur, as well." Carter suggested.

"You think Jerry might send reinforcements from there?"

"It's a possibility. They may already be on their way."

"Surely he'll recall them to defend Honfleur, once the main assault starts."

"He might, but he might not. We can't take the chance."

"You're right Steven. Can't have Jerry sneaking up behind us when we're not looking. Well, that doesn't leave us with any sort of reserve."

"No one said it would be easy, Dickie."

"It was never supposed to be this hard. But you're right, we have to do the best we can with what we have. We can't patrol the roads the way the original plan required. All we can do is protect the battery."

"Are you spiking the guns[2]?"

"We haven't got any explosives, it was all in the second wave of LCs., so we'll have to do the best we can with trenching tools or whatever we can find in the huts. The Germans must have some sort of tool box. After all, the guns have to be maintained. They're big weapons, it won't be easy."

"If we can put them out of action, at least the enemy won't be able to use them, even if they regain control of the battery

The other three officers, Kasmire, Fraser and Motson, had arrived and were listening in, keen to ask questions. Bird quickly brought them up to speed with the plan.

"Can't we just spike the guns and leave?" Kasmire asked.

"We have to make some attempt to prevent the area being reinforced, at least delay an advance on Honfleur by making it deal with us along the way. So, no. We're staying put for as long as we can. If I think our position is no longer tenable, then we'll leave."

"What about keeping one gun in working order?" Motson asked. "We could use it to shell the enemy. With the range these weapons have, even if the Jerries were miles away they would be forced off their line of advance to come and deal with us, just to prevent us shelling them."

"Not a bad idea. Do we know of any gunners in the commando that might be able to operate one of these things?"

"My Troop sergeant, Thorpe, used to be an instructor at Larkhill[3]. If he doesn't know how to fire one of these, no one will." Motson replied.

"OK, get him to take a look. If he thinks it can be done, give him whatever men he needs to do it."

"What do we do about prisoners?" Carter asked. "We must have about forty or so."

"We'll lock them in one of the huts for now. When we leave, we'll strip them to their underwear and send them down the road. We can tip their weapons over the cliff so they can't shoot us in the back. Any officers we take with us, though. They'll need to be interrogated when we get back."

"How do we communicate between positions?" Motson asked.

"A good question, Ian." Bird frowned, looking skywards for inspiration. He was pleased to see that it lay in that direction, where the sun was already climbing above the eastern horizon. "See if any of the men have shaving mirrors in their kit. Use them to flash signals between sites. Let me see, we'll have one flash for each cardinal point of the compass, starting from north and going clock wise. That will indicate in which direction the threat lies. Then a pause, followed by an estimate of numbers, one flash for a platoon or less, two flashes for a company, three for a battalion. Then another pause. One flash for infantry, two for armour, three for artillery, four for a mixed force. How does that sound?"

Carter finished jotting the code in his note book. "We'll need an initial signal, so that whoever is watching has time to respond."

"OK. Two flashes starts every message, then followed by the code we just agreed."

"What about the recall signal?" Kasmire asked.

"We're due to start the withdrawal at eleven hundred hours. That's still my plan, so keep an eye on your watches. But if we're forced to move before then I still have my Very Pistol." Bird replied. "Two flares of any colour means get back to the beach. The group on the road will have to act as the rear-guard and cover everyone else's withdrawal. But act on your own initiative as well. If the situation looks bad, withdraw to the next nearest position and re-group, continue fighting if you can, but if not, continue to withdraw. If the worst comes to the worst, six or more flashes means get back to the battery."

Bird paused as he considered what else he needed to do.

Kasmire's jaw dropped in amazement at the Heath Robinson[4] nature of the communications system. Carter noticed his expression and gave him a friendly punch on the arm. "In the commandos you learn to improvise, Kas. If you can't do that, you'll never get the job done."

"There's improvisation and there's improvisation." Kasmire protested. "I've never heard of anything so …"

"Improvised?" suggested Carter, with a chuckle.

"Steven, I want you on the hill with one section of men. Your other two sections can cover the road from Honfleur. Ian, 5 Troop can take the road. Andrew, I need half of 3 Troop to help with the defence of the battery alongside 2 Troop, and the other half will provide the link between us and the hill. Kas, you can make yourself useful and take command of them. 5 Troop to move out ASAP, 4 Troop to follow, then 3 Troop as soon as we have the defences around the battery dug. Any questions?"

As plans went it was skimpy, to say the least, but Carter knew it was the best they could hope for. But the Germans didn't know the plan and even if they did they would try to do something to disrupt it. What that was, they would have to wait and see.

[1] O-Group – Orders Group, an informal tactical briefing to assess a situation and decide what will happen as a consequence.

[2] Spike the guns – In the days of muzzle loading artillery, the main gunpowder charge was ignited by lighting a hollow quill filled with gunpowder that had been inserted into a touch hole at the rear of the cannon. The simplest way to disable that sort of gun was to hammer a soft copper spike into the touch hole in order to prevent the quill being inserted. Even though the gun could still be loaded, it couldn't be fired. Hence the term "to spike the guns". It is now used as a metaphor to refer to any act of sabotage. Guns were spiked only

when they couldn't be dragged away for use by their captors, such as during naval raids. They were also spiked if they had to be abandoned in the face of an enemy attack, so that the enemy couldn't use them.

[3] Larkhill. – Located on Salisbury Plain in Wiltshire, Larkhill was established in 1915 as the School of Instruction for Royal Horse and Field Artillery. By 1939 it had developed into the main training school for all Royal Artillery gunners and trained over a million men during World War 2. It is still in use as a training school today.

[4] W Heath Robinson (31st May 1872 – 13th Sept 1944) was an English cartoonist who specialised in drawing cartoons of complex machines containing day to day objects (kitchen equipment, bicycle parts etc) and held together with bits of string. The simpler the task the machine had to achieve, the more complicated the machine he drew to achieve the task. A device to crack an egg, for example, might fill an entire room. The term "Heath Robinson Contraption" entered popular use during the First World War as front line soldiers improvised ways of overcoming their discomfort or making devices for use against the enemy. It is usually used to describe temporary fixes which require great ingenuity to build. The machines built by Wallace in the Wallace and Gromit films, might have been inspired by the cartoons of W Heath Robinson.

8 - The Hill

To call it a hill was to pay it a very extravagant compliment. It was barely a bulge in the surrounding countryside, hardly thirty feet higher than the surrounding terrain, but thirty feet was a lot when it came to providing visibility. From its summit Carter was certain that he could see several miles further than he'd been able to from the foot of the gentle climb. With basic maths he'd probably be able to work out the precise distance, but he wasn't here for that.

Taking out his binoculars, he ordered his seven-man section to start digging in around the summit while he surveyed the horizon. By piling the soil that they dug out into a parapet, they could double the protection offered by the earth work without having to dig too deep into the ground. It was handy in rocky ground, but not so much of a problem in the chalky soil they were standing on.

It was still early and the only movement he could make out was a farmer, some distance away, walking along behind a horse and cart, heading away from them towards the west.

He swung through an arc and looked out across the Seine estuary towards Le Havre. Spread out across the surface of the sea was an armada of landing ships and what looked like hundreds of LCs moving towards the land, gouts of water rising silently skywards as short-range shore based artillery attempted to sink them. The mutter of the guns discharging followed a few seconds after the gouts of water erupted. Probably 88mm anti-aircraft guns, which the soldiers in the Western desert were discovering also made an excellent anti-tank gun. As Carter watched, a shell exploded on the prow of one of the LCs, stopping it as suddenly as if had hit a brick wall. When the spray settled Carter could see that it was sinking. Tiny figures leapt from it into the water.

There was nothing Carter or his men could do about that. They had done their bit by making sure that the much larger 155mm guns of the Himmler battery hadn't been able to engage as well. At this range they would have been able to target the much larger landing ships.

On the flanks of the fleet destroyers, frigates and corvettes returned fire, concentrating on Honfleur's small harbour, battering the shore defences to make it easier for the Canadians when they reached the beaches. A gout of water erupted close to a second landing craft and Carter was relieved to see it emerge from the spray unscathed.

Carter noticed that there were no capital ships in the fleet. Surely the firepower of a cruiser or a battleship would carry far more weight and do more damage than the smaller guns of the escort ships. Why had nobody thought to assign bigger ships to the operation? Was the same happening at Dieppe, some seventy miles away?

A noise made him look up and he saw a flight of three aircraft above him. From their northerly direction of travel they could only be Germans, but at that height he could only guess at their type. Bombers definitely; Heinkels he guessed. Something small darted across his eyeline, seeking to get behind the formation. The shape of the wing told Carter it was a Spitfire. A second one appeared, diving from height. The two of them opened fire on the bombers. The left hand of the three aircraft turned out of the formation, smoke streaming from one engine. The left-hand Spitfire followed it around, continuing to fire as the other aircraft maintained its pursuit of the remaining pair.

Entertaining as the aerial combat was, Carter had other priorities. He scanned the road that led to Honfleur, the D513 as the French had designated it. About two miles away he could make out the small village of Pennedpie and then the roofs of the houses in the suburbs of the town beyond. If the Germans knew that the battery had been attacked, they weren't making any obvious effort to come to its aid. Presumably any thought to do so had been quickly discarded as dawn had revealed the presence of a British fleet out in the Channel.

He turned through one hundred and eighty degrees. To the right, on the coast and not far away, was the village of Villeville, hardly more than a cluster of houses. Inland there was no significant community within sight, just the odd cottage or farm buildings. Beyond Villerville, but hidden from view, was Deauville, playground of the rich and famous before the war. Now it was popular with German officers, or so they had been told. Inland from that was the airport. Deauville was the most likely place from which to dispatch reinforcements. It didn't have a big garrison, but it was big enough to present a danger to the defenders of the battery. Perhaps the commander would consider it too dangerous to send the garrison. After all, the Germans had no way of knowing where else the British might be planning to strike.

The garrison commander would be only too well aware that many of Germany's senior commanders in France had confiscated luxurious properties in the town for their personal use. There might even be some *Wehrmacht* General or SS *Obergruppenfürher* in residence at that moment.

The D513 wound around the edge of Villeville and continued westwards. There was no sign of movement there, either.

Inland the D62, still only a country road, also ran east-west, joining the D513 close to Pennedpie. It too was empty.

Well, thought Carter, it was still only six o'clock in the morning. Give it time.

* * *

The trouble, when it came, started in the air. A pair of Me 110 fighter bombers skimmed low across the terrain to drop bombs on the battery, not bothering whether they were hitting friend or foe. The explosions ripped through the early morning air before the aircraft turned back and strafed the area with their cannon and machine guns.

Retaliation came quickly. A Hurricane dropped from its patrol height and gave chase, but the Me 110s were faster and soon outran it. Smoke billowed in the air from the damage done, but from where he was Carter was unable to see what casualties the air raid might have inflicted. Even his binoculars failed to reveal any detail.

He returned his attention to the roads, but still nothing moved. With artillery fire rumbling across the landscape the French were wisely staying at home, while the Germans were still considering what action to take.

Carter looked back towards the sea once more, to assess what progress was being made in the assault on Honfleur. The scene didn't tell him much. Smoke rose from the harbour area and landing craft were still headed ashore, but success or failure couldn't be interpreted from such scant detail.

Huge gouts of water still gushed upwards to signify that the German harbour defences hadn't yet been silenced. Carter was able to pick out landing craft that weren't underway, evidence of strikes or maybe engine failure. Small boats, launched from the landing ships, were skimming around seeking survivors that might be in the water. Anyone they found would be fortunate indeed. Weighed down by their webbing, uniform and boots the soldiers would sink quickly if they couldn't get rid of it before they hit the water.

A droning sound grew in volume from Carter's right. He swung his binoculars upwards and picked out a formation of at least a dozen German bombers. Dots appeared above them as fighters swooped down, but they weren't alone. Another formation of Germans appeared, smaller, nimbler. Fighters engaging fighters in an airborne melee. A couple of the RAF fighters got in amongst the Germans, forcing them to break formation and flee. One solitary aircraft maintained its course, its bomb doors opening so that it could shed its cargo.

The tiny black dots of the bombs were almost impossible for Carter to pick out, but he saw their effect. A series of waterspouts rose in a line, stitching their way towards one of the landing ships. The bomb aimer had released the load too soon. Well, not all had fallen too soon. One bomb hit the landing ship on the bow, sending up a blast of flame and debris. Anti-aircraft fire poured skywards from the escorting ships. As the bomber turned for home it was hit, rolled onto its back and dived seaward. Three parachutes appeared. Too few, Carter knew. The aircraft had a crew of five.

As the dogfight continued above his head, a Spitfire screamed earthwards. Carter prayed that the pilot might escape in time, but no parachute appeared. The aircraft hit the ground about a mile away. Flame engulfed it as its fuel supply caught fire, a great boom echoing across the landscape.

An Me 109 skimmed low across the landscape streaming vapour behind it, heading homewards. Whether it made it or not Carter would never know.

"Lucky!" A voice broke into his reverie. "You might want to take a look at this."

Carter turned and looked in the direction which the man was pointing. He picked out the movement easily enough. Raising his binoculars once again, he lost sight of it for a moment and had to scan the horizon until he located the object that had attracted the commando's attention. Objects, he soon realised. There were three vehicles, heading along the road towards them. In the lead was a four wheeled armoured car, a turret of some sort in the middle of the hull. At that distance Carter could just about make out the figure of the commander behind the machine gun. Behind the armoured car were two half-track troop carriers. Between them they would be carrying a platoon of infantry.

The capacity of the vehicles said that the commandos had the Germans outnumbered, but they were probably just a reconnaissance force, sent to find out what the commandos were doing; whether they were even still occupying the gun battery.

Carter pulled out his shaving mirror. A glass mirror was too fragile to survive for long in a soldier's pack, but Carter, and many other commandos had metal mirrors. These were highly polished rectangles of metal, kept in a leather sleeve to maintain their shine and prevent accidental scratching.

Signalling to 5 Troop to the south of them wasn't a problem. It was just a matter of angling the mirror correctly to catch the sunlight. Signalling to the battery to the north, however, required two mirrors. The first angled towards the sun to produce a pool of reflected light, and the second directed that light northwards. It required either two people to make the signal, or on person with very steady hands or nothing would be seen, but eventually his message was acknowledged.

Looking at his map, Carter tried to work out a plan. He couldn't allow that armoured car to get close to the battery. If it did, its' machine gun would wreak havoc, punching a gap through the defences to allow the infantry to flow through behind. The commandos didn't have any armour piercing weapons, so it had to be stopped before it got close.

Carter quickly wrote a message onto a sheet of paper torn from his notebook. He glanced across the heads of his men, dug in below the hill's summit so that they wouldn't be 'skylined'; silhouetted against the sky behind them.

"Mitchell! On me." He ordered. The trooper, one of the faster runners in the troop, crawled out of his fox hole and approached Carter in a crouching run.

"Take this to Captain Bird with my compliments. Quick as you can." The trooper didn't bother replying. He just took the note and ran off down the side of the hill. Burdened with his kit and weaponry it would take him about five minutes to complete the half mile run to the battery, then another five minutes back. Plenty of time for Bird to react to Carter's note. The small German convoy had to travel at the speed of the slowest vehicle and the half tracks could only muster about thirty miles per hour. They were still about five miles away, so it would take them nearly eight minutes to reach the spot that Carter had designated in his note.

Just to make sure, Carter raised his binoculars again to try to assess the German's progress. He was right. They hadn't yet halved the distance since he had first seen them.

Ahead of them was a patchwork of small fields, each separated from the next by high, cattle proof hedges. Gates were set in the corners of the fields, allowing access from the road all the way to the top of the cliffs. It wouldn't be easy for infantry to fight their way across. The advantage was very much with the defenders; the commandos.

The note had said that Carter would make a single flash with his signal mirror when the Germans were almost at the grid reference he had designated as a target. He didn't expect the resulting artillery shot to hit anything, he may be called Lucky but that would have to be one miraculous shot from Sgt Thorpe's hastily assembled gun crew. But it didn't have to hit anything, it just had to make the Germans leave the road.

He handed his mirror to Prof Green to make the signal, while he kept watch with his binoculars, gauging the right moment. The vehicles crawled towards the designated spot, a junction between a cart track and the road, easily identifiable on his map and Bird's.

"OK, Prof. On my count. Ten, nine …" he watched as the armoured car seemed to crawl forward. The commander had his own binoculars raised, but the bouncing of the suspension wouldn't allow him to get any more than glimpses of the countryside around him. If he wanted to make a detailed reconnaissance, he would have to stop the convoy. "… three, two, one, now!"

Green sent a flash across the open ground between their hill and the battery. Had it been seen? It took only a few seconds to find out. The boom of the 155mm gun was closely followed by an eruption of dirt and vegetation where the shell hit.

The French built guns had a range of up to twelve miles, but the distance from the battery to the junction was barely a mile and a half. The gun's barrel would have to be fully depressed in order for the shell not to scream over the Germans' heads and land harmlessly in the fields beyond. But Sgt Thorpe seemed to know his business, if the results meant anything. The blast was within a hundred yards of the target and it brought the armoured car to a halt as suddenly as if it had hit a wall. The driver put the vehicle into reverse and sent it backwards along the road, straight into the path of the first of the half-tracks. Carter's ears were still deafened by the blast of the shell's explosion, so he didn't hear the crunch of metal on metal, but he saw the result as the commander of the armoured car started gesticulating at the driver of the half-track, who rose from behind his steering wheel and gesticulated back.

An officer appeared from the direction of the rearmost vehicle and silenced both men, giving orders, which the soldiers rushed to obey. The infantrymen cascaded out of the back of the half-tracks to take up defensive positions along the sides of the road, while the armoured car crew got to work with crowbars to try to separate their damaged vehicle form the radiator grill of the vehicle with which it had collided.

Thorpe's untrained crew wouldn't be able to keep up the two rounds per minute rate of fire that the original owners of the gun might have achieved, but they did manage to get a second round off after about ninety seconds. They had adjusted the aim and the second round exploded much closer to the armoured car, in a field almost alongside it.

Carter turned his binoculars towards the battery and saw a loan figure standing on the roof of one of the huts; almost certainly Bird, relaying fire orders that would refine the accuracy of the artillery fire. There was a real possibility that the next round would inflict damage on the Germans.

It was something that the German commander must also have realised. He ordered his men into the fields nearest to the battery, running across and taking refuge in the hedge on the far side. The armoured car crew abandoned their rescue attempts and followed suit. Carter wished he had a heavy machine gun. From his position he would have been able to keep the Germans pinned down for the rest of the morning.

But the gun had achieved what Carter had wanted. It had forced the Germans into the fields where the commandos had the advantage. A third artillery round screamed across the sky and exploded so close to the armoured car that it rocked it on its axis, showering it with dirt and debris.

"Send the cease fire signal" Carter told Green. Artillery of that calibre was no use against troops who were spread out. It might demoralise them, but it probably wouldn't kill any. The best result was that the armoured car was out of the game, at least until the crew recovered their nerve enough to go back and try to disentangle it again. If that happened, Carter would ask for a repeat of the artillery barrage.

The sensible thing for the German officer to do now was to send out sections of men in different directions, to probe the commandos defences and try to find a passage through them to the battery. He wouldn't know that the commandos were so spread out that there were several options for him to try. But it wouldn't take him long to find out. Carter gauged the distance between him and the nearest German troops. At least three quarter so of a mile. The range was too long for his Bren guns to have any real impact. In theory they had a range of over a mile, but realistically they weren't effective at anything much above six hundred yards. But if they got any closer, the height advantage that Carter had would pay off. The German officer must at least guess that he was up here. It was the only possible location from which the convoy could have been observed.

That meant that the weak point, from the German's point of view, was the gap between the hill and the battery. The gap in which two sections of 3 Troop were positioned, under the command of Kas Kasmire.

The runner, Mitchell, puffed his way back to the top of the hill, but Carter took pity on him and waved him back towards his foxhole. "Glass!" he called.

"Yes Lucky."

"Take a jog down to Lt Kasmire's position. Give him my compliments and ask him to come up and join me."

"On my way." Carter watched as the commando climbed out of his fox hole and trotted down the rear of the hill, out of sight of the Germans. He raised his binoculars and tried to pick out the seventeen men, but they had concealed themselves well. Glass would have to find them from memory.

A group of Germans appeared at the gate of the field in which they had taken refuge, crawled under it and started to inch their way across the next field. It was as Carter had suspected. The German officer seemed to know what he was doing and, judging by their field craft, so did the section of soldiers who were advancing towards him.

Carter crawled forward until he reached the Bren gun team, who were positioned on the right flank of the hill. "Pearson, can you see that patrol that's just set out from the German positions?" LCpl Adam Pearson was Easy section's second in command and their Bren gunner.

"I can see something. Looks like half a dozen men crawling across the field."

"That's them. When they get in range, give them a few bursts from your gun. Send them back where they came from."

"No problem, Lucky."

He turned and went in search of Tpr Vardy. He was Easy section's best shot. He asked Vardy the same question he had asked Pearson. "See the old dead tree?" Carter had to guide him a little. His fox hole wasn't positioned quite so well as the Bren gun team's.

"Got it."

"Right, now, one field across, you should be able to see some Germans moving forward at a crouch."

"Yeah, I see them."

"OK, I'll leave it up to you, but when you think you can get a shot off, try your luck."

One Troop, designated as the reconnaissance troop for the commando, had properly trained and equipped snipers, men who could shoot a fly off a pig's back at a mile distance, but they weren't here. Carter wondered where they actually were and said a silent prayer for their safety. Interesting, he thought. For someone who didn't really believe in God, he was doing a lot of praying that day.

His eye was attracted to movement down on the road, where Ian Motson's 5 Troop were positioned. The binoculars showed him three commandos carefully making their way down the hedge line towards the stopped vehicles. It was a risky move and Carter wondered if Motson had ordered it, or if the commandos were acting on their own initiative. Getting men into the armoured car would allow them to fire the vehicle's heavy machine gun into the rear of the Germans.

They would create havoc. But if they were spotted, they would be easily beaten and might also give away the presence of Motson's men.

Well, there was nothing Carter could do about it, even if he wanted to. If he sent a runner to recall them it could give them away. If he asked Motson to withdraw them, Motson could ignore him.

Carter realised that it had been several minutes since he had last checked the approach from Honfleur. The sound of the big gun being fired must have attracted some attention. The town's commander would be wondering what it might mean. He might decide that having enemy controlled heavy artillery on his flank was dangerous and he should do something to remove the threat.

The binoculars revealed no movement on the roads out of the town on this side. So far so good then. He took the opportunity to see how things were progressing with the landing.

A landing craft was lying alongside one of the landing ships and stretchers were being lifted aboard. Casualties, but Carter couldn't see how many. Streaks of blood down the solid sides of the bigger craft suggested that there had been several badly wounded soldiers lifted out already. Lifeboats still chugged around the open area of water between the landing ships and the shore, looking for survivors from craft that had been hit earlier. The sound of small arms fire was a constant crackle from the town, though it told Carter nothing other than there was fighting there. But the 88mm guns seemed to have fallen silent, suggesting that the harbour defences had been silenced at last. It wouldn't be possible for the artillery to fire over the houses to reach the ships. The 88mm gun wasn't designed to do that. It could propel a shell upwards towards an aircraft, or in a flattish arc towards a ground target but, unlike a howitzer, it couldn't propel a shell over obstructions to land on a distant target.

Kas Kasmire appeared at the top of the rear slope, accompanied by Glass. Kasmire was breathing heavily, Glass less so. That would change after Kasmire had been through Achnacarry, thought Carter. He thanked Glass then drew Kasmire forward into the shelter of the windswept bushes just below the front edge of the hill.

"See there." He directed Kasmire's gaze towards the German patrol. It had advanced as far as the edge of the field. No doubt the Germans were looking for a route into the next field that didn't use the gate, which would give away their presence. It was a hard place for the Germans to defend, Carter realised. The hedges provided far too much concealment. Would the Germans react to that after the British had departed? The sensible thing to do would be to rip the hedges up, removing the protection they offered. It would also open up the ground for use by tanks. Carter knew that a lot of that sort of cover had been removed in southern England back in '39 and '40, when the threat of invasion from the European mainland had been at its height. It left clear lines of sight from the hastily constructed concrete pill boxes and gun pits that had been built from the Thames Estuary to The Isles of Scilly.

"Yeah, I see 'em."

"Fancy a flanking attack on them from your position?"

"Will you give me cover from up here?"

"Of course."

"In that case I fancy it." He did his best to copy Carter accent as he pronounced the last two words. He failed, but Carter rewarded him with a smile for his effort.

"Where are your men right now?"

"Are they're my men?" Kasmire asked. "I wasn't sure if I had any official status."

"If you ask those men to follow you, they won't refuse." Carter reassured him. "Especially if they're following you into a fight. But ask the Sergeant's opinion. He'll appreciate it and whatever he says will be good advice."

"What route do you suggest?"

"Where are you right now?"

Kasmire studied the terrain, looking for landmarks that he could recognise. "There." He pointed, "Just by that rusted old piece of junk."

Carter recognised what might once have been a four wheeled trailer but was now overgrown with weeds. He scanned the ground ahead of the position, picking out the best route. The line of advance of the Germans, who were now crawling beneath a hedge, would take them diagonally across the front of Kasmire, but one field to his right, closer to the battery. It left another hedge between his men and the advancing Germans, which would obscure their view. But if they advanced down the side of the field that the Germans would have to cross, they would be able to lie under the concealment of that hedge and fire into the German flank.

"I'd move straight ahead from where you are." Carter advised. "Go straight across that field and into the next. Settle your men into cover then open up when the time's right. At the rate the Germans are advancing, I'd say you had about ten to fifteen minutes."

"In that case I'd better get going."

"Good. Go back the way you came and keep your head down. If the Germans see you, they'll suspect something's happening."

"No problem. Wish me luck, Lucky."

Carter did wish him luck. It would be Kasmire's first proper combat. He had been held back in reserve with 5 Troop during the assault on the battery. Now he would lead this ambush.

Carter faced the front again and re-focused his attention on the German patrol. They were down on their bellies, crawling through the long grass, but from his elevated position they were still visible. The Germans didn't seem to be in any hurry to reach the battery; but then again, haste could lead to them exposing themselves and a counter move being set up to thwart them. Which was just what Carter was planning.

There was the crack of a rifle from Carter's left as Vardy decided he had a clear shot, but if he hit any of the Germans it wasn't evident. They may not even know that they had been shot at. Vardy cranked another round into the chamber of his Lee Enfield rifle and waited for another opportunity. Carter shuffled down to find LCpl Pearson and brief him on the plan. He didn't want the Bren gunner shooting at the wrong side.

9 – Kasmire's Ambush

Carter didn't have to wait long for Kasmire's section to move out. They had either been located in a place where the hedge wasn't so thick, or they had already done some work to clear a way through the base of it. Either way, they came through quickly, taking up a firing positions as they waited for their comrades. Carter counted them, just fourteen. He was sure there had been sixteen, plus Kasmire himself. That meant he had left someone behind, or perhaps sent them by a different path. Yes, he would send a two-man Bren gun team out onto his flank to provide covering fire. Good thinking, or perhaps the Troop Sergeant had suggested it.

The men moved faster than the Germans, crouching low to make best use of the cover of the tall hedges, moving along the side of the field, not across the middle. When they got to the far corner they lay on their bellies and crawled through a gap. It couldn't have been wide, because they were restricted to one man at a time, but they did it quickly, risking whatever scratches and scrapes the thick vegetation inflicted. In the next field they took up their position along the hedge line, burrowing deep into the roots to give themselves clear shots through to the other side. The base of the hedges would be thick with nettles at this time of year. There would be a lot of sore hands and faces.

The Germans had reached the far end of the same field and were now trying to find their own way in. They seemed more reluctant to risk injury, taking their time to probe along the base of the hedge, looking for a weakness.

How long would Kasmire wait? Carter wondered. Would he fire as soon as they were through, or would he give them the chance to get into the middle of the field, where there was less possibility of them retreating to safety and perhaps turning the tables on his men?

What would he himself do? Carter wondered. He would wait, he decided. The enemy would either be pinned down, to be picked off one at a time by the commandos, or they would have to turn and charge the ambush, hoping to overcome the British soldiers. With Carter's own Bren gun team firing downwards into them it meant they would have to try to charge and that meant just as certain a death.

A momentary distraction was provided by another pair of Me 110s flying low overhead to bomb the battery a second time. The German commander must have reported it as being still operational and it was a threat the Germans were taking seriously. Their 250 kg bombs sent shockwaves across the landscape. The German infantrymen used the distraction to rush to the corner of the field and use the gate, before running back to form line abreast in front of the hedge. They dropped to their bellies and started to crawl carefully forward again, but Pearson, the Bren gunner, had seen them and reported the movement to Carter.

"Good man." Carter replied, refocusing his binoculars on them. The Me 110s continued to zoom and roar over the battery, strafing the men on the ground. Carter hoped they were well dug in.

"There's more movement on the road." Mitchell announced from his position at the far end of the hill's summit. There was little point in him trying to keep his voice down. The roar of the Messerschmitt's twin Daimler-Benz engines drowned out most other sounds.

Carter hurried across to him, Things were getting a little hectic already, with more things happening in the countryside in front of him than he could really keep track of.

The road swam into focus in the twin discs of his binocular eyepieces. Carter raised them factionally until he could see the far end of it, where it emerged over the horizon. The movement wasn't difficult to pick out. This column was considerably longer; at least half a dozen half-tracks with a couple of armoured cars, one at the front and another at the rear. Probably the rest of the company, hurrying to the aid of the platoon that was already deployed in the hedges below. No tanks yet though. That was a relief. There was nothing the commandos could do in the face of tanks, except retreat, surrender or die.

"Time for you to take another trip to the battery, Mitchell." Carter informed the sharp eyed commando. "Another fire order for Capt Bird." To send a runner would allow him to convey far more information than their system of flashing shaving mirrors would allow. He would reserve that method of communication for Ian Motson to the south of him.

He wouldn't allow this new convoy to get so close before he ordered the artillery to fire. Keeping that number of men at a distance would give them more time. More time for what? He wondered. It was a numbers game now, the commando's eighty men, give or take casualties, against about a hundred and twenty Germans, plus their armoured cars. Military doctrine held that the defenders always had the advantage, that three times as many attackers were needed to overcome defenders, if they were well dug in. But military doctrine wasn't in the fields west of Honfleur. The commandos were too thinly spread, there were too many gaps between their positions for the Germans to sneak through. It was inevitable that they would have to fall back to the battery at some point and probably withdraw completely before the casualty rate rose too high.

The main part of their task, the destruction of the battery, had been successful. The secondary task of keeping reinforcements away from Honfleur had always been a much trickier prospect. If the full commando had made it to shore, they might have had some chance, but with less than two complete troops they didn't really stand a chance.

With Mitchell on his way back to the battery once more, Carter returned to the Bren gun position to see how the Germans were progressing. There was no sound of small arms fire from the ambush site, so Kasmire had obviously not engaged yet.

The Germans were about a quarter of the way across the field. They seemed to sense something wasn't right, because they had stopped where they were. All but one was lying on his belly. The remaining soldier was carefully approaching the hedge at the end of the field closest to the battery, peering beneath it, looking for any sign of an enemy. Perhaps the presence of the commandos in the hedge had caused the birds to go quiet. It wasn't unknown. Nature had its own alarm system.

As though reading Carter's mind, a hare leapt from the grass at the feet of the advancing soldier. It was difficult to tell which was the more surprised. The solider went bolt upright, firing his rifle into the air as his finger tightened reflexively on the trigger. At almost the same instance Vardy fired and the German dropped into the grass and lay still. It seemed to galvanise both sides into action. The line of the hedge erupted in fire as Kasmire's men picked out their targets. The Germans replied but they were firing blindly, having not had time to locate their enemy.

A Bren gun opened up from the distant corner of the field, obviously where Kasmire had sent it. One of the Germans rose and tried to retreat, But Pearson was ready for him. Firing his Bren gun he dropped the man where he stood, with a short controlled burst.

The remaining Germans resorted to crawling backwards, pushing with their arms and legs while trying to stay as low to the ground as they could. The length and thickness of the grass was all that's stood between them and death. The text book manoeuvre now would be for Kasmire's men to rise and charge the Germans, but the thick hedge prevented that. If they tried to break through they would expose themselves.

A Germans machine gun opened up from where the rest of the platoon still lay in concealment, but the gunner could have no idea where Kasmire's men were. He was as likely to hit his own men as anyone. The German commander must have realised that as the gun fell silent after a few bursts.

As far as Carter could see, none of the German section made it back to the safety of the hedge behind them. They may not all have been dead, but there was no sign of movement. The firing ceased and Carter watched as Kasmire led his men back to their original defensive position.

At best it was a short respite. Help was coming and the Germans now knew which route not to take to get to the battery. They still had plenty of other options.

Carter tapped Pearson on his steel helmet. "Keep an eye on them. If you see any movement, fire. They may just be playing dead."

Pearson grunted an acknowledgement but didn't raise his head from the Bren gun's rear sight. His loader would scan the ground that wasn't in his direct field of vision.

Carter returned to the south side of the hill. There was no sign of the three men who had been moving forward towards the crashed armoured car. That didn't mean much. Commandos were good at moving without being seen. He raised his binoculars and watched the progress of the enemy convoy. His new aiming point for the 155mm gun was about two miles ahead of him. The convoy was still about a mile short. They were moving slowly, cautiously. The sound of small arms fire would have drifted towards them but had probably been drowned out by the sound of their vehicles' engines. Were they close enough to see the misty grey smoke of the discharge of the rifles and Bren guns from the ambush? Difficult to know. They must have seen the smoke from Pearson's Bren gun and Vardy's rifle though. The hill was the only high point for miles around.

The lead armoured car pulled to a halt, the other vehicles obediently doing the same behind it. Carter focused his binoculars on it. He could clearly make out the figure of the commander, peering through his own binoculars. Carter felt that they were staring at each other, even though he knew he would be hard to pick out at that range. Just his imagination working overtime, Carter knew.

The commander climbed out of the vehicle's turret and jumped down off the hull. He walked back towards the first half-track, in no obvious hurry. A figure climbed down from the passenger seat beside the driver and met him half way. Carter could make out the peaked cap of an officer. Right then the convoy was a sitting target, but it made no difference. There was no way to get a message to the battery in time to take advantage of their lack of movement.

The armoured car's commander pointed and Carter was certain that he was indicating the hill. Not really a surprise. If you wanted to position an artillery spotter, it was the only place he could be. The question was, what would they do to counter him? They didn't know that he had no means of speedy communication with the battery. Or maybe the silence of the gun told them otherwise.

They reached a decision and the two men re-took their places in their vehicles. The armoured car moved forward. They had decided to stick to the road for the moment.

10 – The Battle For The Hill

The first shell exploded in a field some way from the convoy. It didn't even slow down. As the smoke billowed across the road the armoured car reappeared, followed by the first of the half-tracks. This officer wasn't going to be diverted as easily as the platoon commander.

Carter swung his binoculars towards the battery and saw the figure once more on the roof of the hut. Well, a figure was on the roof of the hut, but whether or not it was the same one, Carter couldn't tell. A white smudge on the figure's head suggested the presence of a bandage.

The gun crew were quicker both reloading and adjusting the aiming point this time. A second shell followed the first. It overshot, landing in a field beyond the convoy and showering it with dirt. Still the convoy didn't slow. But there was a cork in the bottle and the commander of the armoured car hadn't yet seen it.

Rounding a slight bend the convoy started to slow as the Germans realised that the road was blocked by the earlier convoy. The high hedges prevented the vehicles from going around the obstruction. The 155mm gun fired a third time and convoy was once again showered with dirt. The soldiers in the open rear of the closest vehicles must have been peppered by debris.

But something else was happening. The turret of the abandoned armoured car was rotating, turning to face the vehicles behind. Carter could just make out the soup bowl shape of a British commando. For the 20mm machine gun the range, now less than a mile, was almost perfect. Carter saw sparks flying from the armour of the leading vehicle, its commander ducking down to take cover.

But the German soon recovered his composure and started firing back. Soldiers were ordered out of the first half-track and into the fields on either side of the road. The machine gunner couldn't tackle all the targets at once. It was only a matter of time before the

German infantry were alongside him and able to kill or capture him. It was brave, but also foolhardy.

The commando kept firing for several minutes. He knew how long it would take the Germans to reach him and he wasn't going to withdraw until he had to.

The 155mm gun fired again and, miracle of miracles, hit one of the half-tracks. The affect would have been devastating on the unprotected infantrymen. It forced the Germans into making a decision. Soldiers poured over the sides of the vehicles and scattered into the fields beyond. All except for the ones in the armoured car. The vehicle inched forward, its machine gun firing, keeping pace with the soldiers in the fields. There could be only one outcome of the exchange and the commando knew it. He allowed his opponent to get within half a mile and abandoned the vehicle. Carter couldn't see which way he went, but there was no sign of him on the nearer side of the road.

Again the artillery fired, this time the shell landed in the middle of the road, opening up a crater that the armoured car wouldn't be able to cross. But it could get into the field on its left flank by smashing through the gate. With the armoured vehicle providing cover, the Germans were able to speed up their advance. It didn't stop for the hedge at the end of the field, it just used its four ton mass to smash its way through.

Moving in that fashion it would soon by-pass the stricken armoured car and endanger Motson's men in their roadside ambush. Although it was only travelling at about ten miles an hour, it would be too fast for the artillery to track it. Besides, a stray shell might now hit 5 Troop, or even Carter's own position at the top of the hill.

Suddenly the armoured car stopped. The German infantry caught up with it and surrounded it in a defensive ring. The commander evidently had a plan, or perhaps he was consulting his superiors. A long whip aerial extended above the rear of the vehicle, meaning it had a radio on board.

The Germans that had been advancing on the far side of the road crossed over and joined their comrades. Carter estimated their strength at about sixteen men, plus the powerful presence of the machine gun on the armoured car.

The vehicle started to move and it was soon apparent what the commander's objective was. He wasn't going to bother with the road any more. He was heading towards the hill on which Carter and Easy section were currently the occupants. There was no way for them to defend the hill as they were. Carter considered abandoning it, but it wasn't in his nature to give up so easily. What he needed to do was even up the odds a little.

"We could do with a mortar." Prof Green observed, seeming to read his mind. He scanned the horizon towards Honfleur, the direction that Fox and George sections were covering. There was no sign of any enemy from that direction. Keeping two sections of men covering that approach was a luxury he couldn't afford right then.

"Good idea. Fox section has a 2 incher. Get down to their position and request that Fox and George sections join us up here."

There was about three hundred yards between the hill and the two sections behind them. It wouldn't take long for Green to reach them, but would they get back in time? Carter had to make preparations, just in case they didn't. "Pearson, get your gun team onto the left flank, where you can fire on those Jerries that are with the armoured car."

They would be exposed, he knew. The defensive positions they had dug were all facing west, towards Deauville, but the Germans were coming from the south west. "Everyone get to the left hand end of the hill. Start digging as though your life depends on it." Which it does, he didn't add. The men would be as aware of the dangers as he was himself. His section didn't need telling a second time. Within moments their trenching tools were slamming into the earth, piling soil up to provide a low barricade as they dug down behind to increase the depth and therefore the commandos' chances of survival.

The 155 mm gun fired again, pouring high explosives into the German convoy. Whoever was spotting for it must have lost sight of the armoured car, probably now hidden by the hill. It forced the

German infantry further from the road, but apart from producing several tons of scrap metal the barrage served no other purpose.

Carter considered bringing Kasmire's men up onto the hill as well, but that would open up too big an undefended gap between the hill and the battery. If he needed to withdraw, it would be useful to have someone behind him to provide covering fire. He decided that they should stay where they were for the moment.

Carter checked his watch. It was only eight o'clock. According to their timetable they still had three hours to hold out. He wasn't too worried about the infantry that hadn't followed the armoured car. They were still two miles away and would be nervous about advancing into the unknown without support. Carter wondered why they hadn't called up the second armoured car, the one that had been at the rear of the convoy. He raised his binoculars to take a look. There it was just sitting there on the road. But there was a clue as to why it was still there. Hanging over the side of the small turret was a body. By itself that didn't mean that the vehicle was disabled, but it was a strong hint. One of the 155mm shells had done Carter a vital service.

He turned back to watch the advancing Germans once more. The armoured car had smashed its way through another hedge and the infantry were pouring through behind it. From his position Carter realised that he could see a little bit of the open interior of the turret, which meant that the body of the commander was exposed.

"Pearson! Open fire on that armoured car." Carter ordered. "Aim for the commander."

The Bren gun started to fire almost at once. The Germans went to ground but the armoured car kept moving forward. The commander swung the turret to aim up the hill and opened fire in retaliation. 20mm rounds cracked above Carter's head; he was aiming far too high. It was a common fault when firing up hill. Firing down hill had the opposite effect, with soldiers aiming too low. Pearson, however, knew all about that. Sparks were flying off the metal of the turret, forcing the commander ever lower as he tried to avoid being hit. The lower he crouched, the higher he aimed and the less danger Carter and his men were in. But he didn't stop firing and the armoured car kept moving.

Whoever was leading the German infantry ushered them to the far side of the vehicle where they were protected by its bulk. They crouched low, giving Carter's men nothing to aim at, as they kept pace with it. All they had to do was follow the vehicle up the hill and they would soon be in amongst the commandos.

Prof Green came puffing up and threw himself down beside Carter.

"They're on their way, Lucky. Right behind me." Boots could be heard pounding up the rear slope of the hill to back up Green's words.

Carter got up and went to meet them in a running crouch. "Fox section take the left flank." He ordered. "Dig in. I want that mortar firing as soon as possible. There's German infantry on the far side of that armoured car below us and I want them stopped." With the mortar bombs falling almost vertically out of the sky, there was a real possibility of hitting the Germans. "George section, take up positions between Easy section's foxholes to strengthen the line."

Carter felt a little bit more comfortable. With twenty four men now on top of the hill, there was a good chance of repelling the attack, providing they could neutralise the armoured car.

"Got him!" Pearson's triumphant shout would probably have been heard back at the battery.

Carter looked forward and saw that the armoured car's commander was indeed lying slumped in the turret. But he wasn't alone. A second figure had appeared from inside and was trying to pull his comrade out of the way. Finding it impossible to do, he got underneath and boosted him upwards until he hung over the side. Pearson gave him a short bust of Bren gun fire, just to make sure he was dead. The second German gave another mighty shove and his commander slid out of the turret, bounced off the hull and hit the ground. With the obstruction in the turret now gone, the other crewman was able to grab hold of the machine gun and bring it back into action again. But he was no better placed to fire on Carter's men and the rounds continued to zip harmless across the sky.,

But they would soon be at the bottom of the slope. With the vehicle angled upwards, Pearson would lose his height advantage and the machine gunner would be better protected by the armour of his turret.

There was a cough, or at least that was what it sounded like. A familiar sound to any soldier, it announced the firing of a mortar. With a range of five hundred yards, the Germans were already in danger of being hit. The good thing was that the mortar could be elevated to ninety degrees, meaning that it could keep firing until the enemy were inside the defences.

The chances of the mortar bomb hitting its target at the first attempt were negligible, so Carter wasn't surprised when the bomb exploded harmlessly about fifty yards behind the approaching Germans. It was just a ranging shot. The loader dropped a second bomb down the tube and the operator pulled the trigger.[1] It struck closer, no more than twenty yards away this time. Some fine adjustment and the third bomb hit the armoured car square on, just behind the turret.

The armour protected both the driver and the vehicle's engine, but the machine gun stopped firing, suggesting that the gunner was at least wounded; probably concussed by the explosion a few feet from his head. But it was the unprotected infantry that suffered the worst damage. Bunched up behind the armoured car the shrapnel from the bomb scythed through them, cutting down those in its path. The loader sent another bomb down the tube. It fell beyond the armoured car this time, which had moved forward, but again the shrapnel did its deadly work.

Something must have been said, shouted above the noise of the engine and the screams of the dying and injured, because the armoured car stopped then started to reverse back the way it had come. In its wake it left four bodies. Two more could be seen being dragged away by their comrades. Even at that distance Carter could hear their cries of pain. "Cease firing with the mortar." Carter yelled at the two-man crew. The loader was in the act of dropping the next bomb down the tube, but the operator heard the order and didn't pull the trigger. With the larger 3 inch mortar it would have been too late, as the bomb would have fired as soon as it hit the pin at the base of the tube.

They only had a limited number of mortar bombs and Carter wanted to preserve them until they were really needed. With the enemy withdrawing, the operator would be unable to keep the weapon on target and they would probably fall short.

The Bren guns kept up harassing fire until the Germans were back through the hedge and then they fell silent.

"Well done men." Carter shouted across the hilltop.

There was a ragged cheer, which Carter allowed, but he knew the Germans would be back. Already he could see some of the original reconnaissance platoon, the ones attacked by Kasmire, making their way forward to join up with the armoured car. Once the reinforcements arrived the Germans would try again.

Carter surveyed the horizon from the west, around in a southerly arc and ending up looking to the east, searching out any fresh threat. There was nothing; just the company of infantry still working their way through the fields towards the battery but too far away for any of the defenders to take any action against them that wouldn't leave them exposed and vulnerable to a counterattack.

There was something wrong, Carter knew. There should be armoured columns heading towards the banks of the River Seine, intent on preventing the British from getting a toehold on mainland France, which would turn into a beachhead which, in turn, would become a fully-fledged invasion. But the Germans weren't co-operating.

Which meant that the deception had failed. It didn't take much imagination to work out how the Germans had discovered the limited scope of the raid. Their bombers, operating at a height of ten thousand feet or more, would have been able to see a long way across the English Channel even before they crossed the coast to attack the landing ships and their escorts.

From that height they would have seen that there were no LS(T)s[2] behind the infantry landing ships. Indeed, there were no more infantry landing craft carrying a second, third and even fourth wave of attackers, who could exploit the gains made by the first wave, passing through them to capture fresh objectives and consolidate the ground already captured. Behind them were no logistics ships bringing in the fuel, the ammunition and the food which any invading army would need. And, above all, there were no capital ships that could fire high explosive shells several miles inland to disrupt any attempt to reinforce the town.

So the reports of the bomber crews, made when they returned to their bases and were debriefed, would have been passed up the line and a senior officer would have collated the reports, read them and drawn the conclusion that the attack on Honfleur wasn't an invasion, it was just a large scale raid.

Which meant that the armoured columns could be kept away from the coast to avoid the attention of any RAF Bombers. They would wait close to their barracks, on a high state of readiness, just in case. But in the meantime, the Honfleur garrison would deal with the attackers and the company of infantry from Deauville would deal with the commandos at the Himmler battery. The *Luftwaffe* would bomb the ships because they were an easy target and the German fighters would try to shoot down the RAF fighters, but that was as far as the senior commanders would commit themselves that day.

But the Germans weren't yet finished with Carter and what remained of his troop.

[1] Unlike the larger 3 inch mortar, the 2 inch was fired by a trigger on its base, exploding a shotgun sized cartridge that propelled the bomb out of the barrel. This allows the user to take more careful aim and time their shot better. In extremis, it has been known for a 2 inch mortar to be fired from the hip, like a rifle.

[2] LS(T) – Landing Ship (Tank) - A larger vessel than a landing craft, with a shallow draft for inshore work. It could carry between

18 and 22 tanks at a time, plus their crews, depending on size, depositing them on shore using clam shell bow doors with ramp that unfolded. There were also LC(T)s, landing craft (tank), which could carry up to 5 tanks at a time.

* * *

The next attack on the hill started ten minutes later. It was preceded by an airstrike. A pair of Me 110s screamed across the countryside at treetop height, firing all their guns. All the commandos could do was hunker down in their foxholes and hope that the Germans didn't bomb them as well.

Seeing the aircraft approaching, Carter realised that he was in trouble. He hadn't dug himself a fox hole. It had seemed pointless, because he didn't know from which point any assault might come, so he might end up in the wrong place. It had been his intention just to dive into whichever hole was nearest, cramming himself in beside whichever occupant was already there. But the arrival of Fox and George sections meant that all the available holes were already full, with some of the late arrivals as exposed as himself.

But there were empty positions further round the hill, where his men had previously faced due west. He picked out the nearest one and started to sprint towards it. He could hear the sound of cannon shells exploding as they hit the sloping side of the hill as the lead aircraft started firing, stitching a line of bullets up the side of the hill towards the defenders dug in just below the summit.

Halfway to the hole, Carter decided that trying to get close enough to jump into it wasn't going to work. The chances were that he would be hit before he got there. He had no choice. Using a technique similar to that which he had last used at Troon swimming baths, he dived headfirst towards the hole. His right arm scraped against the side, then his left and he was falling. His arms crumpled under him as they hit the bottom of the shallow hole and his helmeted head crashed against the chalky soil, stunning him. His body seemed to crumple up around him in a tangle of arms and legs. But he was alive.

His vision went dark as the aircraft passed over his head, then brightened again. But that was only the first of the pair. He had to keep his head down. The ground vibrated under him as the explosive cannon shells thudded into the ground. He heard a scream of pain, followed by shouts.

Were they gone? he wondered, or just turning to come back for a second pass. He wriggled his body, trying to turn and get his legs below his head. Fortunately it was more of a shallow trench than a fox hole and Carter was, with some difficulty, able to get himself straightened out just in time to see the two *Messerschmitts* returning. White lights twinkled at the nose of the lead aircraft as it opened fire and Carter ducked down to cringe at the bottom of the hole. This wasn't what the commandos were used to. They were used to being able to fight back, but nothing they could do would inflict damage on the two aircraft. He heard a Bren gun open fire, as well as a few rifle shots as the commandos vented their frustrations, but they wouldn't be effective against such fast moving targets.

A cannon shell exploded close by, showering Carter with dirt, as the aircraft's machine guns raked across the hillside. The fire wasn't accurate enough to cause a lot of casualties, especially amongst those men who were well dug in, but that wasn't its purpose. The air attack was keeping their heads down so that they couldn't defend against the infantry that Carter knew must be starting to approach the base of the hill once more. If they had replaced the gunner in the armoured car, it would mean the end for the troop if the Germans got to the top.

As the shadow of the second aircraft passed over his head, Carter raised it and watched the Germans as they overshot and started a turn that would bring them back for a third time. Their turning circle was wide and it took them several seconds before they were once again lined up on the hill. The lead one had just opened fire when it suddenly turned away, the second one following in its wake. There was a thunderous roar as two aircraft passed low over Carter's head. He was able to make out the RAF roundels on the underside of their wings. They were two-engined aircraft with machine guns mounted in their noses. And they were fast. Already the gap between the two RAF aircraft and the Me 110s was closing and the Germans were jinking left and right to try to put the pilots off their aim.

Carter looked to his left to see where the German infantry were and was alarmed to see how close they had managed to get during the air attack. The infantry must have been sprinting across the fields in the wake of the armoured car.

"Look to your front" Carter yelled, climbing out of his foxhole. There was nothing he could do for any casualties right then. They would have to wait until the immediate threat had passed. If it passed.

"Mortar!" he called. "Fire when ready."

The weapon coughed almost at once, sending the first bomb towards the enemy. The Bren guns also opened fire, but Carter could only hear two, when there should have been three. In a crouching run he went looking for the missing Bren. When he found it he had to lift the bodies of its gunner and loader off it, killed by the same cannon shell. What were their names? He had to remember their names. LCpl Grant, George section, first name Wilfred, he recalled at last. And his loader, Porret. What was his first name. Something odd, not normally associated as a name. he should be able to remember it, but no. It would come to him. Later, when he had to sit down and write the letter to Porret's family, explaining how he had got their son killed on top of a stupid hill in Normandy.

He pulled his hanky from his pocket and wiped the gore from the Bren gun's butt and pistol grip. The haversack containing the spare magazines was lying next to Porret's body. Carter would have to load for himself. He threw himself down behind the gun and lifted the butt, pressing it into his shoulder. He reached forward with his right hand to take hold of the pistol grip and inserted his index finger into the trigger guard, feeling for the curved metal of the trigger itself. His left hand he placed on the butt of the weapon just in front of his face. The sights were set for three hundred yards and Carter had to adjust them down to their minimum of two hundred. He scanned the advancing German formation, looking for a target.

There, out on the left, a light machine gun crew, trying to get into position to provide fire support for the final charge up the hill. Moving at a crouching run, diagonally across his front. Carter squeezed the trigger and felt the Bren leap under his hands. One and two and three, he counted off the short burst before releasing the pressure on the trigger and re-adjusting his aim. The Germans threw themselves to the ground. He doubted he had hit either of them, but he had got close enough to scare them.

They must have decided they had gone far enough and settled behind their weapon to return fire towards Carter. Bullets whipped and cracked about his head, but Carter kept firing. Short, controlled bursts to prevent the weapon from overheating or from vibrating itself sideways on its bipod. There was a spare barrel strapped to the back of the loader's pack, but to swap the hot one over would put the gun out of action for vital seconds.

The weapon fell silent with a click as the hammer fell on an empty chamber. Remember the drill, he counselled himself. Reach forward with the left hand, press the magazine release catch. Slide the thumb up, pushing the rear of the magazine out of its housing and letting the rest of it follow. Don't jerk, you'll just end up breaking your fingernails. Drop the magazine on the left so that the loader can insert a fresh one from the right. Except he didn't have a loader. He had to release the pistol grip and scrabble around in the haversack to find the next magazine. It came out the wrong way round. Which idiot had packed it? he asked himself, before remembering that the … man … who had packed it now lay dead. He fumbled it around the right way and slotted the front edge of the magazine into the housing on top of the Bren. Make sure that the lug on the magazine engages with the recess in the housing, then push the rear down until you hear the solid click of it engaging with the locking mechanism. Let go with your right hand and return it to the pistol grip, then reach forward with your left hand to find the cocking handle, fold it outward so that you can grip it with your fingers, palm upwards, curl them around to get a secure grip. He heaved backwards until the firing mechanism locked in the rearward position, then pushed the handle forward again and folded it back into place.

The whole manoeuvre had taken less than ten seconds, but it seemed like a lifetime to Carter. He started firing again. Three round bursts, ten bursts to a magazine.

A mortar bomb hit the armoured car. Perhaps the earlier damage had rendered it weak, or perhaps this bomb had hit a vital spot, but the vehicle stopped, it's gun silent and pointing skywards. But the German infantry kept coming, around thrity of them, in an extended skirmish line, spaced well apart. Dashing and dropping, dashing and dropping, exposing themselves for the minimum possible time, but getting closer with every dash forward. His men were good shots, but they weren't getting enough opportunities to prove their skill. There was only one possible way for this attack to end, Carter knew. If they were caught in their foxholes the commandos would be killed. He had to take the fight to the enemy. But not yet.

"Fix bayonets!" Carter roared above the crackle of small arms fire. He heard the command relayed along the hilltop from man to man. Carter kept up his fire on the German machine gun, keeping it silent. "Pearson!"

"Yes Lucky."

"Can you see that Jerry LMG[1]?"

"Yeah, I see it."

"When I shout charge, you stay put and keep it engaged. It must not be allowed to fire."

"Got you Lucky."

There was no way Carter could allow his men to charge down the hill without him in the lead. It just wasn't what commando officers did. They led from the front – the very front.

Carter wondered where his Tommy gun was. He'd put it down somewhere, probably while he was watching the enemy manoeuvres, but where was it now? He'd have to use the Bren gun, firing it from the hip as he ran forward.

He changed magazines once again, even though the one on the weapon wasn't empty. When he got up he wouldn't have time to lift the haversack with him, so he would need to keep the weapon firing for as long as possible. After that all he would be left with was his Webley.

The Germans were close enough for the commandos to start lobbing grenades down the hill at them. Carter thanked his lucky stars that some of his men were cricket lovers. They got maximum distance for minimum effort.

But the Germans were still coming. A few had fallen and now lay still in the grass or were trying to crawl away to safety, but Carter estimated that there were at least twenty still in front of them. About the same number as his men on the top of the hill. But once the commandos broke cover, they would start to fall victim to the Germans small arms fire, especially the *Schmeisser* machine pistols that some of them were carrying.

He gauged the distance, it was down to fifty yards. Time to do or die, Carter thought, quite literally. He draped the sling of the Bren gun around his neck and made ready to stand up.

Rising onto one knee, bracing his bent leg ready to push himself upright and launch himself down the hill, Carter filled his lungs with air. "Charge!" he bellowed at the top of his voice. The hill erupted with commandos as they burst out of their holes and slit trenches. The Germans seemed to hesitate in front of them, one even took a step backwards. But a voice rang out below them and the Germans also started to run forwards. They would meet in the middle in a tangle of rifles and bayonets.

Carter couldn't run and fire at the same time, but he walked steadily down the hill, firing his Bren gun in short, controlled bursts. He saw one German fall, then second. Bullets cracked around him, but he seemed to be under some protective charm as none got close enough to hit. He felt something pluck at his trouser leg, but he ignored it.

Behind him he could still hear Bren guns firing, one he knew was aimed at the German LMG, the other must be giving cover fire to the commando advance. The two sides seemed to slam into each other half way down the hill. The momentum of the British pushed the Germans back, like a well-controlled rugby maul.

Carter's Bren gun clicked as the magazine emptied. He threw the now useless lump of wood and metal to one side and reached to draw his Webley from its holster. He didn't get a chance to complete the move. A German ran towards him at full tilt, screaming a war cry, his rifle and bayonet held forward in the regulation field training manual manner. Carter knew he would get one chance and one chance only. He ran towards the German and watched his face form into a sneer of triumph as he saw the apparently stupid, unarmed British officer run straight onto his bayonet point.

With timing honed for many hours on the training ground of the university rugby club, Carter stepped off his right foot and swayed to the left, the German's rifle slipping harmlessly by two inches away from Carter's side. Grabbing the weapon as the German careered forward under his own weight, Carter swung the man round, pulling at the rifle at the same time. The German instinctively pulled back, pressing the trigger to discharge the rifle. What, if anything, the bullet hit, Carter would never know. Using the German's own weight to keep his balance, he swung his right boot towards the soldier's groin.

The German was only human; faced with a choice between his rifle and his testicles, the soldier chose his testicles. He released his weapon and took a step backwards, covering his groin with his hands at the same time. Carter didn't bother to try to reverse the rifle and use the bayonet, he just jammed the butt straight into the face of the German, the jarring of its connection running through Carter's arms to his shoulders. The German fell backwards under the blow, stumbling as he went. Carter sent the butt of the weapon crashing into the German's throat, sending him the rest of the way to the ground.

Now, at last, Carter had time to reverse the German's rifle. He stabbed downwards, thrusting the bayonet hard into the soldier's chest until he could push no more, stopped either by rifle's muzzle or by the ground beneath the German's body. He lay still on the ground, sightless eyes staring upwards. Carter placed one foot onto the dead German and used it to lever the bayonet free, before turning to find another enemy to attack. Around him the combat had broken down into individual fights, but the sheer aggression of the commando's charge had unnerved the enemy and they were giving ground, foot by foot.

Nearest to him a commando and a stocky German were fencing with their bayonets, each trying to find a way to break through their opponent's defence to strike the winning blow. Carter settled the matter by stabbing the German under his exposed arm. He left the trooper, he thought it might have been Prof Green, to finish the matter.

Carter cranked a bullet into the rifle's chamber, but held the weapon in the guard position, ready to use the bayonet as well. He found himself alongside the stranded armoured car. A pool of black oil was soaking into the grass of the field. Whatever the mortar bomb had struck, it had terminally wounded the vehicle. Carter wrestled a grenade from a loop on his webbing harness, pulled the pin with his teeth and lobbed it into the vehicle's open turret.[2] He heard it rattle on the floor inside and a muffled shout as the vehicle's driver came to a sudden and very short-lived realisation that the armoured walls of his vehicle would now contain the explosion that would kill him, magnifying the grenade's power.

The grenade exploded, jetting smoke and shrapnel upwards through the turret.

The Germans had had enough. Several were retreating across the fields, the commandos following at a distance, stopping to take pot shots at them as they fled. Silence fell as the fighting came to an end, the remaining Germans either surrendering or turning to run after their comrades. It was time to stop the killing.

"Cease fire!" Carter commanded. "Corporals on me!"

Porter of Fox section was first to arrive. He was dishevelled, they probably all were, but he had a cheery grin on his face. "Take Fox section forward and set up a defence about fifty yards in front." Carter ordered. There was probably no risk of the Germans returning, at least not immediately, but they should be prepared in case they did. Fox section by itself wouldn't be able to see them off, but they would be able to give a warning. Porter trotted dutifully away to round up his men.

Franklyn and Macmillan arrived together. "George section can look after the wounded. Give them first aid then get them back up the hill and onto the reverse slope." Carter had a second thought: the possibility of the *Luftwaffe* returning. "Cancel that. Get them into slit trenches or foxholes. Then gather up our dead, collect their ID[3] tags and then wrap them in their gas capes."

"Will we be taking them with us, Lucky?" MacMillan asked. It was a tradition amongst the commandos that they took their dead home with them if they could.

"Depends on the circumstances when we leave. If we can take them, we will." The answer seemed to satisfy the corporal, because he changed the subject. "What about the German wounded?"

"Any that are fit to walk can be disarmed and sent on their way. Let the Jerries look after their own. Give the rest first aid and set them alongside the German dead. Which brings me to you, Franklyn. Your men can gather up the German dead and lay them together. Treat them with dignity. They may be the enemy, but they fought bravely. Then collect up the German weapons and put them in the armoured car and set fire to it. I don't want the Germans to be able to get it started again and use it against us. Make sure you remove the driver from inside."

"There's a couple of prisoners as well, Lucky." Franklyn reminded him.

"Yes, tie them up and leave them next to their dead. Once we've gone the Germans will come forward to clear up and they'll release them." It would have been normal to take the prisoners back to England for interrogation and imprisonment, but Carter couldn't spare any men to guard them.

With his men now occupied in activities that would divert their minds from the horror of the hand to hand fight, Carter was able to take stock of the small battlefield. A half dozen Germans lay dead, not counting those that the commandos had shot as they retreated. He could also count four wounded and two prisoners. That made the German casualty rate about thirty percent. It would be suicide for the remainder to try another attack, but that didn't mean that their commander wouldn't send fresh troops to try to take the hill again. But it would take them a while to get there.

Of his own force Carter knew he had two dead at the top of the hill and another lying not far away, the victim of a German bayonet. Another soldier lay halfway down the slope where he had been shot as he charged. Carter could see one trooper being treated for a nasty looking stab wound in his leg, and another couple with less serious wounds, though Vardy would probably have a scar on his face, from eye socket to jaw, for the rest of his life. He had been lucky. If the bayonet that had slashed him had been a fraction of an inch higher it would have taken out his left eye.

Carter suddenly felt tired. The combination of the adrenalin draining from him and a lack of sleep made him feel weary beyond just fatigue. He felt he could have closed his eyes where he was standing and not woken for several hours. He checked his watch, noticing that it was nine fifteen. He hadn't slept since the previous afternoon, before they had boarded the landing craft. Even then the tension he had been feeling had allowed him only a fitful doze.

Plenty of time to sleep when you're dead, he chided himself, remembering what the instructors used to say at Achnacarry. He turned and made his way up the hill, intent on surveying the terrain to identify the next threat that he might need to counter. He had heard nothing from 5 Troop during the short battle. He hadn't expected to. It was the job of soldiers in ambush to keep themselves separate from anything else that was going on. If they gave away their presence the ambush would be useless. But if Carter was right about the Germans not having been tricked into believing that the invasion had started, it meant that no more troops would advance along the road and Motson's troop would remain unemployed.

At the top of the hill Carter was surprised to be greeted by Andrew Fraser, 3 Troop's temporary commander. He was flanked by two soldiers carrying rifles, acting as his personal bodyguard.

"Lucky! Still living up to your name, I see." His Lowland Scottish drawl making him sound slightly bored.

"Come to see how real commandos do things, have you Andrew?" Carter replied with a broad grin.

[1] LMG – Light machine gun. In this case it would have been an MG 34, a belt fed weapon that was the equivalent of the British Bren gun at platoon level. The "34" in its designation refers to its year of introduction into the German army, 1934. Like the Bren gun, it had a folding bipod stand to give it stability. The Germans also deployed many MG 42s, which were the same calibre but mounted on tripods. An additional man was required in each crew to carry the tripod, but it had a 30% higher rate of fire.

[2] It isn't actually possible to pull the pin from a grenade with the teeth, because it is a split-pin and the ends are bent apart to prevent it from being extracted by accident, so please forgive the author for this little bit of Hollywood imagery.

[3] ID tags – Each British soldier wears two compressed fibre identification discs on a thin chord around their neck. Both are marked with their service number, rank, name and religion. If the soldier is killed, one disc is left with the body so that it can be identified and the Red Cross notified, so that details can be sent back to the soldier's government and his next of kin can be informed of his death. The inclusion of religion on the disc ensures that the soldier is buried in accordance with his beliefs. The enemy will then mark his grave with the details inscribed on the disc, but the disc will remain with the body. Whenever possible the second disc is removed by the soldier's own side so that his death can be recorded. The two disc system is designed to make sure that no soldier's death goes unrecorded even if his own side has to retreat. The scene in the film

"Saving Private Ryan" that shows Captain Millar's men sorting through ID tags hanging on chains is inaccurate because the chains would have been left on the bodies and just one "dog tag", as the Americans call it, would have been removed. The reason that so many First World War graves in Commonwealth War Graves Cemeteries in France bear the legend "Known Unto God", rather than a name, is because the bodies were sometimes so damaged that their ID discs couldn't be found or were illegible.

11 – The Defence Of The Battery

"Dickie sent me to get a sitrep[1] from you." Fraser explained his unexpected arrival, "and to discuss your views on what the enemy might be planning."

"We're holding on, but if the Jerries make a concerted attempt to take this hill, then we'd have to withdraw. We've no real protection for our flanks. Casualties so far are four dead and another four wounded, three of those can fight on if need be, but the fourth really needs to be evacuated. He wouldn't be able to keep up with a fighting retreat."

"That may not be a problem. Dickie has his view on what may happen next, but he'd appreciate your input, as you can see better from up here than he can from the battery."

Putting his binoculars to his eyes once again, Carter made a point of scanning the fields in front of them. The enemy seemed to be massing in the fields immediately to the front of the battery. The survivors from the assault on the hill were now also heading in that direction.

Beyond them was a strip of wasteland that stretched as far as the cliff tops, in places as much as a hundred yards wide, but elsewhere as little as ten, but in the direction of the battery it was generally quite wide. The thin soil at the top of the cliffs only supported scrubby sea grass and gorse. It was possible that the French farmers grazed a few sheep or goats out there, but the soil wouldn't support the lusher grass needed for cattle farming.

Around the battery a clear zone had been established to provide the defences with an uninterrupted field of fire, what was known as a killing zone. At its southern extremity it wasn't far from Kasmire's position, about half way between the hill and the battery.

"I'm guessing that they'll attack along the cliff tops, using them to protect their left flank. They'll probably aim for the seaward side of the battery and try to force a gap in the defences on that side. If they succeed, they'll cut off our way back to the landing craft and we'll probably have to surrender."

"That was Dickie's thinking as well. But we can't withdraw with so many enemy close at hand. The men waiting to descend the cliffs would be a sitting target for mortars and machine guns. We'd also be thinning the defences, giving the enemy the chance to rush us."

"So what does he plan to do?"

"Let them attack. He wants you and 5 Troop to withdraw and prepare for a flank attack on the Germans, from this side. As they charge, you come in from their right. With the element of surprise, they'll be caught in the open with nowhere to go but forwards or backwards. With us in the defences and you on the flank, forwards would be suicidal, so they'd have to withdraw. In the ammunition bunkers we found a couple of Jerry 8cm mortars and a whole load of bombs. They'd have to pull back quite a long way to get out of range of those. That should give us the breathing space to withdraw. What do you think?"

"It's as good a plan as anything I could come up with."

"That's what I said. We probably haven't got much time. Do you think you could get into position in the next ten to fifteen minutes?"

"I could, but 5 Troop may need a little bit longer."

"Well, the Jerries are in control of the timetable, so we'll have to hope for the best."

"How are things at the battery? Did those air raids cause any problems?"

"Not for us, but they killed a lot of their own. The first raid went for the big guns and our men had time to get into the Jerry air raid trenches behind them. One man caught some shrapnel and we've evacuated him to the LCs. But the second raid, a bomb landed right next to the hut where the prisoners were being kept. Damn near blew the place to smithereens. There was a dozen dead and a whole load more wounded, mainly from flying glass and wood splinters. We've done what we can for them but some of them won't make it unless the Jerries can get them to hospital pretty soon, and we're not about to allow them to do that."

"Has Dickie thought about offering them a truce to come and collect the casualties?"

"Yes, but that would mean letting them into the battery and they'd see how small our defence force is."

"They'll probably have already worked that out. Those one-tens went out over the sea to turn, so they'd have seen how many landing craft there are on the beach. They can do the sums."

"True, but Dickie won't consider a truce. They don't know where all our men are, other than us, you and Kasmire. If they knew there were so few men in the battery, they'd already be attacking."

Carter had to admit that was an appropriate conclusion to draw. Having finished the clean-up operation below, his men were starting to arrive back at the top of the hill, a column of smoke rising from the burning armoured car. The crackle and pop of small arms ammunition cooking off could be heard from inside the burning vehicle, but the armour of the hull would prevent any of it from escaping in any direction other than upwards and causing injuries to the commandos.

He called the corporals over to him and instructed them to take their men straight down the reverse slope of the hill and start moving back towards the battery. He pointed to a prominent tree where he wanted them to stop and wait so he could brief them on what would happen next.

"I'll take your wounded back with me and collect Kasmire on the way. We'll get the wounded down to the LCs if the Germans give us time to do so. We'll need Kasmire's men to strengthen the defences.

"OK, I'll send Ian Motson the recall signal, then meet him at the foot of the hill and let him know what's planned."

"You have a plan already?"

"We're going to sneak up as close as we can without giving ourselves away and when the enemy charge, we're going to lay into them from the side." Carter grinned. "If you want to call that a plan, then yes, I have one already."

Fraser gave a chuckle. "Yes, I suppose we haven't time to strive for perfection right now. I'll get going then."

Fraser didn't waste any time on goodbyes. Signalling to his bodyguards he turned and started to make his way back down the hill, calling the wounded commandos over to him as he did.

Carter spotted two familiar figures from Easy section, just about to follow their corporal's orders and start their own descent.

"Green, O'Driscoll, stay here. You're my escort."

"How come we get all the shit jobs?" O'Driscoll grinned.

"Because you're stupid enough to follow orders." Carter retorted in kind. He spared a glance towards the small group of bodies lying wrapped in their gas capes. It didn't feel right to leave them there, but he didn't have any choice. Taking the dead men with him would only slow them down at a time when speed was of the essence. He pocketed the four ID discs handed to him by Cpl MacMillan, wondering if he would himself survive to write the letters of condolence to the men's families. Or maybe someone else would have to write to Fiona and his parents telling them about his own brave death in this corner of a foreign field[2]. He wondered who it would be. By rights it should be the CO, but he might be dead himself by now, depending on how devastating the E-Boat attack had been. It had been devastating enough to prevent any more LCs making it ashore, he knew that much.

He shook his head as though he might shake the thought from his mind. Focus was what was needed now, if he was to avoid leaving more gas cape wrapped bodies behind.

Taking his shaving mirror from his picket, he slid it from its leather pouch and sent the recall signal to Ian Motson. He got an acknowledgement immediately and after only a few seconds the first commandos emerged from their hiding places and started to work their way along the hedge line towards the bottom of the hill.

"Come on, Mutt and Jeff[3]," Carter said to Green and O'Driscoll, "Let's go down and wait for 5 Troop."

Green stepped off in front of him and O'Driscoll brought up the rear as they wound their way down the slope. Carter gave the four bodies another regretful glance, then did his best to push them from his mind.

[1] Sitrep – Situation report. A brief summary of events and proposed remedial action.

[2] A phrase from the poem "The Soldier" by First World War soldier and poet Rupert Brooke. The poem is sometimes also known as "Nineteen-Fourteen: The Soldier." Brooke died on 23rd April 1915 from sepsis caused by an infected mosquito bite, while on his way to take part in the Gallipoli landings.

[3] Mutt and Jeff – Popular characters from an American newspaper comic strip, first created in 1902, that was syndicated worldwide. Mutt and Jeff were both a bit dim and easily confused, hence the use of their names as a mild insult. The names were also used as the codenames for two captured German agents, Helge Moe (Mutt) and Tor Glad (Jeff), who surrendered to the British as soon as they landed in Scotland. Their radio transmissions back to Berlin deceived the Germans into believing that there would be an invasion of Norway. The operation was given the codename Omnibus and took place from June 1941 until 1943. This belief was reinforced by a series of commando raids on Norway. Operation Archery, which the author fictionalised as Operation Absolom in the first book of the Carter's Commando series was one of the most significant raids. To give the pair's radio transmissions added credibility, MI5 carried out realistic sabotage attacks, without causing serious damage, that were supposed to have been carried out by the two agents.

* * *

It wasn't long before the forward scouts from 5 Troop arrived, moving carefully along the hedge line at the foot of the hill.
"Willow!" challenged Carter.
"Witch" the leading soldier replied from the other side of the hedge. The passwords were chosen because of the alleged inability of Germans to pronounce the letter w in British words.
"Where's Lt Motson?" Carter asked.

"At the rear." Came the reply.

"OK. Keep going until you catch up with my troop, then wait there for me and Lt Motson. We'll brief you on what is going to happen."

"OK." The soldier replied, leading his section off once again. The brief exchange had been heard and word was passed along the line that there was someone looking for 5 Troop's commander. Motson hurried forward until he was crouching opposite Carter.

"Hi Ian. Come through and we'll take a look at the German positions." Carter greeted him.

Motson pushed his way through a slender gap in the hedge and followed Carter, Green and O'Driscoll back to the top of the hill. He brought his own bodyguard with him. Arriving at the top, the four troopers took up positions in the abandoned fox holes left by Carter's men. "Smoke if you want to." Carter told the men. The Germans knew where they were, so a bit of cigarette smoke would harm nothing more than the men's lungs and after squatting in a hedge for several hours Motson's men would be suffering severe nicotine deprivation if they were smokers. In fact, a little puff of cigarette smoke on the breeze might help to persuade the Germans that the hill was still fully defended.

Motson himself looked as though he had just stepped off the parade ground, if the camouflage cream streaked across his face, neck and hands was ignored. Carter felt like a bit of a tramp by comparison. But then again, Motson and his men hadn't been involved in hand to hand fighting.

"You did well with that German attack. If it looked like you were going to be over-run I'd have come and helped out."

"You did the right thing." Carter told him. He wasn't resentful that Motson's troop had stayed out of the fight. He had a job to do and giving away his position wouldn't have allowed him to do that job if it had become necessary. "Things have changed though. The Germans are massing for an attack on the battery." He pointed to where the enemy were gathered in the fields, still making their preparations for the assault. Motson viewed the scene through his binoculars.

"I take it we're not going to allow that to happen."

"No, Dickie wants us to flank them and push them back out of range, so that we can withdraw without the Germans interfering. I propose that we get ourselves to the edge of the cleared zone, then work our way down until we're forming a line along the hedge. The Germans looks as though they're crossing over to the clear stretch along the cliff tops."

As they watched a man pulled at the base of the hedge, drawing the severed trunk of a hawthorn to one side to create a hole through which another man wriggled. He reappeared, crawling out into the middle of the waste ground, taking cover behind a gorse shrub. All along the hedge line other soldiers were working to create passages through the vegetation. The difficulty of the task was why the Germans weren't already attacking. Further back, in the middle of the field, a group of four Germans were digging a hole large enough to form a mortar pit. Carter made a mental note to assign a section of men to eliminate that when the time came. Somewhere the German commander would also be setting up machine gun positions to protect his right flank, but from where they were Carter couldn't see where those positions might be.

"OK. I think I have the lay of the land." Motson said. "Given that my men haven't been engaged, can I suggest that we take the end of the line furthest from the battery. We'll try to get behind the Germans and create some confusion."

"That's fine, but don't get sucked into a pitch battle. In the end numbers will tell and we can't afford to lose any men." If Motson wanted to win himself a VC that was his affair. The majority of the medals were awarded to men already dead and Carter had no great desire to be the posthumous holder of a bit of old Russian cannon.[1]

"I'll be careful. I don't have your legendary luck." Motson gave his colleague a mighty slap on the shoulder. "Bunting, Grint, let's catch up with the rest of the troop."

He started to head down the hill with his bodyguard, Carter, Green and O'Driscoll following close behind. Their distance from the enemy made it possible for them to jog, though they had to take care crossing any openings in the hedge, just in case the Germans had a machine gun zeroed in on it. It was a normal tactic to keep such obvious features under observation. More than one man had been killed by a machine gun or mortar round when he wandered into the middle of a crossroads to decide which direction to take.

They found the rest of 4 and 5 troops lounging around the base of the tree that Carter had designated as the rendezvous, a small defensive ring covering the approach lines.

Scraping a rough map of the terrain onto a patch of dried mud, Carter explained what they would do. As he had explained to Fraser, there was no finesse about the plan. "If we're discovered," he finished, "before the Germans start their assault on the battery, we just break cover and attack before they have time to get organised."

Carter detailed his sections to specific tasks. Fox section, the only one not to have suffered casualties, was given the job of taking care of the mortars, but without their Bren gun, which Carter would keep with him. Easy and George sections would accompany Carter in the charge into the flank of the German's advance. Ian Motson led his sections along the side of the hedge, but he was only half way to his intended position when a machine gun opened up on them, sending them diving into the roots of the hawthorns.

That seemed to galvanise the Germans into action. Realising that their flank was under threat the mortars started firing and the Germans rose in a *Feldgrau* wave and charged the battery from a distance of about two hundred yards. Bren guns opened fire on them and the first infantrymen started to fall, but the rest kept going, their own machine guns chattering a defiant reply.

The German mortars burst about in eighty yards front of the battery's defences, the bombs sending out clouds of smoke to cover the German advance and putting the Bren gunners off their aim. By the time the Germans broke through that cover they would be within fifty yards of the battery's defences.

As they reached the open area in front of where Carter's men had taken refuge, he drew a great breath and shouted "Charge!". The commandos slammed into the side of the German attack like an out of control bus, stabbing with their bayonets at the soldiers unlucky enough to be closest to them. Behind him, Carter could hear Pearson's Bren gun open fire, pouring lethal bursts of point three-oh-three bullets into the Germans that manged to get beyond Carter's skirmish line.

The first Germans started to waver while some threw themselves to the ground behind the illusory protection of gorse bushes. Those that kept their feet started to step backwards, firing their Karabiner 98k rifles at the closest commandos. Carter saw Cpl Franklyn go down, hit but not dead so far as he could see.

Carter swept his Tommy gun back and forth, firing until the magazine was empty. He went down onto one knee while he changed the mag and heard the crack of a bullet pass the place where his head had been just a split second before. Such were the fine margins between life and death on a battlefield. Rising again he saw a knot of Germans trying to mount an MG-42 on its tripod. Carter charged towards them, firing his Tommy gun. One dropped where he crouched and the other two ran away, leaving their weapon where it was.

Carter was tempted to try to grab the weapon and turn it on its former owners, but it wasn't loaded and he didn't have time to try to work out how to fit its belt of ammunition.

Mortar bombs, fired from the battery, were falling on the far side of the waste ground, closest to the cliff tops. It was the final straw for the Germans. They broke and ran, Carter's men firing after them as they threw themselves through the gaps in the hedges, trying to put something, anything, between themselves and the commando assault.

"Cease firing!" Carter yelled. "Cease firing." He took a quick look around to try to assess the amount of damage his men had inflicted. Three Germans lay dead, another two wounded too badly to move without assistance. One was hobbling after his comrades, casting fearful looks over his shoulder, but the commandos let him go. He was unarmed and in no condition to fight. It wasn't a heavy toll, but faced with the naked aggression of the commandos, the Germans had fled rather than face them. Having a bit of a reputation had paid off as the first to have run would have been those that had already faced Kasmire's men or Carter's men on the slopes of the hill.

An eerie silence had fallen over the battlefield, quiet enough for Carter to hear the angry cries of gulls as they swooped low over the cliffs, disturbed from their nests. "OK, men. Back to the battery." Carter ordered. They needed no second bidding.

Green and O'Driscoll came past him, supporting a wounded Cpl Franklyn between them, their rifles held in the free hands. Franklyn was hopping, his left trouser leg soaked with blood.

"Glass, Mitchell, give a hand over here." Carter called over two more of his men. Between them they made a crude seat for Franklyn out of Green's and O'Driscoll's rifles, each man holding either the butt or the barrel of the two weapons. With Franklyn sitting on the rifles they were able to make far quicker progress.

Carter knew that the German commander would already be planning his retaliation, gathering his men together and threatening or cajoling them into making another charge. But Dickie Bird understood that as well and the sound of mortar bombs exploding assaulted Carter's ears, keeping the Germans at a safe distance. They would attack again, but first they would find a route hidden from the mortars. Carter estimated that they had a reprieve of no more than thirty minutes.

Passing through the battery's defences, Carter heard the voices of the defenders coming from weapons pits and slit trenches. "Well done 4 Troop." And "Good on yer, lads." And similar. Sgt Thorpe, the gunnery expert, was there directing the new arrivals to the positions that he wanted them to take.

Carter sought out Dickie Bird, who was just climbing down from the roof of the HQ hut. He had a bandage around his head beneath his steel helmet.

"Andrew didn't tell me you'd been wounded." Carter observed.

"Just a scratch, more blood than anything else. You know how head wounds bleed. Anyway, well done with that flank attack. None of the Germans got within a hundred yards before they withdrew." Carter was distracted by the cough of mortars as another salvo of bombs was fired.

"This must be 5 Troop." Bird said, looking past Carter. Carter turned to see a file of men approaching across the killing zone in front of the defences.

"I didn't see what happened after the German MG opened up on them. I was too intent on what my own men were doing."

"It looks bad." Bird said. "I can only count about a dozen men."

Carter did his own count and saw that Bird was right. Of the dozen, two were clearly wounded. "I can't pick out Ian."

"No, neither can I." A gloomy silence fell between them. If Motson wasn't leading his men back to the battery, it was for the worst possible reason.

"What should I do with these?" Cpl Porter asked, pointing to two mortar tubes being carried by two of his men."

"What are you doing with those, Porter?"

"You said you wanted the Jerry mortars put out of action. The easiest way to do that was to bring them with us." Carter couldn't deny the logic of Porter's action.

"Well, just dump them over there." Carter pointed at an air raid trench, "Did you suffer any casualties?"

"No. As soon as we broke cover the Jerries ran for it, leaving the tubes behind."

"OK, that's good. Ask Sgt Thorpe where he wants you."

The first men from 5 Troop were just filing through the defences. Bird signalled for one of them to come over and report.

"Where's Lt Motson?" he asked without any preamble.

"Dead, Sir. When the Jerry machine gun opened up on us, he didn't hesitate. He charged straight at it. Didn't even wait to see if we were following."

"Were you?"

The soldier gave an affronted look. "Of course. We spread out and did our best to outflank it, but a second gun opened up, so we were caught in a cross fire. There wasn't much we could do. Lt Motson, though, he was like a demon. He ran straight at them firing his Tommy gun. He got right into the gun pit before one of them got him with a bayonet. We kept going, despite the other MG, and we took out that gun pit, but we had to withdraw. We couldn't bring Lt Motson with us though. There were Germans everywhere, running from the flank attack and they would have caught us."

"How many men did you lose?"

The soldier's face fell. "Five that I know of. Three more we couldn't account for. They may be dead, maybe wounded."

"If they're wounded, I hope the Jerries look after them." Bird said. "OK. Well done. Go and find Sgt Thorpe and tell him he's acting troop commander."

The soldier returned to his comrades and they went looking for their sergeant.

"What's the plan now, Dickie?" Carter asked. "We must be starting to run short of ammunition."

"There's plenty of Jerry ammo if we need it. Plenty of their rifles to fire it as well. We haven't been able to find any machine guns though. They must have them but if they have, they've hidden them well but we haven't the manpower to do a full search of the battery and the ammunition bunkers. We interrogated a prisoner that speaks English, but he just shrugged his shoulders and pretended not to know anything. So I've assigned all the three-of-three ammunition to the Bren guns and most of 2 Troop are now using the German 98k rifles.

With the Germans pushed back and significantly weaker than they were, I think we can start the withdrawal. Once we get the wounded down to the LCs we'll pull a troop at a time out of the defences and send them down the cliffs. We'll need someone to act as rear guard, though."

"I'll do it if you like." Carter knew he shouldn't have said it. His men had seen more action than any others that day. They deserved to be first out of the battery, not the last.

"I won't hear of it, Lucky." Bird agreed with Carter's unspoken rebuke of himself. "My troop will act as rear-guard. I think what's left of 5 Troop should probably go first. They've been weakened the most. Then your men, followed by Kasmire's and finally mine."

"If you're sure?" Having been let off the hook, Carter was happy to accept Bird's decision, but a token protest was always appreciated.

"Thanks for the offer, Lucky, but I am sure." Bird turned to locate Fraser and Kasmire and waved them over so he could complete their briefing.

[1] The Victoria Cross, Britain's highest military award for bravery, is made using metal taken from Russian cannons captured during the Crimean War. The cannons were the ones attacked by the ill-fated *Charge of the Light Brigade*, on 25th October 1854. It was that act which persuaded Queen Victoria to instigate a new award for bravery, which would carry her name. Carter is wrong to think that most VCs are awarded posthumously. Of the 1,358 VCs to have been awarded to date, only 295 were posthumous. Of the three soldiers who have been awarded a second VC (a "bar" as it is known), two were doctors who received them for rescuing wounded soldiers. Three fathers and sons and four pairs of brothers have been awarded VCs. Two of the brothers were Major John Gough and Major Hugh Gough, who both won their VCs during the Indian Mutiny (1857 and 1858 respectively) and Major John Gough, son of Charles, won his in 1903 during the Third Somaliland Expedition.

* * *

"Aren't we a bit exposed, stood out here in plain sight of the Germans?" Kasmire asked as he joined the O-Group.

"It shows the men that we aren't worried about the enemy." Bird explained to the American. "It gives them confidence to see that we have confidence."

"Shouldn't we be worried by the enemy?" Kasmire persisted. "At least a little bit."

"Of course we should and I am, but it doesn't do to let the men see that. They take their cue from the officers, so we have to appear fearless even if we're quaking in our boots."

Kamsire muttered something that might have been "Crazy limeys" but let the matter drop.

Once Bird had explained what was to happen, the officers went to brief their men. Fraser was given the task of supervising the evacuation, using a Very Pistol to let Bird know that each section had reached the beach and he was ready for the next. They couldn't risk more than a section at a time being at the top of the cliffs. It would have made too tempting a target for the German machine guns and mortars.

Carter was given the task of re-organising the defences. At that time the men were still in their troops, so removing a troop would leave a massive gap in the defensive positions. Carter was to space the men out, making sure that no two men from the same troop were side by side. They had just agreed this when a great tearing sound, like huge sheets of cardboard being ripped apart, split the sky above their heads. It was followed immediately by an explosion, the blast from which knocked the officers off their feet.

Shrapnel buzzed through the air above their heads before clumps of soil and chalk started to rain down on them. Something hit Carter on his backpack, knocking the air from his lungs.

"Damn, that's awkward." Bird understated as he regained his feet. "Looks like they've brought up some artillery."

"Could it be a tank?" Kasmire asked.

"No. If it was a tank they'd bring it up to the front to fire from point blank range while the infantry advanced behind it, using it for cover. Did anyone notice how long the gap was between the explosion and the sound of the discharge?"

They shook their heads. Just as with thunder and lightning, the distance between the gun and the battery could be estimated using the time delay between the shell exploding and the sound of the gun's discharge reaching their ears. If there was no discernible time lag, then the gun must be less than a mile distant.

"OK, that changes things. They'll use the gun to keep our heads down while they advance. I think we can expect another attack within the next ten minutes, so better get the men moving. Let's go."

Fraser jogged off to the northern side of the battery where the remains of 5 Troop had been sent, while Kasmire went to the south to re-join his men. Carter's men were between Kasmire's and 2 Troop, who were mainly on the western side, facing the direction from which the enemy was expected to approach. He was almost at the nearest gun pit when there was another huge explosion. Carter was lifted off his feet and thrown into the air, landing heavily in the pit on top of a protesting Bren gunner. More soil and chalk clods rained down on them, peppering Carter's shoulders and his steel helmet like heavy rainfall.

That had been a close one. Close enough for it to have killed him if he hadn't moved from the place where the O-Group had been held. With a sudden realisation, Carter stuck his head up and searched out the other officers. Fraser was just picking himself up off the ground again, wiping debris off his uniform in a rather theatrical manner. Kasmire's head could be seen poking out of a slit trench, also looking to see what had happened. Of Dickie Bird there was no sign.

Shit! Carter thought. Bird hadn't moved from his spot and not being able to see him suggested the worst. Carter pushed himself out of the gun pit and ran to the crater created by the shell. Scraps of bloody flesh lay around the edges, On the far side was what looked like a leg, the foot still encased in its boot. It was all the evidence that was needed to tell him of Dickie Bird's fate. At least it had been quick.

Fraser arrived at the run, Kasmire not far behind. They surveyed the scene for a moment, their faces registering their shock. Carter knew he had to do something before they all froze into inactivity.

"The plan goes ahead just as Dickie briefed it." Carter's voice was firm, decisive. "I just want to make a couple of minor alterations. We can't risk re-organising the defences. If we start moving the men around, they'll run the risk of being hit by the next shell. Also, Andrew, I want a mortar down on that beach to cover the final withdrawal. Make sure it has smoke as well as HE[1] bombs. I'll keep Sgt Thorpe with me till the last. The last section of 2 Troop to leave will be under his command. They've got to provide covering fire for me and my men. As soon as Sgt Thorpe arrives, you get down to the LCs yourself. Make sure they get off the beach as soon as they're full. They're to head for the landing ships lying off Honfleur."

"You're not evacuating in the same order?"

"Mostly we will be, but I'll keep a section of my men back till last. No offence intended, but I'm happier with my own men around me. Any questions?"

There were none. There was no time left to think of answers even if there had been. "OK, Andrew, get 5 Troop moving, right away. Have you got a Very Pistol?"

"No, but Sgt Thorpe has. I'll borrow that."

"OK, then send him over to me. I'll need to brief him on what happens when I start getting my last section out."

There was the sound of tearing cardboard again and the officers threw themselves to the ground. The shell over shot by some margin and landed on the eastern side of the battery, where there were the fewest defenders.

[1] HE – High explosive. Artillery shells and mortar bombs come in several different types. Smoke is used to provide cover for advancing troops, high explosive rounds are for destroying visible targets, armour piercing rounds are used against tanks and air burst shells propel shrapnel down onto men who may be lying in the protection of slit trenches.

12 – The Final Fifteen Minutes

Carter could see Andrew Fraser guiding the remnants of 5 Troop back towards the cliff tops where the ropes they had used to ascend the cliffs would now be used to abseil back down them. It was the quickest way of descending, but it meant that only one man could be on each rope at any time, until that man reached the bottom and let it go slack so the man waiting at the top could wrap the rope around his body and commence his drop. They also couldn't use all the ropes that were available, because some of them lay in the direction of the Germans. Anyone approaching them would make ideal targets for snipers.

Carter estimated it would take about thirty seconds for each man to descend, about two minutes for a complete section given the number of ropes available, if any of the sections were still complete. With the time taken to cross the ground to the top of the cliffs, the total time for the evacuation might be fifteen minutes. If the Germans allowed them that much time.

The answer wasn't long in coming. Smoke bombs started to explode along the length of the killing zone, providing a screen behind which the enemy could advance. Carter's own mortar stopped firing as the operator adjusted his angle, increasing it so that his bombs would drop between fifty and a hundred yards in front of the defences. The Bren gunners didn't need orders. They started to fire as soon as the smoke started to billow outwards.

"Stand-by!" Carter yelled, not that it was necessary. Every man still in the defences knew what was coming.

Carter spotted movement on the left of the smoke screen, quickly hidden as another mortar bomb erupted. It had been fleeting, but there was no doubt that the enemy were moving on that side.

"Kasmire!" Carter yelled. The American's head popped into view above the parapet of his slit trench.

Carter clenched his fist, thumb pointed downwards, the signal for enemy sighted. He then pointed towards the place where he had seen the enemy movement. Did the Americans use the same hand signals? Carter wondered. But there would be someone close by who understood it. That was all it needed.

Kasmire raised his own hand, thumb and forefinger forming a circle, the universal sign for "OK". Another mortar bomb erupted, even further to the south. The Germans were attempting a flanking attack on that side. It was sensible if they had worked out how thinly the defences were spread. If Carter moved any of his men to counter the attack, it would leave the centre or northern flank weakened, no doubt what the Germans were hoping would happen.

Another Very flare hissed upwards from the cliff top and Sgt Thorpe sent the next section back towards the ropes. The northern flank was now almost undefended. Carter called Cpl Porter across to him and ordered him to take his men to fill the gap, then spread the other two sections across the space that had been created.

Carter looked back to see what the Germans were doing to the south. He had no tactic he could use that would prevent the attack. The only thing that stood a chance would be a head-on charge from the southerly defences, pushing the Germans back before they got too close, but there weren't enough men to do that. The Germans would have sent a full platoon to make the assault and Kasmire had barely two sections. He would outnumbered at least two to one.

"Easy section." Carter called. "Covering fire to the left." At least he could make life uncomfortable for the Germans by firing into their flank as they advanced. But firing blind through the smoke, the chances of hitting anyone were slim. By the time they appeared through the smoke it might already be too late to chase them off.

Then Kasmire acted.

The rattle of small arms fire prevented Carter hearing Kasmire's shouted order, but he was up and out of his slit trench, firing a Tommy gun from his hip. Briefly Carter wondered what had happened to Kasmire's M1 rifle, but he pushed the thought from his mind. Kasmire's two depleted sections were following him, charging towards the smoke. The only ones not present were the Bren gunners, who were firing ahead of them.

The first commando fell after about twenty yards of running, the second a few yards later, but the commandos didn't stop. They extended their bayonet tipped rifles ahead of them, their mouths wide open as they screamed their defiance at the enemy. It was hopeless, Carter knew. They could never hope to defeat a stronger enemy that way.

They disappeared into the smoke, leaving Carter wondering about their fate. "Easy section Bren gun; cease firing." Carter called, at the same time tapping the gunner on the top of his steel helmet. He was at risk of hitting friends as well as enemies if he continued.

The gunner took the opportunity to uncouple the barrel of his Bren gun and replace it with the spare. As he laid the used barrel on the sand bagged parapet of the gun pit, the brown hessian started to smoulder with the heat from the metal. There were some soldiers that said they had seen Bren gun barrels glowing red, but Carter didn't believe it. It would mean their bullets would explode as soon as they were pushed out of the magazine and into the chamber and that was more of a danger to the gunner than to the enemy.

The change took only seconds, so good was the design of the Bren, then the gunner was back in action, aiming at the main body of the smoke where he could be sure of only hitting enemies.

No more mortar bombs fell, meaning the Germans were just about to break through the smokie barrier. That also meant that the Germans would switch to HE rounds, adjusting the aim of their mortars so the bombs fell within the defences.

Carter braced himself, taking a tight grip on his Thompson sub machine gun. The enemy would be within the effective range of the weapon, so he would soon be firing it once again. Had he changed the magazine after their last engagement? He couldn't remember. He released the one that was fitted' letting it fall to the bottom of the gun pit and slotted a fresh one into place. The commandos used the long box magazines, rather than the drums that were usually seen in the gangster movies.

Time dragged on with the Germans making no appearance. Carter's jaw started to ache with the tension and he had to force himself to relax a little, before his teeth started to crumble under the force.

The smoke gradually drifted away across the killing zone, to leave no sign of the Germans other than the bodies they left behind. To the left Carter could see where Kasmire's attack had ended. A cluster of bodies in khaki and *Feldgrau,* some entwined in what could have been imagined as a loving embrace, but which had been deadly hand to hand combat. There was no movement; no hope of survivors. Carter picked out the olive drab of Kasmire's uniform, lying further forward than any of the others, his arms outstretched, his Tommy gun still held in his right hand.

Kasmire's charge had forced the flanking Germans to withdraw and with that the rest of the attack had faltered. The Germans had fled back to the protection of the hedgerows while their commander thought again.

In front of them there were fewer bodies, one here and another there, where an unlucky German had been hit by Bren gun fire from a luckier Bren gunner. Carter did a few quick calculations, based on what he could see and the estimates of Germans killed or wounded in previous attacks. If the Germans had deployed a full company against them, he thought that the German commander might still have seventy percent of his men still combat fit. A thirty percent casualty rate was high, but not enough to prevent another attack. It was more than enough to take the battery against Carter's much depleted force. And his force was getting smaller as each section withdrew towards the cliff top.

Which brought a new problem for Carter. Without the concealing smoke, the activity at the cliff top was clearly visible. It wouldn't be long before the Germans positioned machine guns to fire along the line of the cliffs, backed up by more mortar fire.

Carter climbed out of the gun pit and scuttled across the ground in search of Sgt Thorpe. His skin crawled as he imagined a sniper picking him out and trying to end his life. The attack might have been repulsed, but that didn't mean that the Germans had all retreated. There was plenty of concealment in the French hedgerows for a sniper to ply his trade. Carter recalled his father saying how demoralising a good Jerry sniper could be, sapping the men's morale as he picked off any man not switched on enough to keep his head down. They had been remorseless, operating day after day, night after night, the Tommies never knowing who the next victim might be.

"Over here, Lucky!" Thorpe had seen Carter approaching and guessed his purpose.

"I need you to send a message back with the next section. The mortar operator on the beach needs to start sending up smoke bombs." The mortar in the defences had ceased firing as its last operator had withdrawn with his section.

"I'm ahead of you there, Lucky." The sergeant grinned. "The first bombs should be arriving any second now."

Right on cue, the first one exploded in front of them, about a hundred yards away. Of course it was a double edged sword. If the enemy couldn't see the defenders, then the defenders couldn't see the enemy. But Carter thought that Kasmire had bought them enough time.

"How many sections to go?" Carter asked.

"The next ones out will be your three sections, in whatever order you want, then the last two sections from my troop."

"I'm staying till last and I want my Easy section with me. I'll send Fox and George sections next, then you can send your two sections. Keep hold of the Bren guns and any remaining ammunition. I want you to use them to give us covering fire from the top of the cliffs as we withdraw. We'll go back across the middle of the battery to keep your field of fire clear. Once we get to the other side we'll turn north and sprint for the cliffs. When we get there, we'll cover you as you go down the ropes."

"The Jerries will know what we're up to. They'll attack, for certain. They'll want one final chance to kill us."

"Which is why I want you to leave your Bren guns behind. We'll take hold of them as we arrive and keep shooting until they jam or we run out of ammunition, then we'll follow you down the ropes. If we can keep them back, then we'll just have time to get down the ropes. If necessary you can take the last landing craft out far enough so it can use its Lewis guns to keep the cliff tops clear. We'll dump our kit and swim for it. It won't be the first time."

"So I've heard." The sergeant's face grew serious. "You know you probably won't make it."

"But the rest of you will. That's what's important." Carter slapped the sergeant on the shoulder. "Now, you know what to do. Just give us whatever covering fire you can. We'll do the rest."

Carter didn't allow time for any further discussion. He scuttled back to Easy sections' part of the defences once again. Was this how it had felt at Rorke's Drift? Carter wondered. Faced by overwhelming enemy numbers, had Lieutenant Chard[1] been this cool, calm and collected? Chard had survived against those fearsome odds; maybe Carter would too.

The artillery bombardment started up again, shells landing randomly across the battery; some falling short, other missing it completely. The smoke was concealing them from the German forward observer, which was something. But a lucky, or should that be unlucky, shot could land at any moment, just as Dickie Bird had discovered. Carter's heart lurched at the thought. His mind went back to the day he had first reported to the commando at Troon. Dickie Bird, the harassed Adjutant, searching for his posting order amongst the chaos of his desk. He might have been a lousy administrator, but he was an excellent leader.

It would be an uncomfortable few minutes as Carter waited for 2 Troop's sections to make their way to the cliff top. Not all the retreating commandos had made it to safety, he knew. There was a body hanging over the barbed wire and others would probably have been wounded. And that didn't include those accidental injuries caused when anxious men are abseiling down a cliff face. Had they thought to attach safety ropes, to prevent severe falls? Carter hoped so.

But he would be the last man down. He wouldn't have a burly commando at the top with a safety rope wrapped around his body. If he slipped it would probably be the last thing he ever did.

Carter pushed the thought from his mind, telling himself to concentrate on the task in hand. If the Germans broke through now, all thoughts of plummeting down the cliff face to this death would be irrelevant.

There were explosions off to his right and Carter saw that mortar bombs had exploded close to the withdrawing troops. So the Germans had switched the focus of their attention.

"Easy section." He called above the noise. "We're moving to the northern sector. Come on, let's go."

If the Germans wanted to cut off the retreat, they would have to pass in front of the defences on the northern side of the battery and Carter would be able to fire into their flanks. With Cpl Franklyn and Tpr Vardy wounded and already, Carter hoped, on board the LCs, there would be just seven of them to hold the battery while the last of 2 Troop withdrew. Seven against seventy, maybe eighty Germans. The odds weren't good, but he wasn't going to feel sorry for the Germans. He chuckled at his silent joke, attracting a sideways glance from Paddy O'Driscoll.

"Something funny there, Sorr?" The Irishman asked.

"Just a stray thought." Carter replied.

Between the German mortars and the artillery shells exploding, the noise was almost constant. How had the men in the trenches of the First World War put up with it for days at a time? The truth, he knew, was that many hadn't. Many men had come back from France with broken minds, destroyed by the ceaseless noise of the German artillery barrages. He supposed it had been the same for the Germans. He had been told that one point five million shells had been fired in the artillery barrage ahead of the start of the Somme offensive. The noise must have been unimaginable.

Figures flitted through the edge of the smoke barrier. The enemy were coming once again. The mortar on the beach was still sending bombs over the top of the cliff, alternating HE with smoke, but they were landing too far away to do any harm and Carter had no way of correcting their aim.

The German lead units were much closer to the edge of the cliffs, trying to rush the gap between the battery's defences and the cliff tops. If they succeeded, the men still descending wouldn't stand a chance and Carter and his men would be cut off. But they were crossing in front of both the Bren guns that Carter had available, which meant that the Germans were vulnerable.

"Pearson, Green, keep your guns firing on the right, the rest of you keep up fire to your front." The smoke was masking any view to the west, but Carter knew that the Germans would be approaching from there as well. It was the only way to silence the Bren guns.

The larger artillery piece had fallen silent, not doubt to prevent injuries to the advancing Germans, but mortar bombs were still falling inside the battery. Most were harmless, landing too far away to worry them, but the occasional one would spatter them with soil and stones. It was the shrapnel that was the problem. The razor-sharp shards of bomb casing were lethal. The only way to avoid it was to keep their heads below the parapets of the gun pits and the slit trenches, but that meant they couldn't fire their weapons with any accuracy. Which, of course, was the German intention.

Out of the smoke came a section of Germans, running full tilt towards them. Carter's riflemen opened fire, picking off targets. All commandos were good shots, they had to be, but the Germans knew what they were doing, zig-zagging to put the defenders off their aim. But in doing that they couldn't return fire for fear of hitting one of their own. One German went down and the others faltered. Carter suspected that it was the leader, probably a corporal, who had been shot. Without anyone to shout encouragement, the bravery of the others started to ooze away. The hesitation was costly as Paddy O'Driscoll put another one down.

Carter pulled the pin on a grenade, drew his arm back and launched the small bomb in the general direction of the attackers. It fell well short but bounced and rolled a little closer before exploding.

It was enough to persuade the remaining attackers to withdraw back into the smoke.

Carter looked across to the cliff tops. The Bren guns had succeeded in slowing the German advance. Instead of continuing, most of the Germans had gone to ground and were trying to pick off the defenders. Someone must have ordered a section attack, because a handful of soldiers got to their feet and rushed forward, before dropping into cover again. A second group rose and did the same.

The outcome was inevitable. If the Germans continued with that tactic, enough would reach the defenders to over run them.

"OK. Time for us to go." Carter ordered. He tapped the nearest man on the top of his steel helmet and pointed towards the rear of the battery, before moving to the next and repeating the gesture. The men needed no second bidding. They clambered over the sandbags at the rear of the gun pits or they crawled out of their slit trenches and scuttled across the battery, using whatever cover they could find.

One of the sections of Germans had just dropped to the ground. Carter waited until the others started to rise, then pulled the trigger of his Tommy gun, traversing it from left to right until the hammer clicked on the empty chamber. One German fell and another used it as an excuse to stop and help his comrade. But the remainder came on. Bullets cracked around Carter's head. As the last of his men left his position, Carter threw the Tommy gun down, its empty magazine rendering it useless. He drew his Webley. Six rounds was all he now had. He, too, made his withdrawal. He leapt over the sandbags and started zig-zagging his way across the battery. The grass clad bulges of the ready use ammunition bunkers offered some protection and allowed him to straighten his run, speeding up his escape. A mortar bomb exploded to his left, but Carter ignored it. He just kept his head down and sprinted for the far side of the battery.

Ahead of him he saw the gun pits and slit trenches of the eastern defences. Beyond that his men were turning northwards, looking in his direction to make sure he was still with them before they continued their own escape. He could pause there, in the nearest gun pit, he knew. Maybe he could take a out a couple more Germans as they came across the battery in pursuit. He abandoned the idea. It would mean his certain death, or capture. He didn't particularly want to die and he certainly had no desire to spend the rest of the war in a PoW camp.

He leapt across a gun pit, his feet landing on the sand bagged parapet on the far side. He jumped down and started to turn towards the north, the direction in which the cliffs lay.

He didn't hear the explosion. All he saw was the earth in front of him erupting. He felt the chin strap of his helmet tighten as the blast pulled at it. It slipped from his chin, scraped over his nose and the helmet flew backwards. Something large and solid looking was flying directly at his head, but there was no time for him to duck.

Bright lights exploded in Carter's skull and, for a fraction of a fraction of a second, he felt an excruciating pain, then the world went black.

[1] Lieutenant John Chard of the Royal Engineers was the senior of two Lieutenants at the South African missionary outpost of Rorke's Drift when they were attacked by the Zulus of King Chetswayo between 22nd and 23rd January 1879. Chard took command of the defences. Chetswayo's Zulus had already massacred the 1,700 soldiers of the military commander, Lord Chelmsford, at the Battle of Isandlwana. The other officer at Rorke's Drift was Lt Gonville Bromhead of the 24th Regiment of Foot (South Wales Border Regiment). A force of 150 British soldiers and Colonial militia faced about 4,000 Zulu warriors. Eleven VCs were awarded to the defenders, with both officers receiving the honour. The action was immortalised in the 1964 film "Zulu"

13 - Nurse Duckworth

A bright light pierced Carter's eyelids. Was this it, he wondered? Were these the gates to Heaven, and the blinding light the aura of St Peter, waiting to greet him and make him account for his sins? That was what the Vicar had said arriving in Heaven was like, in all those interminable childhood sermons about repentance and redemption.

He squeezed his eyes together to resist the glare. A shadow fell across his face and he felt hands under his head, adjusting whatever it was that he was lying on. He got a smell of soap as whoever it was leant close to his face. That was interesting; the Vicar had never mentioned a smell of soap or his pillows being adjusted. Maybe this wasn't Heaven after all. Maybe this was Hell. But if it was Hell, he should be able to smell brimstone, not Sunlight[1].

Carter allowed one eye to open and he made out a shape in front of him. The shape was clad in white and, judging by what was hovering a few inches from his nose, definitely female. It wasn't impossible for Satan to be female, in fact Carter's uncle Arthur had insisted that his wife was the devil incarnate, but it was unlikely that St Peter would be female, unless the Bible had got things very wrong.

The white clad curves moved away from him and his view was enhanced by the face of a rather attractive woman. Heart shaped face, dark hair pulled back into a severe bun, topped by a stiffly starched white headdress. So, neither St Peter nor Satan, but a nurse.

"Ah, Lt Carter, you're awake. Good, the doctor will be pleased." Her voice sounded hollow, as though she were speaking through a drainpipe. He also became aware that his head was pounding and there was a sharp pain above his eye, with more pain running down the side of his face. He raised a hand to touch the source but felt crisp bandages rather than his own skin. "You've had a bit of a bang on the head." The nurse continued, "but nothing too much to worry about. It's left you with a black eye and some severe bruising, but it's not as bad as it looks. The doctor will be along a in a little while to take a look at you. Any questions can wait until he sees you."

Questions such as 'What happened?' and 'Where am I?' Carter assumed. But the Nurse would surely know the answer at least to the second one. She must know where she worked. A realisation dawned on him that the nurse was not only speaking English, but she also had no trace of any accent other than one that spoke of sheep grazing in rolling fields. So he wasn't a prisoner of war.

He tried to speak. "Wh …" was as far as he got. His throat was so dry it felt like it was lined with sandpaper.

"Hang on." The nurse said. She lifted a glass from somewhere out of his sight and touched it to his lips, letting a drop of water seep into his mouth. Carter swallowed thirstily and opened his mouth for more, taking so much that some slopped over to run down his cheeks and chin. "Steady there. A little bit at a time will work much better." The nurse chided gently. Carter followed her advice and he soon finished the whole glass.

"Wh… where am I?" he tried again.

"The Royal Sussex County Hospital." The nurse replied.

"Where is that. Sussex obviously, but where in Sussex?"

"Brighton."

"Never been to Brighton before." Carter replied.

"Not the best way to make your first visit, I suppose." The nurse gave him a smile that would have melted icebergs, let alone hearts.

"My men …."

"That I can't help you with. If the doctor is happy with your condition then you'll be allowed to have visitors and then perhaps your questions about your men can be answered."

"Are there many soldiers in here right now?" Carter asked.

"Too many. Most of them are Canadians. They say that the queue of ambulances waiting at Newhaven was a mile long." She paused, not sure whether to ask a question of her own. "Was it bad over there?"

"The last time I remember anything, it was getting pretty bad." He replied. But she wouldn't have meant the Himmler battery. He doubted she would have heard of it. She would have meant at Honfleur or maybe Dieppe. "You're not Canadian though, are you? I saw the commando flash on your uniform when I hung it up."

It took a moment for Carter to realise that she meant that she must have undressed him and got him into the hospital issue pyjamas that he saw, for the first time, he was wearing. He felt his cheeks redden.

"Shy, Lt Carter?" the nurse gave him a cheeky smile. "One of our big, brave commandos can't be worried about a nurse seeing him in his birthday suit, surely?"

Carter's cheeks were now starting to burn. The nurse laughed. "Sorry, I shouldn't tease. In fact it was an orderly that put you in those pyjamas; a male orderly. I just hung up your uniform, that's all. In truth, there's not actually much of your uniform left, it looks as though it's been through a threshing machine. And it's filthy."

"I'll ask my unit to arrange for my kit bag to be sent. I've got a spare uniform in that." Carter said, happier to be off the subject of who might or might not have undressed him.

"Now." She was all business like again. "I've got other patients to attend to. You soldiers have created an awful lot of work for us girls." Giving him another dazzling smile, she turned on her heel and left the room.

For the first time Carter was able to take in his surroundings. He was obviously in a private room. One of the privileges of rank, he supposed. It wasn't a large room, just space enough for his hospital bed, a locker and a bedside table and a little bit left over for the staff to work around him. There were no pictures on the institutionally plane green walls. In a way he would have preferred to be in a ward with other men like himself, so he could talk, but then he'd be reminded of the horrors of what had happened to them and that wouldn't be so good.

Feeling drowsy, Carter allowed himself to drift off to sleep. It was a sleep troubled by explosions and small arms fire, bodies dropping around him like flies. Dickie Bird's body flew apart in front of his eyes, even though Carter knew that he hadn't witnessed it happening in real life. As a German soldier charged towards him, intent on stabbing him with his bayonet, Carter jerked awake once again, sweat pouring off his bandaged brow.

"You seemed to be having something of a bad dream." A white coated figure said from the end of Carter's bed. He was holding a clipboard in his hand, writing something on it. Around his neck hung a stethoscope. He was elderly, well over sixty, probably called back from retirement to fill the gaps in the medical ranks left by the younger doctors who were now serving in the armed forces. "We've seen a lot of that in here over the last couple of days. If you'd like, I can arrange for you to see one of our psychiatrists. Can't say I'm keen on all that mumbo jumbo, but some people say it helps."

"No, that won't be necessary." Carter replied and then regretted it. Perhaps it might help to talk to someone. It wasn't the first nightmare he'd had recently, just the most violent so far.

"As you wish. Now that you're awake I can take a proper look at you." He drew an ophthalmoscope from the pocket of his white coat and switched it on, holding Carter's head still with one hand while he examined his eyes. He hummed and hah'd for a bit then straightened up.

"How many fingers am I holding up?" The doctor asked.

"Two." Carter said without looking.

"How did you know that? Your eyes were closed."

"It's always two." Carter replied with a grin. His rugby coaches had asked him the same question after more than one bang on the head, following an over enthusiastic tackle. It had always been two fingers.

The doctor allowed himself a small chuckle. "Nothing obviously wrong, so far as I can see and your sense of humour is a good sign. You took a pretty nasty blow to the head, so you're certainly suffering from concussion, but that seems to be all the damage we could find. Your X Ray pictures don't show any sign of a fracture, which is good. We'll keep you under observation for a few days, but that's just precautionary. Are you suffering from a headache?"

"A bit."

"I'm not surprised. I'll prescribe an analgesic for that. If you start feeling nauseated, tell someone at once because that's not a good sign. The swelling on your bonce will start to go down in a couple of days, and the bruising will clear up, but there'll be some tenderness for a while."

"Do I really have to stay that long, just for a knock on the head?"

The doctor gave Carter a stern look. "You were unconscious for about twenty four hours. I was worried you might slip into a coma, but you woke up and that was quite a relief for everyone, but that doesn't mean you're out of the woods yet. I know all about you commandos. If I let you out of here, the first thing you'll do is start dashing around the fields like a lunatic again. I'm not risking you getting another bash on the head right now, so you'll stay here for as long as I think it necessary. And before you think about appealing to the War Office, they'll back me. The army can manage without you for a week or so, I'm sure. Now, have you any questions?"

"Can I have visitors?"

"I don't see why not. But don't tire yourself out." The doctor was about to leave when he had another thought. "I don't know what happened over there, but whatever it was, it filled this hospital and every other one from Dover to Portsmouth. It would be natural to have some sort of reaction to that. I treated a lot of very fragile young men when they came back from France after the last war. Don't feel you have to put on a brave face."

"Thanks, Doctor, but we commandos are tough up here …" He tapped his bandaged head, suppressing a wince of pain, "… as well as here." He concluded by tapping his chest.

"All men have a breaking point, Lt Carter. And no man knows where that breaking point lies. Just remember that."

The doctor did finally depart, leaving Carter thinking about his words. The thought of another nightmare was enough to keep him awake for several hours before he finally slipped into a fitful sleep.

[1] Sunlight – A brand of household soap manufactured in the UK by Lever Brothers (now Unilever), from 1884 onwards. The small

town of Port Sunlight in Cheshire was built to house Lever Brothers employees and was named after their most successful (at that time) product.

* * *

It came as no surprise to Carter that his first visitor should be his commanding officer, Robert Vernon. Nurse Duckworth, as Carter had found out she was named, had just left after taking his morning observations, as she called them. She was originally from Yorkshire and had moved south at the start of the war, but that was as much information as Carter was able to get from her.

"I thought, not for the first time, that I was going to have to replace you, Steven." Vernon greeted him with his customary good humour.

"I'm afraid you'll have to put up with me for a bit longer, Sir." Carter struggled to try to sit more upright, but Vernon waved him back down.

"You stay comfortable, old boy. It looks like you've just gone ten rounds with that big Yank up at Prestwick. What was his name? Oh yes, Johanson."

"You should see the other chap." Carter quipped.

Carter wasn't sure what else to say. There were so many questions he wanted to ask, but he was afraid of the answers. He went for something safe, instead.

"Does my wife know I'm OK?"

"Yes, I phoned her as soon as South East Command reported you safe and in here." Carter noticed that the smile had slipped from Vernon's face at the mention of his wife.

"What is it?" Carter asked, a rising feeling of panic in his voice. "Is it the baby? Is Fiona ..."

Vernon raised another hand to halt Carter's flood of words. "Fiona and the baby are just fine, so far as I'm aware. But there is something. I'm afraid it's your father-in-law. When you were going ashore in France he was being rushed into hospital in Irvine. I'm sorry to have to tell you that he died later the same day." He paused to let the news sink in. "I'm sure you'll understand that Fiona has quite a lot on her plate right now, having to organise the funeral and such like. She won't be down to see you for a day or two."

"I understand." He felt deflated that he wouldn't see his wife for a while, but his heart went out to her. She had nearly lost him as well. It would have been a cruel blow if it had happened on the same day as John Hamilton died.

"In fact, you may be up in Scotland before she can get away." Vernon added.

"Are we going back to Troon?"

"No, but the whole commando is stood down for a month, so you'll be able to take some leave."

"A month. That's a long time." There could only be one reason why the commando would be given such a respite. They weren't combat fit any longer. "How bad was it?" he asked, not really wanting to know the answer but at the same time desperate to know.

"Three hundred and fifty five men left Newhaven with the commando on the 18th. Only one hundred and ninety four made it back. 6 Troop are intact, of course, They didn't suffer a scratch thanks to that Ack-Ack boat they were on. My gunboat was shot out from under me and I had to transfer to it after the E-Boat attack was beaten off. About eighty men made it back even though their LCs were damaged. There were a lot of dead and wounded amongst them of course. Those Eurekas can't stop a bullet worth a damn. I'll have to insist that Combined Ops get rid of them if they want to stop men dying before they even get ashore. We picked a few men up from the water, but not many. We didn't know that you had made it to shore, of course. That came as a nice surprise. Combined Ops are singing your praises for silencing that battery and holding out there for the whole morning. You did us proud."

"It was at a high cost, though."

"It always is in the commandos. But the cost would have been far higher if you hadn't got ashore. I was dreading what I might hear when I got back. It was bad enough as it was."

"There are a lot of wounded Canadians in here, I know. The nurse told me that much."

"There are more spread along the whole South Coast. But they're the lucky ones. There were hundreds killed at both Dieppe and Honfleur, maybe thousands taken prisoner. It was carnage. Probably the worst disaster since the Charge of the Light Brigade."

"As bad as that?"

"I don't know if the Germans knew we were coming, but they certainly seemed ready. One thing we can now be sure of is that trying to capture a French port is a nonstarter. Someone said you could almost have walked ashore across the bodies of dead Canadians."

"How did 16 Cdo do?"

"Not as badly as us. They made it ashore and managed to capture their objectives, but the street fighting was cruel and they hadn't done the right training for it. Now there's an almighty row over whether they should have ignored their objectives and helped clear the shore defences instead. The Canadians are saying they should have, but as 16 Cdo's CO is pointing out, their orders specifically prohibited them from doing that. No doubt it will all come out in the wash. Combined Ops are setting up an inquiry to see what can be salvaged from this shambles. Not much, I fear. I would like to say that Operation Jubilee, at Dieppe, went better but it didn't. The Canadians ran into the same sort of stiff resistance as the chaps at Honfleur, with pretty much the same result."

"So where's the commando now? Back at Bishopstone?"

"No, they've given us the drill hall in Worthing. There were Canadians living in it until the other day, but they don't need it anymore, poor sods. We'll stay there until we're told otherwise." He paused, then fished around in the pocket of his battledress blouse. He unfolded his hand to reveal two Bath Stars nestling in the palm. That was the official name given to the 'pips' that were worn as badges of rank. "These are for you, *Captain* Carter."

"Which dead man's shoes am I filling?" Carter picked up the two stars and put them on his bedside locker. In peacetime a promotion would have been something to celebrate, but Carter knew that wasn't the case for him.

"Martin Turner didn't know it, but he was just about to be promoted to Major and was going to be posted. You were his natural successor, as I told the War Office and they agreed."

"I notice your choice of tense there, as in 'going to be posted'. Is that no longer the case?" If it was, then there could only be one reason that Carter could think of.

"I'm afraid that Martin is one of those not accounted for amongst the living. He may have been picked up by the Germans …"

"But that is something of a forlorn hope." Carter finished the sentence.

"I would say so, yes."

Getting a promotion was supposed to be a happy thing, Carter knew. But this one was tinged with so much sadness. "I suppose I'm not the only one who has taken a step up thanks to Operation Dagger."

"No, you're not. And there are too many that will never take any steps again. It's what we do, Steven. You knew that when you volunteered."

"I did, Sir. There was never any secret made of the dangers. And I don't regret it, honestly I don't. It's just so … I don't know. Such good men, good friends. And what a way to go, not facing the enemy, as we're trained to do, but trapped in a sinking LC because no one thought about the possibility of us running into E-Boats." A thought struck him. "What happened to the Tyndal? She was supposed to be looking after us."

"Rest assured, that is a question I shall be asking the inquiry."

"What about the rest of the men in 4 Troop?"

"One of your LCs is amongst those that made it back. Charlie and Dog sections suffered a few wounded but none killed. I'm afraid Able, Baker and How sections in the third LC, with Martin Turner, weren't so lucky."

"So, Fred Chalk went as well?" Carter's sergeant had been with How section.

"Actually, no. We found him swimming the Channel in just his underwear. I'm making him your Troop Sergeant Major, so you won't be losing him. I've also promoted Green to full Corporal to replace Franklyn and Glass is now a Lance Corporal."

"Nothing for O'Driscoll?"

"I offered him a Lance Corporal's stripe in another Troop. But he said he wanted to stay with you, so he turned it down."

Carter nodded his head. That sounded like O'Driscoll. He had no real interest in promotion. "Franklyn must be severely wounded if you've replaced him."

"Yes and no. He is wounded but he'll recover, but I need experienced NCOs so Franklyn gets his third stripe. I'm moving him to 1 Troop. Well, the new 1 Troop. There's nothing much left of the old one. Being on the left flank of the flotilla they got it worst when the E-Boats attacked."

"I think on future ops we should wear life jackets." Carter suggested. "We can take them off just before we land."

"I think you're right. If the men had been wearing them this time, more would have undoubtedly survived."

"So what happens to the commando now?"

"We go on, Steven. We go on. The first replacements are due in from Achnacarry in a few days' time. 6 Troop will take on the job of training them to our standard while the rest of the commando enjoys some leave. I've also been promised some seasoned veterans from other units. We'll probably get the ones they want rid of, but beggars can't be choosers. We should be fully up to strength and ready for another operation by Christmas."

"Well, I'll be ready when you need me, Sir."

"You just enjoy the rest. And keep your hands off that pretty nurse I saw on the way in. I doubt Fiona would be too pleased to find you with lipstick on your pyjama collar when she arrives."

Carter laughed dismissively, but he had entertained a few naughty thoughts about Nurse Duckworth; something he would only admit to himself, of course. What was it about nurses that did that to a man? he wondered.

Vernon stayed for a few more minutes chatting and exchanging other gossip, but then took his leave. He had other men in the hospital whom he had to visit, so couldn't stay chatting with Carter all day.

* * *

The next visitor that Carter had was more of a surprise. Reading an out of date newspaper that Nurse Duckworth had found for him, Carter looked up to see an American officer in the doorway of his room, just about to knock at the open door. The silver leaf on the officer's shoulders showed him to be a Lieutenant Colonel. Carter struggled to sit upright.

"You stay where you are, Son." The American drawled. "I'm not here in an official capacity. Well, maybe that's stretching things a little, but I'm mainly here just to talk to you and find out about how Lieutenant Kasmire died."

"If I can tell you anything useful, Colonel. I will."

"Sorry, I haven't introduced myself properly. My name is William Darby and I'm responsible for recruiting and training the US Rangers. Specifically, I'm the commanding officer of the 1st Ranger Battalion.[1] I take it you've heard of us."

"Of course, some of your men took part in the recent Dieppe operation."

"Yes, we lost some brave men there. And we lost Kasmire at Honfleur, where he shouldn't have been."

"I'm sorry about that, Sir. Kasmire …"

"Don't worry, son. I've already spoken to your CO and he told me how persuasive Kasmire was. And he was right, his orders didn't prohibit from going on the raid. If we give our officers leeway to act on their own initiative, we shouldn't be surprised when they do. I suspect that even if Col Vernon had refused to take him, Kasmire would have found some way of getting aboard those landing craft. No, I just want to know how he died, so I can write to his family."

"He died bravely, Sir, is the best I can say. He took command of men he didn't really know and he led them in the true commando spirit. If he hadn't done what he did, we might have been over-run."

"What did he do?"

Carter described the operation, firstly describing Kasmire's ambush of the German patrol and then the way Kasmire had led a handful of men out into the killing ground and taken on the flanking Germans, meeting them head on with bayonets, knives and fists. How Kasmire had actually died, Carter couldn't say. As far as he knew, none of the men had returned to the British line to tell the tale. "He was a good solder, Sir." Carter concluded.

Darby fell silent for a moment, taking in what Carter had told him. "I wonder if you might put all that in the form of a letter. It would be good for his family to hear the story first-hand. At least as first-hand as it can be, under the circumstances. I'll enclose it with mine."

"Of course, Sir. I have a few letters of my own to write. In fact, I must ask Nurse Duckworth for some paper. I may as well make good use of my time in here."

"Thank you, Lt Carter."

"Actually, it's Captain now, Sir."

"Congratulations, though I suspect that your promotion has come at a cost."

"It has, I'm afraid, Sir. A lot of promotions in the commandos are the result of someone else not making the journey home."

"I guess I'll have to get used to that myself. My men will be going into combat soon enough."

"If they're half as good as the commandos, they'll do well, Sir."

"Half as good? They're already twice as good." Darby laughed.

"I'm afraid you won't really find out how good they are until the first bullet is fired, but if they remember their training, they'll do alright."

"I've got a couple of my guys in here I've got to go see now, but before I go, is there anything you think you've learnt from this operation? You know, something I can use when I'm taking my boys ashore for the first time."

It was a question Carter had been asking himself since he had woken up in hospital. Anything that doesn't kill you makes you stronger, he knew. But the main trick was to stop the same things from killing you the next time. "There are two things, Sir. The first is about making sure that anything that can jeopardise the operation has been taken into account in the plan. That coastal convoy we ran into shouldn't have been a surprise. The Jerries run those convoys along the coast every few nights, but nobody considered the possibility that we might run into one and what might happen if we did. If our escort ship had been with us they would have had the firepower to smash those E-Boats into matchwood, but because nobody had spotted the possibility, it had gone off to do its own thing somewhere else."

The American nodded his head, taking heed of the advice. "Yeah, we call it the six Ps."

"I think you actually got that from us, Sir, but it was seven Ps[2]. In this case the planning was less than perfect and we paid a high price for that."

Darby seemed unwilling to argue whether the saying was British or American, but he recognised the point being made. "You said there were two things, so what was the other."

"Make sure you spread your critical resources around so if anything does go wrong, you don't lose all your vital equipment. For example, none of our supplies of explosives made it ashore, so it made it hard to disable the guns.

But worse was the lack of communications. We ended up with only one radio and because it couldn't make contact with anyone, we had no idea if it was still working. If we could have communicated with the Navy, we could have found out what was happening and if the CO had been able to make contact with us, he might have made different decisions. We had an entire troop completely uncommitted, our floating reserve, who could have come ashore, but nobody knew that we had made it ourselves so the Colonel couldn't reinforce us.

It's been a problem that's plagued us since we were formed and I think it probably cost us lives this time."

"I have to say that we're a bit light on radio sets ourselves right now." Darby commented. "I'll look into that when I get back to Northern Ireland." He stood up and replaced his hat. "You take care of yourself now, son." He said, before leaving.

[1] William Orlando Darby was a real person. On 19th June 1942 he established the 1st Ranger Battalion at Carrickfergus in Northern Ireland. He led his unit during the invasion of Tunisia in 1943 and for the Sicily and Italy landings later that year, before being promoted to full Colonel and transferred to a regular infantry brigade for the Anzio operation (commenced 22nd January 1944). He was killed in action by an artillery shell on 30th April 1945 while serving in Northern Italy. He was posthumously promoted to Brigadier General. Col Darby's presence at the hospital and the words that he speaks are entirely fictional.

[2] 7Ps – An old adage from the British Army: Perfect Planning and Preparation Prevents Piss Poor Performance. It is a lesson drummed into all trainee officers but is still forgotten when enthusiasm to get the job done is allowed to take priority over making a good plan.

* * *

There was a pile of half a dozen letters sitting on Carter's bedside locker by the time his next visitor arrived. It had been a strain writing them, but it was vital that the families of the men that had died knew that they had died bravely, serving their country. The official telegram said so little that it could offer no comfort. Not only did he have to write to the families of the men of his own troop, but as one of only two officers that had survived the fight at the gun battery, he had also to write to the families of Ian Motson's and Dickie Bird's troops.

But when Fiona walked through the door, all thoughts of France fled from his mind. She was dressed in sombre black to show she was in mourning. He got out of bed an met her halfway, pulling her in, to give her a huge hug. Her face fell as she saw the bruising on his face. The worst of it had started to fade, but it still had the bright colours of a Turner seascape.

"Oh, my poor darling." she said, raising her hands to touch the marks. Carter pulled back, knowing that they were still tender to the touch..

"It's not as bad as it looks." Carter tried to reassure her. He squeezed her close to him.

"Careful, now." She scolded as their kiss came to an end. "Mind the babies."

Carter stepped back to take a good look at her, holding her at arm's length. "You would hardly know you were expecting. You still look so slim."

"This coat hides a lot." She smiled back at him, unbuttoning the coat and taking it off. She folded it carefully and laid it across the bottom of Carter's bed. But Fiona was right, without the coat she was far more obviously pregnant.

"I see what you mean." A penny dropped in Carter's mind. "Hang on a minute, did you say 'babies'?"

"I did. The doctor thinks we might be having twins."

It took a moment for the idea to sink into Carter's brain. "Wow." Was all he could think of to say. "You're going to have your work cut out looking after the farm and two babies at the same time."

"I've taken someone on. He worked on a neighbouring farm until he joined the army. He was wounded in Libya, he lost a foot, but that shouldn't be a problem, not with the two Land Girls as well. He's on leave right now, waiting for his discharge papers to come through, but that's just a formality."

"Well, a helping h… I mean someone to help around the farm will be welcome and I'll be a lot happier knowing that you'll have a man about the place." He paused, turning his attention to the reason for her wearing mourning clothes. "I'm so sorry about your dad." Carter said, pulling a hard backed chair across to the side of the bed for his wife to sit on. He sat down on the edge of the bed, so as to be as close to her as possible.

"He'd been ill for a long time and was getting weaker by the day. But even when you know the end is coming, it's still a shock when it finally happens."

"He was a fine man. He made me feel very welcome after we were married. How's Mary holding up?"

"She's putting a brave face on things, but I can tell she's taken it hard. They were married for thirty years and courting for five before that. They were devoted to each other." Tears sprang from Fiona's eyes and she reached into her bag for a handkerchief, dabbing her cheeks with it.

"Give her time. She'll never get over it, but she'll learn to live with it."

"I hope so. So, what about you? How did you end up in here? Your CO didn't say much."

"I got a bit of a bump on the head, but it isn't that serious." Carter decided not to tell her that he had been unconscious for almost twenty four hours. "The doctors are only keeping me in as a precaution."

"I know it must have been bad. There are several women in the town who got telegrams with worse news than mine. There will be a couple of babies that will grow up never knowing their father."

"I know. I'm writing letters to the families of the men I lost. None of them were married to Troon girls though."

"The radio said the raid was a great success." She said, the tone of her voice suggesting that she didn't quite believe the official version of events.

"You can't believe everything you hear on the radio." Carter confirmed "The government has a duty to maintain morale, so you will hear what they want you to hear, which isn't always the full story."

"So, what is the full story?" She probed.

"I can't tell you that. Not because I don't want to, but because I don't know it myself. We were bounced by E-Boats on the way over, which is where we suffered most of our casualties. Part of my troop, me included, made it ashore, along with another sixty or so men from other troops and there was a bit of a fight, which is where I got my knock on the head. But the Canadians suffered much worse. All the hospitals along the couth coast are full of their wounded."

"So many wasted lives." Fiona said sadly.

"That's not the way Mr Churchill would put it, I'm sure. They gave their lives protecting our shores."

"By attacking France?" Fiona scoffed.

"The best form of defence is attack." Carter replied, calmly. "That's what the commandos are all about. We attack the enemy on their own soil, so that they can't sleep comfortably in their beds at night."

"But it costs so many lives." Fiona said.

"All wars cost lives. If we want to beat the Germans, to put an end to their evil fascism, we have to be prepared to make sacrifices." Carter decided that a change of subject was called for. "Now, tell me, how are things on the farm?"

Fiona brightened a little, happy to chat about something less contentious than the war. She shared some of the gossip from around the town. "An RAF squadron has moved into the old sweetie factory." She said, unexpectedly. "They fly sea planes, great big four engine things called Sunderlands. They sit out on the water and make a heck of a stooshie[1]."

"I'd heard we wouldn't be going back to Scotland." Carter confirmed. "They've put the commando in Worthing for the time being."

"So when will I see you again?"

"When they let me out of here, I'll be given some leave. We can travel back up to Troon together."

"And after that?"

"Who knows. We've got to rebuild the commando, so we won't be going on any more raids for a while, probably not this side of Christmas. But after that, well, the Jerries are still in France and

Norway, so we'll probably carry on trying to keep them awake at night."

"Well, I've got you to myself for a few days anyway. Your Col Vernon has found me a room in a guest house here in Brighton. I'll be back this evening to see you again, but I'll leave you to your letter writing for now." She stood and put on her coat before picking up her bag from the floor. Feeling its weight reminded her of something. "I nearly forgot. Mother sent you this." She reached inside and pulled out a bottle, handing it to Carter.

He looked at the label and gave an appreciative smile. It was a bottle of single malt whisky. It had been opened, but only a few drams were missing. Carter had shared them with John Hamilton the night before the commando had left Troon. "Mum doesn't drink whisky and I'm not drinking alcohol right now, so she said it would only go to waste now …"

"Tell her thank you very much. It's greatly appreciated. I'll raise a glass to your father's memory with it. But I'd better hide it for now. I don't think Nurse Duckworth would approve."

"Is she a bit of a dragon?"

Carter decided it would be better not to correct his wife. She would probably meet the nurse during her visits anyway. "She's a stickler for the rules." He said instead, which was true. He gave his wife a warm kiss, before watching her hips as she swayed along the corridor. Carter decided it might be time for a shower.

[1] Stooshie – Scottish dialect word for a commotion or noise.

* * *

The sound of heavy booted feet echoing along the corridor woke Carter from his nap. Male voices laughed and a female voice, that of Nurse Duckworth, scolded the noisy men. A sort of silence fell, broken only by the booted footsteps, before the light from Carter's door was blocked by the arrival of more visitors. The grinning faces of Cpl Green, LCpl Glass and Tpr O'Driscoll filled the doorframe.

"Well, who do we 'ave ere?" Glass asked the world at large, as the three men moved into single file so they could pass through the door. "Typical officers, lounging about all day in their pyjamas."

"More to the point, who's that pretty little nurse we met in the corridor?" O'Driscoll asked with a leer. "She could take my temperature any day of the week."

"You behave yourself around Nurse Duckworth." Carter pretended to be severe. "She's a very nice girl and I don't want any of you changing that. Anyway, what brings you here?"

"Paddy and me were sent down with the Tilly to bring the Prof back. The CO asked us to drop your kit in at the same time." He hefted a kit bag, showing it to Carter, before dropping it in the corner of the room.

For the first time, Carter noticed the swathe of bandages at the cuff of Green's battledress blouse, covering the palm of his hand and disappearing under the khaki material. Then he saw the bright white of the corporal's stripes on Green's sleeve. Glass was wearing the single bright stripe of a Lance Corporal.

"I didn't know you'd been wounded, Prof."

"It's just a scratch. Nothing to worry about."

"Don't you believe a word of that, Sorr" O'Driscoll protested. "He took a Jerry bayonet through the palm of his hand, fending him off from trying to skewer you. Then Danny got the Jerry."

"I don't remember any of that." Carter said, puzzled.

"Well, Sorr. You wuz having a bit of a nap at the time. The Prof, Danny and me were trying to get you down to the beach when the Jerries finally broke though the defences. I didn't realise how hospitable the Jerries were. They just didn't want us to leave and were trying to persuade us to stay. But you know, we had things to do elsewhere so we politely declined and got the feck out of there."

"So, I owe you my life."

"Sure, 'twas nothing. We'd have done as much for someone we liked. Besides, Danny told us you'd promised to buy us a pint when we got back, so we weren't going to leave you behind."

"I don't know what to say, I…"

"Then say nothing at all." O'Driscoll said.

"Now you've started, I want the full story." Carter waved to the chair. "You can sit on the bed as well, but be ready to jump up because Nurse Duckworth doesn't approve of that. Something to do with germs getting on the sheets. So, tell me, what did happen? I don't remember anything other than running across the battery to get away from the Germans."

Prof Green took up the story. "You ran straight into the blast of a mortar bomb. It's a miracle you're here. By rights the shrapnel should have torn you to pieces, even if the blast didn't. Your uniform was shredded, but the legendary Carter luck seems to have held out. I ran back to see if you were still alive, and sure enough you were, if only just."

"Prof picked you up and threw you over his shoulder and me and Danny tried to cover the two of yez." O'Driscoll continued. "But going back had given the Germans time to get closer and two of the feckers came leaping across a trench at us. Prof fended off the one that tried to stab you with his bayonet, which is how he got his hand skewered. You should have seen it, the bayonet had gone right through so the rifle barrel was one side of his hand and the rest of the bayonet was poking through the other side. But while the German was trying to pull the bayonet out, Danny shot him at point blank range."

"And Paddy put a bullet in the other one." Glass took up the story. "By that time the rest of the section, Pearson, Woodward and Mitchell had seen what we were up to and they started firing at any German who was thinking about having another go. Between us we got you to the top of the cliff. Sgt Thorpe sent you down on the end of a rope and he made Prof go too. He said he'd be useless on a gun with only one hand."

"I would have managed." Green protested.

"Well, maybe yez would and maybe yez wouldn't." O'Driscoll said. "It's water under the bridge now. Anyway, we did just as you ordered. Pearson, Woodward, Mitchell, me and Danny took over the guns from 2 Troop and they started down the ropes while we blasted away. We did our best to keep them back, but every time we stopped firing to change a mag, the Germans would dash forward a few more yards. They were using the trenches and gun pits as well, leap frogging along trying to outflank us. We knew it wouldn't be long before they got round us and with the cliffs behind, we'd have been surrounded."

"Did you all get out?"

Glass shook his head sadly. "No, just as he was getting up to withdraw, Pearson took a bullet in the chest. It sent him back over the edge of the cliff. If the bullet didn't kill him, then the fall would have."

"But you two did make it. It must have been close." Carter was pretty certain that Glass and O'Drsicoll would have been the last two down the ropes.

"It was. You'll remember telling Sgt Thorpe to get an LC offshore so it could use its Lewis guns." Carter nodded his head. "Well, some bright spark decided to take the mortar as well. They started lobbing bombs over our heads. Because of the rocking of the boat they were a bit erratic, some going long, some short, some left and some right. But they helped to keep the Germans heads down. Then Mitchell and Woodward went down the ropes, just leaving me and Paddy. We kept blasting away and the Jerries were getting closer and closer. In the end we just let go of the guns, grabbed the ropes and threw ourselves over the edge."

"We just slid down the ropes." O'Driscoll chipped in. "We tried using our feet to slow us, but we still got some bad rope burns." O'Driscoll held up his hands to show the red welts across his palms.

"It certainly isn't the best way to go down a rope." Carter had to agree. "But I'm so glad you made it. And I owe you so much I …"

Green held up his hands in protest "Now don't you go getting all maudlin on us. You'd have done the same for us and we know for a fact you would have been the very last man down that rope."

The others nodded their heads in agreement.

"We met your good lady yesterday." Glass informed him. "Me and Paddy did, anyway. The prof was still in here. The CO brought her to see us, so she could thank us for taking care of you."

"She didn't tell me that when she visited last night."

"Maybe she didn't want you getting jealous."

"Sure, she said she'd be naming the bairns after us, when they arrive." O'Drsicoll said. "Paddy and Danny if they're boys and Patricia and Danielle if they're girls. If it's one of each then they'll be Paddy and Danielle."

Carter couldn't tell if they were joking or not. He decided to go along with it anyway.

"They're fine names. It will be an honour. But neither of you suggested Archibald, after The Prof. After all, it was him that carried me."

"Oh sure we did, Sorr. But she said she didn't want to saddle either of the little blighters with a moniker like that." They shared a laugh at Green's expense. The name had featured in an old George Robey music hall song and had been regarded as comic ever since.

"But visiting in hospital gives man a bit of a thirst." O'Driscoll said. "I don't suppose there's anywhere around here where a man can get a pint?"

"Not that I know of. But I've got something better if you can find something to drink out of. Prof, reach into my bedside locker. You'll find a bottle there"

Green did as he was bid and withdrew the bottle. "Well, that's a bit of alright." he said after reading the label.

"I saw a tea trolley in the corridor. I'll see if it's still there." Glass volunteered.

He soon returned, carrying four teacups. Glass placed them on the locker and Green poured a generous measure of whisky into each one, then handed them around.

"We should have a toast." O'Driscoll said.

"We'll have the Scottish toast.[1]" Carter decided. He raised his teacup. "Here's to us."

"There's none like us." Green said next, raising his own teacup.

"There's some like us." Intoned Glass.

"But they're all dead." O'Driscoll finished.

They raised their cups in a final salute then placed them to their lips and downed their whisky in one swallow. There was a satisfied smacking of lips as they placed the teacups back on the locker.

Green picked up the bottle once again and the cups were refilled.

"Oh, by the way." Glass said. "We just heard this morning. The Germans have started a major new offensive in Russia, at some place called Stalingrad."

[1] This toast is quite old and is thought to have originated in Ayrshire, where 15 Cdo was supposed to have been based prior to Operation Dagger. It may have been penned by Robbie Burns. It is used by many Scottish regiments when they drink to the memories of fallen comrades.

This ends the third story in the "Carter's Commandos" series.

Historical Notes

Like previous books in my "Carter's Commandos" series, most of the military action portrayed in this story is based loosely on real life military operations of World War II. In this case I named the specific operation, which was code named Jubilee.

On 19th August 1942 a Brigade of infantry from the 2nd Canadian Infantry Division, supported by 40 RM Commando and elements from the French Troop of 10 (Inter Allied) Commando, raided the port of Dieppe. Along with Dunkirk and the attack on Arnhem bridge it was one of the most costly operations of the war in Europe, especially in comparison with the numbers of troops involved. The fact that it isn't better known is probably because the man behind it was the King's cousin and therefore not likely to be publicly criticised at the time. He later claimed that the lessons learnt from this operation saved lives on D-Day, but that was an easy claim to make after the event.

The political background to the raid was confused. The Canadian government was pressing for more involvement in the war for their troops based in Britain; more so because soldiers from Australia, New Zealand and South Africa were so heavily engaged in North Africa. A major raid on the European mainland seemed to provide the ideal opportunity for the Canadians to get involved. The United States army in Britain were not impressed by the British tactics of hit and run raids and were pressing for a full-scale invasion of France, which the British knew would be unsuccessful at that stage of the war. The British may have been hoping to impress the Americans with the value of their raids with the Dieppe operation.

In Russia, Joseph Stalin was concerned that his country was bearing the brunt of Germany's war effort and demanded that the Western Allies open a second front to draw German troops away from the east. Given that Germany was succeeding in its eastern offensive at that time, Stalin probably had a good case (the decisive Battle of Stalingrad would start four days after Operation Jubilee and continue until February 1943). Finally, the RAF were having to fly deeper and deeper into France to tempt the *Luftwaffe* into combat and that was proving costly in terms of aircraft losses. A major raid on the coast, especially if it had the appearance of a full-scale invasion, would be bound to draw the Luftwaffe into the skies over the English Channel, where the RAF could engage them.

That complex background seems to have been behind the decision to attack Dieppe, which was authorised at the highest level.

The idea to carry out a large-scale raid on a French port had originally been that of Lieutenant General Bernard Law Montgomery, at that time in charge of South East Command, covering Kent, Surrey and Sussex. In fact he had cooled on the idea by the time he went to take command of 8th Army in North Africa and it was revived by Commodore Louis Mountbatten, at that time Chief of Combined Operations. Montgomery's original target had been Honfleur, which is why I have used that location for the fictitious Operation Percival and 15 Cdo's Operation Dagger. It was Commodore Mountbatten that changed the destination to Dieppe.

In support of Operation Jubilee, the Army Commandos mounted two additional simultaneous operations, to land before dawn on 19th August. Operation Cauldron was carried out by 4 Commando, against a coastal artillery battery nicknamed the "Hesse Battery" at Varangeville to the west of Dieppe. Operation Flodden was mounted by 3 Commando against the "Goebbels Battery" at Berneval le Grand to the east of Dieppe. 3 Cdo were selected for this more difficult target because of their proficiency in rock climbing, which was an essential for the raid. Both batteries could have inflicted severe damage to the Naval forces supporting Operation Jubilee had they not been neutralised.

The attack by E-Boats I have described as being suffered by 15 Cdo was in fact suffered by 3 Cdo during Operation Flodden. The E-Boats had been escorting a coastal convoy that had departed from Boulogne on the evening of the 18th August. Its presence had been detected by British shore radar but had not been reported to the ships at sea. Just as in my story, the warships assigned to protect 3 Cdo's landing craft, the Free Polish ship the *ORP Slazak* and Royal Navy ship HMS Brocklesby, were nowhere to be seen. It turned out that they were about four miles away to the north west and believed that the gun fire from the E-Boats was actually from the shore, so they didn't intervene.

Only four landing craft made it to shore to attack the battery. My father took part in the operation but, for a change, drew the long straw as his troop were the floating reserve and were on board a sturdy and well-armed Landing Craft Ack-Ack, which was able to engage the E-Boats and accounted for the sinking of at least one of German vessel, the armed trawler UJ-1404. Not knowing that four landing craft had made it to shore, they later sailed to the main operating area off Dieppe and rescued two downed RAF aircrew before returning to England with the rest of the survivors from the main force.

Lt Col John Durnford Slater, CO of 3 Cdo, had made his HQ on board the Steam Gunboat SGB Grey Owl (SGB 5). It was severely damaged in the E-Boat attack and he had to transfer his command to the Landing Craft Ack-Ack that was transporting the floating reserve. He was able to maintain contact with the commander of the seaborne operation, but lost contact with his men in the landing craft. The reason is not given in his account of the raid, but it was probably the result of losing his radio set. Durnford-Slater was forced to request permission to withdraw the remains of 3 Cdo in order to retain some semblance of a force on which to rebuild. He wasn't aware, at that time, that some of his command had broken free from the E-Boat attack and had made it to the French shore.

Captain Richard Wills took three landing craft into Yellow 1 Beach but their assault was held by the German defences. After several hours of fighting only one man, LCpl Vince Sinclair (uncle to singer Isla St Clair) made it back to the landing craft and escaped. The rest were killed or captured.

Captain Peter Young and eighteen of his troop of 3 Cdo landed on Yellow 2 Beach, climbed the cliffs, worked their way along a gully and around to the rear of the battery, engaged it with small arms fire and kept it silent for three hours, before returning to the beach and boarding their landing craft. They all made it safely back to England. Peter Young was awarded a DSO for his leadership as was Lt Buckee RN for his command of their landing craft. Lt John Selwyn and Lt Anthony "Buck" Ruxton were awarded the Military Cross.

Over half of 3 Cdo were killed, wounded or taken prisoner during Operation Flodden. Of those that made it to the beaches, 37 were killed and 81 taken prisoner. These casualties were higher than the commando later suffered on D-Day, or in any other operation and it is for this reason 3 Cdo veterans always considered Dieppe to be their most significant action. The survivors returned there each year on the anniversary of the operation until old age and infirmity took its toll. The last visit was in 2011. After D-Day and the breakout from the Normandy beachhead, John Durnford Slater was able to visit Berneval le Grand and view the defences from the German side. He concluded that had his commando made it to shore in high enough numbers, they would undoubtedly have captured the Goebbels Battery.

In total 275 commandos from 3 Cdo, 4 Cdo, 10 (Inter Allied) Cdo and 40 (RM) Cdo, were killed on 19th August 1942.

Lt Edward Loustalot, who was among 50 United States Rangers who had accompanied 3 and 4 Cdos, was one of those killed on Yellow 1 Beach, the first American to die in land combat in Europe during World War II.

As for operation Jubilee itself, the casualties were significant. Of the 5,000 Canadians who took part, 907 were killed, 586 wounded and 1,946 captured, a casualty rate of over 66%. The Royal Navy lost 1 destroyer, 33 landing craft and 550 dead or wounded. The RAF lost 100 aircraft, with 62 aircrew killed, 30 wounded and 17 taken prisoner. The levels of casualties were considered too high to be made public at the time, so were suppressed and the operation was reported as a success when it had actually been a disaster. German casualties were 311 killed and 280 wounded. The *Luftwaffe* lost 48 aircraft and the *Kreigsmarine* lost the armed trawler referred to above. The Royal Navy had assigned no capital ships to the task force.

For more information about Operation Flodden, I would refer you to the books by Brigadier Durnford Slater and Brigadier Peter Young, listed at the end of these notes.

Sergeant Bill Chitty was a real person and was one of the two the Provost Sergeants for my father's unit, 3 Commando. He was an ex-police officer and former heavyweight boxer who had his own unique way of dealing with disciplinary issues; ways that weren't approved of under Kings Regulations. But they worked and Chitty kept more than one troublesome commando out of the CO's eye, which prevented the soldiers being returned to unit, the standard punishment for breaches of discipline in the commandos. He was taken prisoner at Dieppe and saw out the remainder of the war in a PoW camp. He was replaced by Sgt "Lofty" King, who was as equally efficient in maintaining discipline.

Sporting matches between neighbouring units have always been common practice in the armed forces and the commandos were no different. However, because of their competitive nature most commando units could only find other commando units to oppose them. Most popular amongst the commandos, probably because of its inherent aggression, was boxing. While there is no evidence that 3 Cdo, based in Largs, ever held a tournament against their American neighbours at Prestwick, just 30 miles away, it is not impossible that such an event took place. Similarly it would be quite normal for units such as the commandos to be used to test the military capabilities of neighbouring units in the way I have had 15 Cdo test the defences at Prestwick airfield. It was good training for both sides. While these events may be fictitious, they are within the bounds of possibility.

While it may seem fanciful to suggest that soldiers might have to sleep on a railway station while still in their own country and not under combat conditions, it did actually happen. The small towns (as they were then) of Newhaven and Seaford were the concentration area for Operation Jubilee, with the area being flooded with British and Canadian troops in the weeks before the operation. Due to shortages of barrack accommodation and a lack of civilian billets for soldiers in private houses, there was no accommodation available for the majority of 3 Cdo for most of the period prior to Operation Jubilee, so they spent several weeks sleeping in and around Bishopstone railway station. It appears that no one had considered providing tents and other camping equipment for the commandos.

Trains were prevented from stopping at the station, so travellers had to use neighbouring stations at Newhaven and Seaford. My father recalls the weather being fine and dry, which made the rough living conditions just about bearable. However, the commandos still had to live with the public gawping at them as the trains ran to and fro along the South Coast line.

Leonard A J Peddlesden was the Coxswain of the Newhaven lifeboat, CECIL AND LILIAN PHILPOTT *DURING WORLD WAR 2. HE WAS AWARDED THE RNLI'S SILVER MEDAL FOR HIS EFFORTS IN RESCUING THE CREW OF THE HM TRAWLER AVANTURINE ON 23RD NOVEMBER 1943. THE REST OF THE CREW WERE AWARDED THE BRONZE MEDAL. THE LIFEBOAT WAS BADLY DAMAGED IN THE RESCUE. THE NEWHAVEN LIFEBOAT WAS ONE OF 19 THAT HELPED IN THE EVACUATION OF DUNKIRK IN MAY/JUNE 1940.*

* * *

It was a Royal Artillery officer, Lt Col Dudley Clarke, who had first suggested the establishment of a specialist raiding force to attack German occupied France. This suggestion reached the ears of Winston Churchill, who embraced the idea with typical enthusiasm.

The Army commandos were established in June 1940 on the direct orders of Winston Churchill. It was he who recognised that to maintain the war effort until victory could be achieved, he needed to maintain the morale of the British people following the disaster that had been the evacuation from Dunkirk. The skilful use of propaganda had turned that defeat into a sort of victory, but genuine victories, however small, would be needed if he was to convince the British people that the war could be won.

It would be the commandos that would provide those small victories. Often the targets of their raids were insignificant in military terms but, on occasions, they had a far greater impact than could ever have been imagined. For example, following successive raids on Norway, Adolf Hitler became convinced that they were the prelude to an invasion of that country as a stepping stone for invading Denmark and then Germany itself. No such plan existed, but Hitler ordered 300,000 additional troops to be sent to Norway, where they remained for the rest of the war, along with additional Luftwaffe and naval units. The fact that the invasion of Norway never came about was proof to Hitler that his strategy had worked. Had those troops been available at Stalingrad, El Alamein or in Normandy in 1944, who knows how the outcomes of those battles might have been affected.

15 Commando is a fictitious unit. The Army commandos were numbered 1 to 14 (excluding 13). 50, 51 and 52 commandos were formed in North Africa. The Royal Marine Commandos weren't formed until 1942 and took the numbers 40 to 48. Unlike the Army commandos, only 40 (RM) Cdo was made up of volunteers. The rest were just Royal Marine battalions that were ordered to convert to the commando role. For this reason the Army commandos tended to look down on them, but once they had proved themselves in combat they became part of the commando family.

No 10 (Inter Allied) Commando was made up of members of the armed forces from occupied countries in Europe who had escaped. There were two French troops, one Norwegian, one Dutch, one Belgian, one Polish, one Yugoslavian and a troop of German speakers, many of whom were Jewish. They often accompanied other commandos on raids to act as guides and interpreters, as well as carrying out raids of their own.

If you wish to find out more about the Army commandos there are a number of books on the subject, including my own, which details my father's wartime service; it's called "A Commando's Story". I have provided the titles of some of these books at the end of these notes. These also provided the sources for much of my research for this book.

Achnacarry House is the ancestral home of Clan Cameron and it was taken over by the War Office to become the Commando Training Centre. The original occupants of the house moved into cottages in the grounds. During the course of World War II over 25,000 commandos were trained there, plus their American counterparts, the Rangers, who were modelled on the commandos. Originally each commando was responsible for providing their own training, before the first training centres were set up at Inveraray and Lochailort, in late 1940, before moving to Achnacarry.

Although in use from 1940 onwards, Achnacarry House was a holding centre for volunteers for special service before becoming a formal training school in March 1942.

Should you ever travel to that part of Scotland you will find a small museum to the Commandos at the Spean Bridge Hotel. At least, it was there the last time I visited. If you continue to drive north along the A82 for a couple of more miles you will come across the Commando Memorial, unveiled in 1950. You can't miss it, it's 17 ft high. If you have time, please stop for a moment to remember the men who trained in that rugged countryside. Some of them, including my father, have memorial plaques lodged there in the small memorial garden.

In the fictional world, Captain Carter and Cpl Green, LCpl Glass and Tpr O'Driscoll will soon be reunited with 15 Commando, but they are destined, like my father, to have many more adventures before the war comes to an end.

Further Reading.

For first hand accounts of Commando operations and training at Achnacarry, try the following:

Cubitt, Robert; A Commando's Story; Selfishgenie Publishing; 2018.
Durnford-Slater, John, Brigadier: Commando: Memoirs of a Fighting Commando in World War 2; Greenhill Books; new edition 2002.
Gilchrist, Donald: Castle Commando; The Highland Council; 3rd revised edition, 1993.
Scott, Stan; Fighting With The Commandos; Pen and Sword Military; 2008.
Young, Peter, Brigadier; Storm from the Sea; Greenhill Books; new edition 2002.

For a more general overview of the commandos and their operations:

Saunders, Hilary St George; The Green Beret; YBS The Book Service Ltd; new edition 1972.

Preview – Operation Carthage

(Carter's Commandos Book 4)

1 – Weymouth

The four men lay in the thick heather, waiting. They knew their target was out there, somewhere, but not yet visible. The cloud scudded across the sky, sometimes revealing the moon and providing so much light that it hurt the eyes. Sometimes it was hidden, leaving a blackness so deep it was almost impenetrable.

When the moon was at its brightest the commandos covered their eyes, protecting their night vision. Sound was their best friend. Noise would tell them when their quarry was near. Then they would fall on them like the furies.

Some distance away they could hear voices, but they weren't the voices of the men they were hunting. Their blundering and calling would send their quarry to ground, like a rabbit hearing the rustle of a fox through the undergrowth. The commandos smiled a grim smile to themselves. They would never make noise like that. They were masters of stealth, capable of moving through the night silently, like wraiths. It was how they had got to this position undetected.

While daylight had lasted, they had followed the trail of bent grass, footprints in the soft earth, stray fibres left on twigs. It had pointed in a straight line across the landscape. Leading them through the woods and fields of southern Dorset until they had been sure of their quarry's destination.

Their quarry had done well to get this far, Carter had to conceded, but he knew it was now only a matter of time. The commandos had used their fitness to get ahead of the two men, leaving the slower police officers to act as beaters, sending their quarry into their waiting arms.

They were heading for Taunton, that much was obvious. It was the only place on their route that made sense. What their plan was when they reached the town was another matter. Perhaps they would try to board a train. Twice they had tried to steal a car, but the black market in spare parts, caused by the wartime shortages, meant that most car owners removed a vital part each night before they went to bed, in order to prevent just such an act. Half the cars in the country were up on bricks to prevent the rubber of their tyres from perishing, because there was so little petrol available for private motoring.

A voice called and a whistle screeched, but it was from the wrong direction. Whatever had caused the alarm to be sounded, it wasn't the two men that Carter and his little group were waiting for. Not unless they had changed course for some reason.

There was a sound, the rustling of a bush as the branches were parted to allow passage through to the other side. It was slightly to Carter's left. That was no surprise. No one could keep to a straight line when their course was continually being blocked by buildings, hedges or trees. It didn't matter. When they were as close as they would get, Carter and his men would rise out of the ground and issue their challenge. If the men were sensible, they would stand still and surrender themselves. If they were stupid, they would try to run. They wouldn't get far. To either side the rest of Carter's troop were arrayed in a line. The fugitives couldn't hope get past such a barrier.

Feet scuffed through the heather, the stems swishing against the men's trouser legs. They would be tired by now, having been on the move nonstop for two days, trying to put as much distance between themselves and Portland prison as they could. They had managed to snatch a meal, food stolen from a shop in a village. That had been the act that had given Carter and his men the starting point for the trail that they had then followed.

The cloud parted once again and Carter covered one eye, while the other searched the night for a sight of the two men. They were to the south, as expected, perhaps fifty feet to Carter's left. Danny Glass was on that side. Beyond him was Prof Green.

"Stand still and you won't get hurt." Glass's voice broke the silence of the night.

The men failed to obey. They tried to make break for it to their left, directly towards Carter. As they thundered towards him he rose up and swung the handle of his trenching tool at the nearest man's thigh, making a solid contact. He howled with pain but tried to continue his run, stumbling as his injured leg threatened to give way under him. The other man continued, making it past Carter but not very far past. O'Driscoll rose from where he had been lying and took one mighty swipe at the fugitive, the trenching tool handle making a sickening thunk as it made contact with the man's head. He fell as though pole axed.

"Steady Paddy!" Prof Green admonished as he ran up. "You're supposed to be arresting him, not killing him."

"Sure, haven't I arrested him. In fact, I'd say I've never seen a man more arrested than this one."

The first man was still making feeble attempts to get away, his lurching gait keeping him a fraction ahead of Carter. But Carter was walking.

"You may as well stop now." Carter said quietly. "I've got other men out there and they'd just love have a crack at you as well."

The man stopped and turned to face his tormentor. He took a swing at Carter with his fist, more out of frustration at being caught than anything else. Carter swayed out of reach then used his trenching tool handle to jab the man in the stomach. There was a whoosh of escaping breath and the man went down on one knee.

Satisfied that his man wasn't going anywhere, Carter raised a whistle to his lips and blew three long blasts. The sound would summon his men to him, ending their night's exercise.

The police would also respond, coming to collect the two prisoners that had escaped from Portland Prison two days earlier.

The request to help the police had been an unusual one, but Lt Colonel Vernon recognised the training value for his men. Stalking prey was a useful skill for a commando, transferring to the battlefield in the need to locate the enemy and then creep up on them. It was also a useful diversion for men who had been cooped up in barracks for too long.

After the raid on Honfleur, 15 Cdo had been billeted in the Territorial Army Drill Hall in Worthing for a few weeks before transferring to Weymouth in October. They were replacing 1 Cdo there, who had last been seen heading off to Southampton to board troopships for pastures new. Rumours were rife that they were to take part in a big operation, but no one really knew. Other rumours said they had been sent to Egypt to bolster Montgomery's beleaguered 8th Army, but that might not be true either.

But 15 Cdo now occupied 1 Cdo's former barracks and it was a considerable improvement on the drill hall and the commando's previous accommodation, the platforms of Bishopstone railway station.

Work had already started to re-build the commando after its devastating losses at sea and on land in August. Several new intakes of commandos had arrived from the training school at Achnacarry, including one group made up almost entirely of former police officers. The police had just had their reserved occupation[1] status lifted and many had rushed to volunteer for the armed forces. The commandos in particular had attracted them. Perhaps they hankered after some excitement after spending so much of the war chasing black marketeers and pulling bodies out of the ruins of bombed out buildings.

But for Carter the excitement of the chase couldn't block out his own worries entirely. His wife, far away in Scotland, was heavily pregnant and their last parting hadn't been as fond as it might. Given the choice, he would far rather be in Troon than in Dorset.

[1] Reserved occupations – At the outbreak of the Second World war, several industries were considered vital for the war effort, so people employed in those were exempt from conscription and also weren't permitted to volunteer for military service. These industries included the more obvious ones such as coal mining, steel making, ship building, aircraft production, farming etc. But they also

included some less obvious occupations such as the police. The inclusion of the police may have been a precaution against large scale outbreaks of civil unrest, but in 1942 the restriction on the police joining the armed forces was lifted and many hundreds of police officers rushed to join up. The physical requirements of policing made them attractive to commando units, as their stature was useful in the newly formed heavy weapons troops, where the strength to carry a Vickers machine gun or a 3 inch mortar was welcomed. At that time, you had to be over five feet eight inches tall to join the police, which was above the average height of about five feet six inches at that time. Height restrictions on the police were removed in the 1990s as they were considered to be discriminatory.

* * *

Despite the warmth of her first hospital visit with Carter, the rest had not been nearly so comfortable. Fiona had seemed withdrawn, her anxiety clear. In some ways it had to be expected. Her father had just died and she had nearly lost Carter to the war. It was natural that she should be worried. But there was more to it than that, Carter felt sure.

His service with the commandos had been the cause of their relationship faltering back at the beginning of the year. Now, as the first leaves on the trees were turning to gold, he feared that it might tear them apart again, just as he was about to become a father.

The train journey back to Troon had been frosty. Some of that might have been attributed to the fatigue of a heavily pregnant woman travelling on Britain's wartime rail network, but Carter wasn't foolish enough to think that was the only problem. It was as though Fiona has detached herself from him in some way. She seemed to be keeping him at arm's length, perhaps frightened that she might be committed to someone who might soon be dead.

There was little Carter could do to allay her fears. At every railway station, newspaper hoardings shouted news of the latest German offensive at Stalingrad. The rumours were that the Germans had reached the Volga river north of the city and were threatening to surround it. Everyone was speculating on what that might mean for the British. The words "second front" were commonly heard.

Once at Home Farm, Carter took to turning the radio off when hews broadcasts started. Fiona knew what he was doing but didn't comment on it. Cutting his wife off from the war news wouldn't stop the war from happening. Besides, they both knew the date on which Carter was due to report back to 15 Cdo.

To keep himself busy, Carter occupied himself by helping around the farm. He met Fiona's new farm hand, Sandy MacGregor and had taken an instant liking to him. Despite his injury he had an indefatigable optimism about him.

"Ach, it's only a we scratch" he had said as he hobbled around the farmyard on his crutches. "I'll be getting a new foot afore long and then you'll be thinking they're both real."

He would have made a good commando, Carter thought. But then decided not to wish that on anyone. Had he been a commando he might now be dead. Instead he was doing good work around the farm on any task that only required him to use one foot. He was certainly still able to milk a cow twice as quickly as either of the two Land Girls.

"How did you lose your foot?" Carter asked him.

"Some stupid Sassenach drove a tank over it." he replied. "We were part of Operation Crusader, the force sent to relieve Tobruk. We were moving through some tanks that were holding the line when a shell blast knocked me off my feet. The damn tank drove straight over my left foot and crushed it. He didn't know he'd done it, of course, so I was just left lying there. I might have died if it hadn't been for a Royal Engineers demolition party who were coming back across No Man's Land after blowing a bridge. They found me more dead than alive and got me back to a dressing station."

"That was last November, wasn't it?"

"Aye. I've been in hospital pretty much ever since. They didn't want to let me out until my wound had fully healed. I was sent back to Blighty via a hospital in South Africa, then spent some time in a convalescent home. Then I got news I was being discharged, so they sent me home on leave until the paperwork was done. It just came through this week, so I'm no longer a sojer, so I don't have to call you Sir."

"I wouldn't want you to anyway. Call me Steven."

"I can't do that either. Oot o' respect for Mrs Carter. She's my employer, ye ken. If ye don't mind, I'll call you Mr Carter."

"If that's what you want. Now, have you any jobs you would like me to do while I'm here?"

In many ways Carter's leave of absence at Home Farm had been a pleasant interlude. He was able to immerse himself in physical labour, which kept his mind off his recent experiences, but always the distance between himself and Fiona had nagged at him.

It wasn't until the night before Carter was due to depart that he raised the subject of Fiona's pregnancy. "The chaps were telling me that you've agreed to name the babies after them. Paddy and Danny, or maybe Patricia and Danielle."

"I think they may have been pulling your leg. They did ask if we'd chosen any names, but I certainly didn't agree to any. I do rather like Patricia for a girl though."

"If you want. It is quite nice."

"No, not for the West of Scotland though. Anything that has a hint of Catholicism about it doesn't go down too well in some quarters."

"Even today?"

"I think you need to go to a Rangers versus Celtic match some time to understand how religion still works up here."

Thinking about it, Carter had to concede that in some parts of the country being a catholic didn't go down too well even in England. Indeed, the monarch still wasn't allowed to be a catholic, so until that changed nothing else could be expected to.

"So, what names would you like?" Carter asked.

"If you've no objection, I'd like a boy to be named John, after my father."

"That's a wonderful idea. I can't think of anything better. What about a girl? Mary, after your mother?"

"How about Katherine, after my grandmother?"

"That's nice too. But if its twins, we're going to need two more names."

"What about your father's name?"

"No disrespect to my father, but I'm not keen on Gerald. How about James? It's my father's middle name."

"Given that we've had six kings of that name, I think we could get away with it despite its catholic connections. So, what about another girl's name?"

"How about Elizabeth, after my mother."

"And the name of our future Queen, assuming no boy princes arrive in the meantime. Yes, why not."

The discussion seemed to have thawed relations between them, as Carter had hoped it would. Time for him to broach the subject of his real worries. "You've been a little bit distant for the last few days. Is anything bothering you? Are you regretting marrying me?"

She looked down at her hands, holding the sewing that she had been working on. "No. I love you Steven. I think I've always loved you. But …" she fell silent.

"You're afraid you might be left alone."

She nodded her head. He couldn't think what to say. To mention that she would soon have two children to remind her of him didn't seem appropriate. They would be a substitute, no more. The idea of having children was to make them a family and they wouldn't be that if he didn't come home.

"Would you like me to ask for a transfer to a line infantry battalion?"

"I know you'd do it if I asked, but no. You love what you do, I know that. And I know you're good at it. When I met your men, while you were in hospital, they told me how much you are admired in the commando. All the men want to be in your troop. You have a reputation for being lucky. They think that with you in charge they'll have a better chance of making it to the end of the war."

"It's nice of them to say that, but several of my men were killed on the last raid and others were wounded. And …" he touched the last remnants of the bruises on his face, "… my luck might not be that good. I only just made it back myself. If Prof hadn't come back for me …" he left the rest of the sentence unspoken. It would be too distressing a prospect for Fiona to consider.

"No. You must stay where you are needed most. I'm being selfish."

"No, you aren't. You're being a mother and a wife. There is a big difference."

"I've not been much of a wife while we've been together this past couple of weeks."

"I didn't want to tire you out."

She laughed. "So, you think you can tire me out? I'll put that to the test just as soon as I've finished this sewing."

Carter was pleased to hear her laughter once again. He hadn't heard it since the commando had left Troon at the end of June. But he knew that her better mood would only be short lived. They may have talked about her worries, but nothing he had said had taken them away.

* * *

Aside from the never-ending training, there was little excitement for 15 Cdo. With so many military personnel crowded along the south coast there were the inevitable rivalries. Some were resolved on the sports pitches, others outside the pubs after too much beer had been drunk.

Part of the problem for the commandos was their reputation. Every other soldier, sailor and airman seemed to think it necessary to try to take the commandos down a peg or two. Most of the time they lived to regret it, but from time to time a commando would be found unconscious in an alley, dumped after he had been set upon by a gang of drunken rivals. It didn't help that the single ladies, and a few married ones, found the commando badges on their uniforms something of an attraction. It took only the appearance of a group of commandos at the door of a dancehall for the local women to abandon their escorts and gravitate towards the new arrivals. It did nothing to ease tensions around Weymouth.

Carter was given the job of trying to prevent some of the conflict. The easiest answer seemed to be to limit the number of occasions on which the commandos would come into contact with the members of other units.

There was a NAAFI canteen in the barracks, but it didn't have enough space for real recreational facilities. The bar was tiny, as was the cafeteria. There was no room for a snooker table or a darts board.

But the barracks had been built to house a battalion of six hundred men and the commando was only three hundred and fifty strong. Carter organised working parties to convert some of the space to make it suitable for leisure activities.

The QM had requisitioned a film projector for use in showing training films, so Carter made sure that the room set aside for use as a training cinema was also put to good use for showing more entertaining films. An agreement was made with the projectionist at the local cinema for films to stop off at the barracks for a night when they were being sent to the next cinema on the circuit. By coincidence the projectionist seemed to always have a packet of strictly rationed cigarettes in his pocket and he was seen out in his car more often than the petrol ration should have allowed.

A barrack room capable of housing twenty men became home to a snooker table that had been discovered languishing in the cellar of a mansion that had been taken over by the Navy. As the house wasn't being used as a residence, the table had been in the way in the room set aside for it by its previous occupants. The officers clubbed together and bought darts boards and the Local British Legion club donated a mixture of old darts which were fitted with new flights. Lads from the local area found they could earn a ha'penny a pint taking orders from thirsty commandos and collecting beer from the bar to take across to what had been nicknamed the "Pool hall" after a W C Fields movie in which the game had featured[1].

But allowing the commandos to meet girls was a much harder task. Another spare barrack room served as a dance hall, but there was no money available to hire a band. There were a number of concert parties, groups of enthusiastic amateur performers drawn mainly from military units and they could be persuaded to perform providing transport could be arranged. Carter became adept at negotiating deals with local Service Corps units for the loan of trucks.

The music problem was solved by the commandos themselves. In any large enough group of people there are always a few musicians. All that was needed was the instruments. Carter arranged for the officers' mess piano to be moved across to the designated dancing area and contacted the local Salvation Army citadel to see if they could help. Some battered brass instruments were given on loan, along with well-worn tenor and snare drums and some cymbals. The sound wasn't as tuneful as it might have been, but it was recognisable as music. Letters were written home to ask family to send whatever sheet music they had. What arrived varied from Beethoven to Blues, but the commandos were able to pick out the best of it and turn it into something that could be played at a dance.

The first dance was held at the beginning of October. Nurses from the local hospitals were invited, as were teachers from the local schools. Transport was organised and assurances made to Matrons and head teachers that their charges would be well looked after. Just to make sure, chaperones were provided. The dance was a success and paved the way for several more before the commando moved on. Just as in Troon, weddings soon took place, some organised more urgently than others.

Carter soon found himself being referred to as Billy Butlin[2], a nickname he wasn't quite as happy with as "Lucky".

The concert parties were the biggest success. They varied in quality, but the men liked their informality. The first one was something of an experiment.

It started with a pianist playing the old favourites: Tipperary, Pack Up Your Troubles, Roll Out The Barrel and more in that vein.

The men sang along and it got everyone in the right mood. Next up came a comedian, a corporal, who told the bluest of jokes, much to the men's delight. Carter had heard of comedians like him but had never actually witnessed an act like it. They were certainly jokes that he couldn't tell his mother; his father neither, come to think of it. though they'd have gone down well with some of his friends from his student days.

A rather inept magician came on and was badly booed and heckled.

"Shall I quiet the men down?" Carter asked the fresh faced Royal Signals Second Lieutenant that had brought the party along.

"Oh no. This happens every night and he loves it. In fact he deliberately makes some of the tricks go wrong just to get a laugh."

A male tenor came on and sang some lovely Scottish ballads, mainly on the theme of unrequited love, along with a couple of operatic arias, before the penultimate act of the evening.

A diminutive you ATS[3] woman came on, young, barely in her twenties. She couldn't have been five feet tall in her army issues shoes. The pianist played a few chords then she started to sing. It was the Skye Boat Song, which the men had become familiar with hearing in the theatres they had visited in Scotland. The woman didn't have the best voice in the world, Carter had to admit, but it had a sort of sweetness that caught the ear. The room fell silent, taken under the spell of her rendition.

The next song upped the tempo a bit, a cheerful rendition of the old Harry Lauder favourite, "I'll Tak' the High Road". Then the final song of her set, 'The Wild Mountain Thyme'. Perhaps it was the mood of the song or perhaps it was the way the woman sang it, but Carter would have sworn he saw more than one of the commandos wipe a tear from his eye.

At the end of the piece the room went wild with applause and the compere, the blue comedian, had to calm the men down. "Thank you. Thank you, gentlemen. And thank you to young Kitty Sutherland from Edinburgh."

The compere introduced the final performance of the evening, which was the tenor and the young woman, Kitty, singing duets from pre-war musicals.

Afterwards the commandos surrounded the young woman, all trying to persuade her out on a date.

"Shouldn't you recue her?" Carter asked the signals officer.

"More likely I'll have to rescue the men." He laughed. "No, Kitty can look after herself. And we'll be leaving in a minute anyway."

As they left the large barrack room more than one man gave Carter a thumbs up in appreciation of the evening's entertainment.

[1] Pool Sharks – The first film made by American comedy actor W C Fields, for which he had written the screenplay. It was released in 1915 and lasted only ten minutes.

[2] Billy Butlin – Founder of the holiday camp empire that still bears his name. His first camp was opened at Skegness in 1936. A camp built for him at Dovercourt in Essex was requisitioned in 1938 to house Jewish children evacuated from Germany under the *Kindertransports* programme before the outbreak of the Second World War. His camps at Clacton and Skegness were both requisitioned by the War Office for use as training camps and he built other camps for the War Office on condition that he could purchase them for use as holiday camps after the war. Visitors to the camps who have a military background often remark on their military style architecture.

[3] ATS – Auxiliary Territorial Service. This was founded in 1938 as preparations for war started to be made behind the scenes. It was the women's branch of the British Army and provided female personnel to release men from support roles for service in the front line. Typical duties were clerical, logistics, transport, catering and communications. The ATS became the Women's Royal Army Corps in 1949. The women's branch was disbanded in 1992, along with the Women's Royal Naval Service (WRNS) and the Women's Royal

Air Force (WRAF) when equalities legislation made it necessary to integrate women into the armed forces, rather than treating them differently. From 1992 onwards all women serving in the armed forces served on equal terms with their male counterparts, with the exception of eligibility for combat service.

* * *

As the clock ticked towards eleven hundred hours, the commando stood in their troops, in three ranks, forming three sides of the parade ground of their barracks. Two troops stood on each side of a square that was open on its fourth side. Having just returned from five days training on Dartmoor, where they had bivouacked in tents made from their gas capes, Carter had been surprised to see the order requiring them to parade the next day.

The chill of a late October wind had the men rubbing their hands together in an effort to keep warm. The voice of Sgt Maj Finch rang out across the parade ground, calling the soldiers to attention. This was followed by the arrival of the newly appointed 2IC, Maj Charlie Cousins. He had been posted in on promotion from 6 Cdo. The reputation of the unit and the ribbon of the Military Cross on Cousins' chest told the men of 15 Cdo all they needed to know about his suitability for the job.

The 2IC stood the parade at ease again but didn't allow them to stand easy[1]. Carter wondered about the presence of half a dozen thick cardboard packing cases that were dotted along the open end of the square. What could be in them? No doubt they would find out soon enough. They must be related to the unexpected calling of the parade.

On the front of the Napoleonic headquarters building the hands of the clock ticked around to exactly eleven o'clock. The 2IC called the parade to attention once again and the CO marched to the centre of the open end of the square, made a left turn and continued until he came to a halt five paces in front of the 2IC. They exchanged salutes, the 2IC going first, then the 2 IC marched to the centre of the closed end of the square where he took up a position in between 3 and 4 troops.

"Number 15 Commando!" The CO's voice rang out. "No 15 Cdo, stand at ease! Stand easy."

The CO stood himself at ease before speaking again. "No doubt you came back from Dartmoor last night hoping for a couple of easy days in which to clean your kit and get ready for the next training task." As he spoke he turned from side to side, making sure that all three sides of the square could hear at least some of what he was saying, though the wind whipped much of it away before the sound could reach those furthest from him. "I did have that in mind for you but changed my mind when these …" he indicated the large cardboard boxes "… turned up unexpectedly. I will tell you more about those in a minute.

But first, as you all know, the commandos have often been described as a rag-tag army. It has been said that we look like a bunch of misfits wandering around Piccadilly Circus on a Saturday night. This is because, between us, we wear several different types of head gear. And it's not just you men. I wear a peaked cap, as do some of your other officers. But some wear forage caps, some wear berets and Capt Fraser wears a Tam O'shanter which, as we all know, is a heathen form of headdress worn north of the border." Vernon paused to allow the men time to chuckle at his joke, which they dutifully did. "And I won't even deign to describe the abomination that Tpr O'Driscoll wears." This brought even more laughter. Paddy O'Driscoll's caubeen with its green feathered hackle had been the butt of many a joke.

"For some time now the commandos, with the support of HQ Combined Operations, have been trying to persuade the War Office to issue us with a single form of head dress. This campaign gained some additional impetus this summer when those upstarts in the Parachute Regiment were granted the right to wear a maroon beret." This brought some booing, which the CO tolerated for a few seconds.. "Well. We finally won the battle."

There was a ripple of voices around the parade ground as the commandos shared the news with those who hadn't quite heard it. The CO allowed it to continue for a few seconds, then raised his hands for silence.

"Sadly, we have still not been allowed to adopt a cap badge of our own. All the suggestions for a suitable design have been rejected. But, from today, all the commandos under my command will wear the same style of hat. In a moment, I will be the first to place one on my head. After that you will be called forward by troops to have yours issued to you, following which any member of this commando who wears any other form of head dress will be regarded as being improperly dressed. Do I make myself clear?"

The was a ragged chorus of 'Yes, Sir.' around the parade ground, which brought a mock stern look from the CO.

"I said 'Do I make myself clear?'" This time there was a wholehearted shout.

"Very well. I will now bring you to attention and the ceremony will commence. Parade! Parade 'shun!"

Three hundred and fifty left boots crashed into the tarmac of the parade square, alongside the commando's right boots. The CO did an about turn, so that he was facing towards the open side of the square.

Sgt Major Finch marched forward with something held in front of him in both hands. It was reminiscent of a Chamberlain bearing a monarch's crown. But this was no crown; this was a beret, but its colour wasn't the familiar black of the Royal Tank Regiment, it was bottle green. A black painted cap badge was visible at the front. The commandos had been painting their badges matt black ever since they had been founded, as a precaution against the enemy seeing them sparkle in the moonlight.

The Sgt Major came to a halt in front of the CO, who removed his peaked cap. Extending his left hand he offered the hat to the Sgt Major, while raising his right hand to take the beret. The exchange completed; he placed the beret on his head. A spontaneous cheer rang out around the parade square.

The CO did an about turn, so he was facing inwards again, and raised his hand in a salute. A second cheer rang out.

After the CO had marched off and the Sgt Major had once again taken charge of the parade ground, the troops were called forward in numerical order to collect their berets. It was a significant moment for them, the unique nature of their role finally being recognised. Finally, they felt as though they really were one family, one band of brothers[2]. A new badge to go with the berets would have been nice and they were aware that the Royal Marine commandos already had that distinction, of which they were envious, but the beret was a start.

[1] Stand easy – Standing at ease is a formal drill position, in which the men are more relaxed than they would be if they were stood to attention, but they are not allowed to move or talk. Stand easy is an informal position, the men can chat and fidget, so long as they stay in their ranks. The command "Stand at ease" would be used when the parade is waiting for a parade to start, or when in front of an officer for a formal interview. Stand easy would be used while the men were waiting for the start of a briefing, the arrival of a train or other routine activities where strict silence or immobility isn't required.

[2] In Shakespeare's Henry V Act IV, Scene 3, King Henry exhorts his men ahead of the Battle of Agincourt, saying "We few, we happy few, we band of brothers. For he today that sheds his blood with me shall be my brother."

* * *

It was in the first week in November that the CO called the officers together for an announcement. "We've just received orders that we're to move overseas." He announced. "I can't tell you where, that will be revealed once we're on our ship, but I think you will have some clue because before we leave we'll be issued with khaki drill uniforms."

This brought some mutterings between the assembled officers. Khaki drill clothing was only issued for hot weather areas, which probably meant that their destination was North Africa or India.

"Firstly, all the men will be given a week's embarkation leave, so they have time to go home and say goodbye to their families. After they report back here, we'll be moving up to Glasgow to board a troop ship. Now, Steven, seeing as you will be up there anyway, there's little point in you coming all the way back down here again. There are another half dozen men who also have wives in Troon or the area around it, so you will form a work party in Glasgow, receiving the kit we send up in advance and making sure that it all gets loaded onto the ship." Dockyards were notorious for 'losing' military equipment and units were often frustrated to find vital equipment missing when they got to their destinations.

There were a few more details about advance parties and rear parties, dates, times and the other logistical information that the officers would need to brief their men, but the main question on everyone's lips was 'where?'.

"There's been a move of commandos to the Mediterranean." Carter commented to Andrew Fraser. "Both 1 and 6 have gone out there. Something big's on the way."

"Maybe they've just been sent to bolster Monty's 8th Army. You know, to prevent Rommel reaching the Suez Canal."

"Could be. Maybe that's where we're going as well. But that would turn us into line infantry, which isn't what we're trained for."

"Not necessarily. We could be used to raid Rommel's supply lines. It would mean him having to commit more men to protesting them, which would weaken his front line."

Carter nodded his head. That would make sense, he thought. The commandos were raiders. Their job was to get in amongst the enemy, create mayhem and then get out again. They all dreaded the day when they might be used as ordinary infantrymen. It would come, of course. If you push the enemy away from the coastline there's fewer opportunities to attack from the sea and that would leave the commandos without a job. It would be inventible that elite troops such as themselves would be found a new job, at the forefront of the war effort.

* * *

Making the best of his short period of leave became Carter's main objective. With Fiona now very heavy with the twins, there was little he could do to distract her. He suggested another stay in Edinburgh, but with winter setting in she said she didn't fancy having to face the east wind that seemed to scour the city of all its warmth. He then suggested Norther Ireland, but the prospect of a sea crossing, however short, was also a cause for rejecting the idea.

So, instead, he settled for a few days of home comforts, fussing around his wife and causing her to get more annoyed with him. She was too independent to tolerate being treated like an invalid and, although she understood what Carter was trying to do, she spent more time snapping at him than smiling.

It was therefore almost with a sense of relief that Carter reported to the Port Liaison Officer at Port Glasgow to start supervising the assembly of the Commando's kit. The majority of the commandos would travel together by train, but individual consignments of stores and weaponry were to be escorted up by smaller detachments of men and held on the docks until their ship was available for loading. With merchant ships in short supply thanks to attentions of the U-Boat packs, the speed of their turnaround was vital and they wouldn't be held back in port waiting for stragglers or late arrivals of equipment.

The commando found that they weren't to be the only passengers on board the ship. Drafts of young conscripts were being sent out to join units weakened by combat losses. They stared in awe at the commando's shoulder flashes and medal ribbons. After work the commandos were stood pints in the local pubs to encourage them to tell their stories. More than one fresh faced conscript regretted asking the question 'What was it like?'.

Over the following days the rest of the commando arrived and the ship was loaded. It was an ancient coal powered rust bucket which would probably have been sent to the breakers' yard had it not been for the war. Even the crew didn't seem to know their destination, though someone must have. On the day before they were set to embark the BBC news carried the story of Operation Torch[1], as it would become known: the United States led invasion of Morocco and Algeria.

Was that where they were going? It only served to fuel more speculation.

In the small hours of the following day the old ship slipped its moorings and made its way down the Firth of Clyde to join up with a convoy that was assembling north of the isle of Arran. From there they steamed down the Irish Sea, across the western end of the English Channel and out into the Bay of Biscay, keeping well clear of the French coast for fear of encountering U-Boats either returning from Atlantic patrols or setting out on them.

After two weeks at sea the commandos leant on the port railings of the ship to take in the sight of the Rock of Gibraltar, shouting abuse. By this time the tiny British outpost was known to be the commando's destination, so they were frustrated that their ship was sailing right past and into the Mediterranean Sea, to the newly liberated port or Oran in Algeria. After disembarking they were told they were waiting the arrival of another ship, which would take them back to Gibraltar.

There was much discussion about why they hadn't disembarked there days earlier, when they had passed it by, but Carter had been in the Army long enough to know that such decisions were baffling and, often, arbitrary. Most of the ship's cargo was destined for General Eisenhauer's forces in Algeria, so that was where the ship was sent. For the conscripts it was worse. They had several more days to wait in a transit camp before being moved on to Alexandria through waters patrolled by both German and Italian submarines and all ships passing through that area risked being bombed by Luftwaffe aircraft operating out of Libya and Sicily.

The ship that took them back to Gibraltar was the Prince Leopold, a well-known and much loved commando landing ship. It had been one of the landing ships that had transported the men of Nos 1 and 6

Cdos, who had participated in the capture of Algiers. They soon discovered why it was necessary for them to be transported by landing ship. The port of Gibraltar was so packed with shipping, both merchant and naval, that the only way to get the commando ashore was in landing craft.

[1] Operation Torch was a significant event during World War 2 and gets very little mention in the history books. Firstly, it was a major logistical challenge, as the whole invasion force had to travel either from Britain or directly from the USA. Such a long sea voyage prior to an invasion had never been attempted before and wouldn't be attempted again until the Falklands War of 1982. The force was split into three elements, spaced hundreds of miles apart. The western most element was to capture Morocco, thereby preventing the closure of the Straights of Gibraltar should Spain decide to intervene on the side of Germany. The other two elements landed at Oran and Algiers, the major ports of Algeria, facilitating the build-up of forces that would eventually meet the Germans in battle at Kasserine in Tunisia. The primary objectives were the capture of port and airfield facilities, which would finally end German and Italian air superiority in the Mediterranean and cut their supply lines to Libya. The Vichy French[2] forces in Morocco and Algeria put up only light resistance, which meant that allied casualties were small, the United States suffering 524 dead and the UK 576 dead with 756 wounded all told. Many of those casualties were actually inflicted at sea, by U-Boats. This was less than had been suffered in a single day at Dieppe the previous August. The immediate effect of the landings was to force Field Marshall Erwin Rommel, commander of the *Afrika Korps*, to split his forces in Libya to face both east and west, paving the way for the British victory at the Battle of El Alamein the following month.

[2] Vichy France – The name given to the puppet French government permitted by a treaty with the Germans to establish itself in the unoccupied part of central and southern France, in the town of

Vichy. From there it ruled what remained of the French Empire until the Germans occupied the area after Operation Torch. Technically it was neutral, but in fact it did what it was told by the Germans. Some parts of the Empire, such as Indochina, remained loyal to the Free French government in London and fought on against the Germans and then the Japanese. The head of the Vichy government was Marshal Pétain, the Hero of Verdun in the First World War.

And Now

Both the author Robert Cubitt and Selfishgenie Publishing hope that you have enjoyed reading this story.

Please tell people about this eBook, write a review on Amazon or mention it on your favourite social networking site. Word of mouth is an author's best friend and is much appreciated. Thank you.

Find Robert Cubitt on Facebook at https://www.facebook.com/robertocubitt and 'like' his page; follow him on Twitter **@Robert_Cubitt**

For further titles that may be of interest to you please visit our website at **selfishgenie.com** where you can optionally join our information list.

Printed in Great Britain
by Amazon